BECAUSE THE BARON BROODS

ROGUE RULES
BOOK TWO

DARCY BURKE

Zealous Quill Press

BECAUSE THE BARON BROODS

ROGUE RULES

When a young lady is ruined, her friends vow none of them
will ever be ensnared by a scoundrel again. They will resist
every gentleman's charms even—and especially—if it means
gaining a reputation for being impossible to woo. It will take
extraordinary rogues to break their rules...

Growing up in isolation in Cornwall, Tamsin Penrose looks
forward to the one month each year that she spends in an
idyllic seaside town with her best friends. She's shocked to
receive a letter from her reclusive father informing her of a
potential groom—they've never even discussed marriage and
she rather expected to be a spinster. But she's met a charming, if serious, baron and now she's dreaming of a romantic,
wedded life.

During his annual trip to a friend's seaside estate, broody
Isaac Deverell, Baron Droxford finds himself in an objection-

able situation: socializing with a group of ladies over several days. He is not prepared for the storm of cheerfulness that is Miss Penrose, nor can he deny that she makes him feel…good.

Because Isaac is an unheroic rogue with a devastatingly sinful secret, he should flee this delightful ray of sunshine. However, he can't keep his distance, and when her overzealous suitor arrives and won't take no for an answer, Isaac protects her in a scandalously public fashion. Now he can't run from her. Can these attracted opposites find a happy ever after, or will the past destroy their chance?

Don't miss the rest of the *Rogue Rules*!

Do you want to hear all the latest about me and my books? Sign up at Reader Club newsletter for members-only bonus content, advance notice of pre-orders, insider scoop, as well as contests and giveaways!

Care to share your love for my books with like-minded readers? Want to hang with me and see pictures of my cats (who doesn't!)? Then don't miss my exclusive Facebook groups!

Darcy's Duchesses for historical readers
Burke's Book Lovers for contemporary readers

Want more historical romance? Do you like your historical romance filled with passion and red hot chemistry? Join me and my author friends in the Facebook group, Historical Harlots, for exclusive giveaways, chat with amazing HistRom authors, and more!

THE ROGUE RULES

Never be alone with a rogue.
Never flirt with a rogue.
Never give a rogue a chance.
Never doubt a rogue's reputation.
Never believe a rogue's pledge of love or devotion.
Never trust a rogue to change.
Never allow a rogue to see your heart.
Ruin the rogue before he can ruin you.

CHAPTER 1

Weston, England, August 1815

Tamsin Penrose adjusted the curl that rested against her temple, wishing it was as springy as the one on the other side of her face. Ah well, she did the best she could and did not bemoan the fact that she didn't have a maid. She didn't really need one, and her illustrious friends, including a duchess and the daughter of a duke, never made her feel that she was any different from them.

Except she was, despite being cousin to a viscount. Her friends came from prominent families and had bright futures with Seasons and advantageous marriages, while Tamsin resided with her hermit father in Cornwall and was lucky enough to spend every August in Weston, where her grand-mother lived and where she'd met her dear friends three years ago.

Still, the differences between them didn't matter to Tamsin any more than they did to her friends. They were simply a group of young ladies who enjoyed each other's company. In fact, today, they would all enjoy an alfresco luncheon hosted by their friend, Lady Minerva, daughter of the Duke of Henlow.

Tamsin adjusted the ribbon of her bonnet and plucked up her gloves before going downstairs. Her friend Persephone, who was now the Duchess of Wellesbourne after marrying last autumn, would be picking her up on the way to the Grove, one of many estates owned by the Duke of Henlow. She would also fetch Gwendolen Price, who hailed from Bristol, from the Weston Hotel, where she was staying with her mother.

Tamsin's grandmother was awaiting her in the staircase hall. Her blue eyes swept over Tamsin as she smiled. "You look lovely, dear. That daffodil yellow is such a brilliant color for you."

"Thank you, Grandmama." Tamsin drew her gloves on. "I take it Somerton left some time ago?"

Tamsin's cousin, the Viscount Somerton, was also visiting. His mother and Tamsin's had been sisters—and Grandmama was their mother—but they hadn't been close, particularly after Tamsin's mother had wed her father and moved to St. Austell. Consequently, Tamsin hadn't grown up knowing Somerton or his older sisters well at all. Indeed, until a few years ago, when her and Somerton's trips to Weston had begun to overlap, she'd met him only a few times.

Generally regarded as a jovial gentleman with rakish tendencies, Somerton was close friends with Minerva's brother, the Earl of Shefford. They, along with a few other gentlemen, also gathered in August, though not for the entire month. Eventually, they grew bored with the sleepy seaside village and moved on to wherever unwed rogues found entertainment.

"He did," Grandmama replied. Petite, with dark blue eyes and light gray hair, she was a force of nature who didn't look or act her seventy years. She held up an envelope. "A letter from your father just arrived."

Tamsin blinked. "How odd. He doesn't ever write to me while I'm here."

"Well, you can read it when you get back."

"Would you mind opening it?" Tamsin asked, since she'd already donned her gloves. "I'm afraid my curiosity is getting the best of me."

Grandmama opened the missive and handed the letter to Tamsin. She scanned the short message, her heart beating faster with each line.

When she finished, she looked back at her grandmother. "He says he's found a suitor for me and is in support of me marrying him."

Moving to stand beside Tamsin so she could see the letter, Grandmama asked, "Who?"

"He doesn't say."

Grandmama's brows pitched down. "That is ridiculous. Why would he leave that part out?"

"It is likely an oversight." Tamsin sighed. He was always so focused on work. The fact that he'd written to her at all was a marvel, and leaving out pertinent information seemed, unfortunately, exactly something he would do.

Since her mother had left them when she was eight, Tamsin had felt the need to watch over her father. She made sure he didn't forget things, such as eating dinner. He'd already been somewhat buried in his work by the time her mother had gone, but her departure had sent him further into seclusion. He spent his days in his study and even some of his nights. Tamsin did her best to bring him cheer as he was very often dour. He did seem brighter in her presence, so she believed she served him a great purpose.

"It's terrible is what it is," Grandmama said with a deep frown. "He's taken almost no interest in your life, particularly with regard to potential courtships or marriage."

That was true. Indeed, Tamsin had expected to end up a spinster and rather thought her father had no quarrel with that. "He doesn't even allow me to attend the quarterly assembly." He didn't see the point in investing in the appropriate clothing. He'd also said on more than one occasion that marriage was not always the best path. But then Tamsin knew why he would say that: because his wife had left him.

Had he changed his mind about her marrying? Had he realized that Tamsin might want to wed? Tamsin hadn't allowed herself to think about it too closely. What was the point when she had no occasion to meet potential suitors? Perhaps that was all about to change. A curious excitement gathered in her chest. "Am I to have a Season?" She felt suddenly breathless at the notion.

"I shouldn't think so," Grandmama said. "Your father is far too selfish and shortsighted for that." Grandmama's description of him did not surprise Tamsin, as they did not get on well. "I do wish you'd decided to live with me when you came of marriageable age."

Though she'd invited Tamsin to move in with her, for years now, Tamsin always declined. She ran her father's household, and while the housekeeper, Mrs. Treen, could do the same, she wasn't his daughter. He needed Tamsin, and in some ways, she needed him too. After her mother had left, they'd only had each other.

"You know why I didn't," Tamsin said in response to her grandmother's suggestion.

"Because he needs you." Grandmama pursed her lips. "He doesn't really, my sweet. And I hope his callousness in this marriage matter will convince you otherwise. I can't begin to imagine whom he wants you to wed."

"He says the gentleman may arrive in Weston to convey me home to St. Austell toward the end of the month." How would she know to expect him? This was all very strange.

Tamsin tried to think of who the mystery suitor could be, but everyone her father knew was, well, old. Or close to his age, anyway. There was a younger gentleman with whom he corresponded. He had sought Papa's counsel on an academic matter, and Papa had spoken highly of the young man's letters. Could he be the potential suitor? Though Tamsin knew almost nothing about him, she couldn't deny a burst of excitement at the prospect of meeting someone who not only wanted to meet her but was ready to travel with her to St. Austell. That sounded promising, didn't it?

If that was the gentleman. She didn't know enough right now to make a judgment as to whether this was good or bad news. And since she never chose to dwell on negative things, she chose to believe this must be good news. It had to be. Even if it meant cutting her annual sojourn short, which, if she were honest with herself, *was* a little disappointing.

"I shall hope he is a splendid fellow, and we will make a brilliant match," Tamsin said brightly, considering, for the first time, the idea of leaving her father's household to have a family of her own.

"While your optimism is always wonderful to hear, I must say that your father did not think this through. At the very least, he should have offered the identity of this gentleman so you aren't kept guessing," Grandmama said firmly. "I'll write to him while you are at your luncheon. I'm also not inclined to let you leave before the end of the month. I only have you with me for a short time as it is."

"You are right. I would like to stay through August." Tamsin so looked forward to this time with her beloved grandmother and with her friends—two things she didn't have in St. Austell. "Thank you, Grandmama." Tamsin hugged her.

"I will always ensure your happiness, my dear," Grandmama said softly as they parted.

Tamsin heard a coach outside and turned toward the door.

"Have a good time, Tam," Grandmama said. "Put your father's nonsense out of your mind."

After blowing her grandmother a kiss, Tamsin walked out into the bright summer day. Securing the door behind her, she saw the Duke of Wellesbourne climb down. He held the door for her. "Good afternoon, Miss Penrose."

"Good afternoon, Your Grace."

"You must call me Wellesbourne. Or Welles. Or Wellesy, I suppose." He grinned, his dark eyes crinkling at the edges.

"Are you encouraging people to call you Wellesy?" His wife, Persephone, called from the interior.

"Why not?" he said with a shrug as he helped Tamsin into the coach.

She sat on the rear-facing seat next to Gwen. The newest member of their group, having "joined" with them last August, Gwen was a year younger than Tamsin's twenty-two years. Her father was a Lord Commissioner of the Treasury, and she had an older brother, a barrister who had recently accepted a position in the same department. Gwen had not yet had a Season, due to her needing more "polish." She was sometimes clumsy and claimed to be an abysmal dancer. These were just two things she was working to improve upon before she had her debut on the Marriage Mart. Though Tamsin was certainly no expert, she found Gwen lovely precisely as she was. Surely, there existed a gentleman who would think so too.

"What a fetching bonnet," Persephone said to Tamsin. At twenty-three, Persephone was the only one of their group who was married. It had been a remarkable turn of events last year when she'd suddenly wed the Duke of Wellesbourne. Her mother and his mother were old friends and had proposed the union. While Persephone had been against it at first—due to Wellesbourne's close association with the abominable Bane, who'd ruined her sister Pandora last August here in Weston—she'd ultimately fallen in love.

Perhaps Tamsin would be that fortunate with whomever her father wanted her to wed. Tamsin hoped so. Indeed, the idea was quickly taking root.

"I've news to share now that we're all here," Gwen said, her dark eyes sparkling. "Except Min. I'll tell her later, for I'm afraid I simply can't keep it in a moment longer!"

They all looked to her, expectant, including Wellesbourne. Tamsin wondered again if she ought to share her news, except she wasn't nearly as enthusiastic as Gwen was. Indeed, she possessed a decided *lack* of enthusiasm.

"I'm to have a London Season!" Gwen said, her shoulders lifting with glee.

"How splendid!" Tamsin was so pleased for her friend. Tamsin hadn't even been to Bath. London seemed so far away. She honestly wasn't sure she ever expected to see it.

Persephone reached over and gave Gwen's hand a pat. "I'm delighted for you. I will support you as much as I can, but I have news of my own to share." She glanced toward her husband, her lips curving into a warm smile. "Acton and I are expecting a child. I will have a baby in my arms before spring."

"Oh!" Tamsin and Gwen exclaimed in unison. They both leaned forward as if they would leap upon Persephone.

"I want to hug you!" Tamsin cried.

"I do too!" Gwen said.

"I will gladly accept your hugs when we arrive at the

Grove," Persephone said with a laugh, her blue eyes gleaming. She tucked a dark gold curl back from her face.

Gwen looked to Wellesbourne. "You must be thrilled."

He chuckled. "I confess I'm still getting used to the idea." He took Persephone's hand and clasped it in her lap. It was such a sweet gesture, and Tamsin couldn't help smiling. "My mother is ecstatic."

"As are your sisters," Persephone said. She looked across the coach at Tamsin and Gwen. "They've written with all manner of advice. They're very sweet."

Tamsin wondered what Persephone's sister, Pandora, thought of this news. They'd become especially close when Pandora had come to stay with Tamsin in Cornwall after Persephone's wedding. Seeking refuge from the scandal Bane had caused when he'd ruined her then fled to marry someone else, Pandora had spent the late autumn and entire winter with Tamsin in St. Austell.

From their months together, Tamsin knew Pandora envied her sister's happiness—primarily because of the acceptance Persephone had received from her husband's family. Pandora was of the mind that she would never wed after what happened with Bane. And since Tamsin hadn't expected to wed either, they'd laughingly planned a spinsters' future where they spent time in Weston and kept goats or cats or both.

Persephone looked to Gwen. "How exciting you are to have a Season. I suppose that means at least one more of us will be wed before next August."

"If I receive any offers," Gwen said with a self-deprecating laugh. Her Season had been postponed for so long that Tamsin understood why she might be nervous.

"Of course you will," Persephone stated firmly. "You are clever and witty, and infinitely interesting to talk to. I daresay you will have *multiple* offers."

"I hope they aren't from rogues," Gwen said, shooting Wellesbourne a nervous glance. "I mean no offense."

"I don't take any," he said pleasantly. "I freely admit I was a rogue. I have known nothing but privilege and excess, and I readily took advantage of those things." He brought Persephone's gloved hand to his mouth and pressed a kiss to the base of her thumb. "Thankfully, my lovely wife saw past my transgressions and gave me the chance to be the man I want to be—a grateful, loyal, and thoroughly besotted husband."

"And father," Persephone murmured.

Watching them together gave Tamsin hope. Being in love certainly looked beautiful. She wondered how it felt. Like being filled with light and joy, she imagined. So full that you nearly burst with the quantity of it. She'd never even considered motherhood, but if she made a match with this mystery suitor, she could very well have a family of her own. A close, loving family that she'd never had. She began to imagine this man she might marry. Perhaps he was tall and handsome, with smiling eyes and a sparkling laugh that made her feel giddy. He would sweep her in his arms, and she would feel wholly loved and protected.

"Are you aware of our Rogue Rules?" Gwen asked, jarring Tamsin from her silly daydream. But was it silly?

Tamsin set her mind to what was being discussed—their Rogue Rules. They'd come about after Bane had ruined Pandora. Outraged, the friends had drafted the rules to keep them safe from rogues. Hopefully, this man she would marry would not be a rogue. She'd vowed to avoid them. How would a rogue make her feel loved and protected anyway? Unless he was like the duke. Persephone was so very lucky.

"I am indeed acquainted with your rules about rogues," Wellesbourne said. "A stitched copy of them hangs in Persey's sitting room."

"I do wonder if the rules were made to be broken, however," Tamsin said. "Looking at Persey and Wellesbourne, it seems a rogue can change." *Never trust a rogue to change* was one of the rules. As was *never show a rogue your heart.* Clearly, Persephone had broken that rule as well.

"I tried very hard to follow them," Persephone said. "Acton, however, was most persistent and demonstrated not only an ability to change, but a sincere desire to reform himself."

"But what if not all men are even rogues to begin with?" Tamsin suggested.

"I do think that's true," Wellesbourne said. "I have several friends who are not roguish, at least what I understand that to be, based on what Persey has told me. In our own group, Droxford isn't particularly roguish."

"I've seen women in London hope to catch his interest," Persephone said. "Though that seems to be due to his title and wealth. He is generally reserved, brooding even. I would not believe him to be roguish, but then, I don't know him very well."

"If anyone will be lucky enough to find a man who isn't a rogue, it will be Tamsin," Gwen said. "Provided she's able to meet someone," she added with a light laugh. They all knew that Tamsin had no occasion to encounter gentlemen or be courted.

Tamsin considered telling them about her father's letter, but she was still getting used to the idea of marriage. She would tell them soon. Today, however, was for enjoying her time with them, which had suddenly become vital if she was to leave Weston early.

She hoped that would not be the case, but if true love came upon her, she feared she would not be able to resist.

CHAPTER 2

Isaac Deverell, Baron Droxford, stepped outside onto a brick patio where the alfresco luncheon would be held. The space had been transformed into an elegant outdoor dining room with a long table set for eight people.

His friend, the Earl of Shefford, whose father owned the Grove, the estate where they stayed every August, stood nearby with the Viscount Somerton and Evan Price. Somerton gestured for Isaac to join them.

Isaac looked at the three of them with their heads bent together. They almost appeared guilty, and Isaac suspected he knew why. Shefford went out of his way to annoy his sister, and she did the same to him. Since Lady Minerva had organized this luncheon, Isaac surmised that Shefford was going to make trouble. "What are you plotting?"

"Nothing terrible," Shefford replied innocently. "My sister knows to expect mischief from me."

Evan nodded. "I can attest to this since I too have a younger sister."

Somerton grimaced. "I had it much worse with *three older*

sisters. Drox, if you'd had a sibling, you would know this sort of thing is a matter of survival."

Isaac didn't have any siblings because his mother had died giving birth to his brother, who'd also died, when Isaac was four. It had been a tragedy, of course, but even more so due to his father, a rector, ensuring the grief of losing them was ever present. Not a day went by that the two of them hadn't prayed—extensively—for his mother's and brother's souls.

Isaac adjusted his hat to more effectively block the sun. "If I had a sibling, I would enjoy their company rather than find ways to annoy or play pranks on them."

Shefford chuckled. "Do you ever tire of being serious?"

"You know the answer to that," Isaac said.

"I do indeed. Serious is probably one of your names. Isaac Serious Deverell." Shefford waggled his brows in jest, but he wasn't wrong. Isaac's father had wanted his son to be like him: serious and joyless.

"Isaac Serious Grim Deverell," Somerton added with a grin.

"Whatever your name, I'm glad you decided to attend the luncheon," Shefford said with genuine warmth.

Somerton brushed something from his sleeve. "I'm glad I didn't take your wager that he wouldn't."

"Is there nothing you won't bet on?" Isaac asked his host.

Shefford shrugged. "It seemed easy money. Except Somerton is more intelligent than his marks at Oxford indicate."

Rolling his eyes, Somerton gave Shefford a light shove. This was normal behavior amongst them. They teased Isaac about his moodiness. Then they made light of Somerton being unserious regarding his studies—and a great many other things. With Shefford, they needled him about his fear of marriage and the impending ultimatum to wed that was surely coming from his father. Isaac wasn't yet sure how they might poke fun at Price.

"Why you thought Somerton would fall for such nonsense is beyond me," Isaac said to Shefford. "It's no secret at all that I would rather be inside working than participating in this luncheon."

Isaac typically preferred to avoid social events entirely, but this one was small, and he could easily escape into the house under the guise of having work to do—which wasn't really a guise, because he *did* have work to do.

"But you do attend some social occasions," Price said. "I know I met you at a rout in London."

"You are correct," Isaac replied. "I allowed these idiots to drag me to several events this past year, starting with a soiree in Bath last autumn and at least *three* routs in London during the Season."

Somerton snorted. "You only agreed to those routs because you were on a mission to discuss certain business with gentlemen who were in attendance, not because you were hoping to enjoy yourself."

"That is precisely *how* I enjoy myself," Isaac said crisply. Working in the House of Lords and persuading others to his causes were the things he relished most.

"Promise you won't work too much while you're here." Shefford clapped him on the shoulder. "We've a great many activities planned for our week together. And please tell me you'll stay for the duration this time."

Isaac had arrived only the day before and typically stayed four, perhaps five, days. By then, he was more than ready to return to the solace of Wood End, the ancestral pile in Hampshire he'd inherited four years ago. "We'll see how long I can tolerate your company." He lifted the edge of his mouth.

"The Droxford Smirk," Somerton said with a laugh. "Closest thing we get to a smile."

"Is that true?" Price asked. He was relatively new to their group after Shefford had befriended him last Season, perhaps as an unconscious replacement for their dwindling numbers now that Wellesbourne and Bane were wed.

"He used to grin and guffaw," Shefford said, referring to when they'd first met, shortly after Isaac had arrived at Oxford. When his uncle, the baron at the time, had sent Isaac off to be educated, he'd experienced joy for the first time. However, he'd found a way to muck it up, just as his father had said he would. He'd advised Isaac that indulging in gaiety and happiness inevitably led to disappointment and disaster, which was precisely what had happened. Isaac had learned that lesson most painfully.

He directed the conversation back to something less personal. "What do you have planned beyond riding and playing billiards?" Those were their primary pursuits during their time at the Grove.

"I'm trying to arrange a boat to take us out to Steep Holm." Shefford referred to an island in the channel with many caves he wanted to explore.

Isaac would find a reason not to go. Though he'd grown up in a seaside village not too unlike Weston, he didn't like boats, and for good reason.

"Brilliant," Somerton said. "Wellesbourne will be game, I'm sure." He paused before adding, "It isn't quite the same here at the Grove without him."

The duke had wed last autumn, and instead of staying at the Grove this year, he'd leased a cottage for himself and his wife, who Isaac believed had arrived at the beginning of the month. Wellesbourne seemed quite changed since marrying, from what Isaac had observed, particularly during the London Season. While the duke had typically avoided Society events in the past to keep himself from the Marriage Mart, he now attended them with his wife. They appeared devoted to one another, as if they were truly in love. While pleased for them, Isaac understood that most people were not that lucky.

Shefford's brow creased. "I do wonder if he'll continue spending time with us here now that he's married. He will no doubt prefer to be with his duchess." He sounded resigned and a trifle disappointed.

"Marriage is not a death sentence," Somerton said. "We know you are averse to the idea, particularly given your parents' continued insistence that you wed soon." The more they pressed him, the more Shefford resisted.

Shefford became visibly uncomfortable, his shoulders twitching and his gaze moving away. "I'm not ready to be leg shackled. It's forever, you know."

Isaac was aware, just as he was of the duties that came along with marriage, namely siring children. He wasn't ready for that specifically and didn't know if he would ever be. He could never be a good father.

"You'll hear no argument from me," Isaac said. "Nor from any of us." He wasn't aware of Somerton or Price harboring a desire to wed.

"You are all fortunate to not have any family members pestering you," Shefford grumbled. "Just look what happened to Bane."

"Nothing happened *to* Bane," Isaac said. "He chose to wed."

Somerton arched a brow. "We don't know that. None of us have seen or spoken to him in months." That was true. Bane had stayed in northern England with his new wife, and none of them had been invited to celebrate their union. "Seems to me he married someone his parents chose."

"It certainly didn't come about naturally," Shefford said. "He didn't tell any of us about her. Not until after he'd already committed to the marriage."

While they weren't necessarily defending Bane, they were not as direct in their condemnation of their friend's behavior as Isaac had been. That was perhaps because they hadn't behaved as badly as—or worse than—Bane, as Isaac had done years ago. "I should like to know why he was carrying on with the Duchess of Wellesbourne's sister if he was already betrothed. It's no wonder he hasn't shown his face in Society since then."

"I doubt he had an ulterior motive," Somerton said. "Bane has simply never been able to ignore a pretty face."

Isaac sent him a dark look. "Do *not* defend him. Unless... Do you find his behavior acceptable?" He looked at both Somerton and Shefford, but not at Price since he didn't know Bane.

"Of course not." Shefford's brow furrowed. "However, I would be a hypocrite if I said I hadn't found myself in similar circumstances—allowing myself to be swept into a romantic moment that I should not have." He gave Isaac a pointed look. "We've all made missteps."

Isaac knew precisely to what Shefford was referring, and calling his transgressions "missteps" was a gross understatement. "Bane's behavior was egregious. He engaged in inappropriate activity with a young lady while apparently betrothed to someone else. That is simply inexcusable." As had been Isaac's actions.

Shefford exhaled. "I can't disagree. However, we don't know precisely what happened between him and Miss Barclay. I am not ready to terminate my friendship with a dear friend, though he's made it damned difficult with his silence. I stopped writing to him a few months ago. There was no point since he never responds."

"It's strange not having him here this year," Somerton said. "Hopefully, when Wellesbourne arrives, it will feel more like years past."

Shefford kicked a pebble off the patio. "Except Welles-bourne isn't staying here. I'm afraid we have only our nostalgia. Marriage is putting an end to our fun. Now you see why I'm avoiding it."

Somerton rolled his eyes, then looked to Price. "Don't listen to Sheff. He's being maudlin. There is plenty of fun to be had."

This perked up Shefford. "Yes, there is. Starting with today. Here comes my sister and her companion now."

Lady Minerva sauntered toward them, the lilac skirt of her gown swaying gently as she moved. Beautiful and charming, she would be married if she hadn't turned down a half dozen marriage proposals during the last Season, or so Shefford had told them.

Dark curls brushed her temples beneath her bonnet as her pale gray eyes focused on them. Her elegant brows lifted slightly as she regarded them. "I hope you have abandoned any plans to sabotage my luncheon."

"We're still finalizing them," Shefford said with a mischievous glint in his eye.

She gave her head a light shake. "I honestly don't know why I invited you."

Shefford grinned. "Because now that Wellesbourne and your friend are wed, we must socialize together."

Lady Minerva rolled her eyes. "Next time, I'll avoid including you just the same, especially if you ruin anything." She glanced toward Isaac. "I'd still invite *you*, despite your perpetual scowl. At least you won't try to add too much pepper to one of the dishes or water to the wine."

Shefford gasped as he raised his hand to his chest. "I would never defile wine in that manner!"

Lady Minerva looked at him with great skepticism. "I think you doth protest too much. The rest of the guests will be here soon. Perhaps you could see where you are sitting at the table?"

She and her companion, who'd come to their household as an orphan, moved in that direction. Somerton and Price drifted after them.

Isaac frowned at Shefford. "Am I really *always* scowling?" His friends liked to jest that he did, but hearing it from someone else felt somehow different.

Somerton lifted a shoulder. "Not always, but I remember when you *rarely* did it. I can scarcely reconcile the man you are now with the lad I met that first year at Oxford."

They'd started together at Christ Church College, and Isaac had been thrilled to meet young men his age and, more importantly, people who were generally happy and liked to laugh. After a childhood in which he was expected to be quiet and sedate, the environment had been heady.

Isaac had thrown himself into the social aspects of being with a group of students and away from his oppressive father. He'd drank too much, behaved obnoxiously on multiple occasions, and started a liaison with the laundress who came to his room to fetch his clothing.

Two years his senior, Mary was sweet and beautiful, with the most delightful laugh. Isaac had been entranced, then smitten, then head over arse in love with her.

"Why aren't you like that anymore?" Shefford asked.

Now Isaac definitely scowled. "Because that wasn't the man I wanted to be. And you know why." He was the only one who did, aside from Isaac's uncle and father.

Shefford's features creased. "That was over a decade ago. You need to stop blaming yourself. Your uncle took care of the matter. The girl was fine, better off than if you hadn't given her a child and necessitated her removal to a faraway place."

Just hearing someone else mention the family Isaac had

abandoned nearly tore him apart. The pain was still sharp all these years later. Isaac knew it would never go away, nor should it. He deserved to live with regret and shame the rest of his days.

And while Shefford's perspective might be true, that Mary's life was likely improved from that of a laundress, it didn't excuse Isaac's actions. He'd behaved like an absolute rogue, without care for Mary. He'd completely surrendered to indulgence and emotions, and the results had been utter ruin. He'd altered Mary's life and fathered a son who would never know his true father. The loss of the family Isaac could have had ate at him.

"I wanted to marry her," Isaac said quietly.

"I know." Shefford nodded faintly. "But that would not have worked. Not for you, and not for the laundress. You came from completely different classes."

"I wasn't even heir to the barony then." At that time, there were multiple people in front of Isaac: his cousin who was the baron's son, another uncle who was the middle son between the baron and Isaac's father, who'd died a few years later on a campaign in Spain, and of course Isaac's own father. Though Isaac couldn't imagine his father, a devout rector, becoming a baron.

"Still, your position was such that you could not marry a laundress." Shefford grimaced. "I know how that sounds, as though we inhabit some pompous, superior space."

"Isn't that precisely what you are saying?" Isaac asked without a hint of irony.

"I was trying to help you then, and I would do it again," Shefford said firmly. "You were seventeen with no means to support a household. She was settled in a nice village as a widow. It's highly likely she wed and has been living a secure life with her family for nigh on a decade. That should make you happy. Or at least relieved."

He wasn't sure what it made him. Isaac had gone to that village—against his uncle's advisement—to see if Mary and their child were indeed living the life they deserved. However, he couldn't find them and assumed they'd ended up somewhere else, not that he'd asked his uncle, for then he would have had to reveal that he'd gone looking.

As much as he longed to know they were safe and well, he accepted his uncle's assurances that they were. Anything else would be too heartbreaking to contemplate.

And he struggled with enough sorrow, as he had to work on not dreaming of the life that could have been his. Regardless of what Shefford said about not having the means to support himself, Isaac would have loved to be the one to care for his wife and child. In any case, that life *hadn't* been his, and he'd learned to not even want such a life. He didn't deserve it.

Before Isaac could head toward the table, Shefford added, "You should also relinquish whatever vow you made to yourself when all that happened."

Turning back to face Shefford, Isaac gave him a cool stare. "What are you talking about?"

"You can't deny—not to me—that you completely changed after the girl was sent away and the situation resolved. You no longer did anything for amusement, at least not in the same way." Shefford stepped closer, his dark blue eyes moving over Isaac's features as if he were trying to discern something. "You've loosened up a little over the years, but you don't drink to excess, nor do you gamble, and you do not indulge your most basic needs, not even at the Rogue's Den, as the rest of us do. You're a bloody saint."

A saint? A man who'd ruined a young woman, got her with child, and left her and the babe to fend for themselves was a saint?

Isaac glared at his friend, who'd made a rare miscalculation and overstepped. "You've no idea what I do or don't do at the Rogue's Den or anywhere else." If Isaac were truly a saint, he would take a true vow of celibacy and deny himself all pleasures of the flesh. Instead, he merely abstained from intercourse in order to avoid fathering another child. He wouldn't take that risk again.

Shefford looked at him with concern. "You are hard on yourself, Drox, and you needn't be. You deserve joy just like the rest of us."

"I'll ask you to keep your counsel to yourself," Isaac said coldly. "I live a comfortable life that is apparently my birthright. I don't need to laugh or gamble or delight in stealing a kiss from some widow in an alcove at a ball. That is *your* life. Leave me to mine." Isaac refused to succumb to the roguery that lurked beneath the wall he'd erected around himself.

Shefford's nostrils flared, but he didn't respond because the other guests arrived just then. Wellesbourne came from the house with his wife, and they were accompanied by two other young women—Price's sister and Somerton's cousin, Miss Penrose.

Moving away from Isaac, Shefford went to greet them.

Isaac's gaze was drawn to Miss Penrose. Petite in stature, she possessed delicate features and warm brown hair. Some of the strands reminded him of dark honeycomb. She was dressed in a cheerful yellow gown that perfectly matched her bright smile. Looking at her, he saw nothing but light and found himself wanting to drift toward it. She was like the flowers his bees at Wood End buzzed toward, an attraction that could not be ignored. Which he found odd, for he'd met her last year, at least, but barely recalled her.

Wellesbourne came abreast of him, smiling. "Good to see you, Droxford. I keep meaning to ask if you wouldn't mind giving me scowling lessons."

The query was made affably, but after his very recent discussion about scowling with Shefford, Isaac made a concerted effort to keep from scowling. "Did Sheff tell you to say that?"

"Er, no. I was joking. Mostly." Wellesbourne shrugged. "Scowling is a useful expression. However, I am not very accomplished."

"Have you not had reason to scowl?"

"I have always found it easier to smile," Wellesbourne said without a hint of irony.

"And you do it so well," Isaac said, glancing toward Miss Penrose who was still smiling quite beautifully. He averted his gaze from her and remained on the periphery as everyone began to mingle.

When, he wondered, would it be too soon to excuse himself?

CHAPTER 3

They were to mingle for a short while before the luncheon, so Tamsin chatted with Minerva and her companion, Miss Ellis Dangerfield. The oldest of them, at twenty-five, Ellis had come to live with Min's family when she was nine. Somewhat reserved, with intelligent eyes and pretty blonde hair, she'd been orphaned, having lost both parents to illness. Her family had, at some point, been close to the Dukes of Henlow, and the current duke had taken Ellis in. She'd been Min's companion ever since.

"Mrs. Ogilvie isn't attending?" Tamsin referred to the ancient woman who acted as Min's chaperone outside London when Min's mother wasn't present. She was Min's mother's great-aunt's cousin or some other far-flung relation.

Ellis shook her head in response. "This is when she takes her first nap. She reasoned that Min didn't need a chaperone since the duke and duchess are here."

Tamsin found it passing strange that Ellis never seemed to be included in the chaperonage, but she was not on the Marriage Mart. Still, as companion to Min, she comported herself with the utmost integrity and propriety. Tamsin wondered what Ellis would do when Min wed.

"Look at Droxford standing by himself, aloof as always," Min said. "I have gathered he does not care for social gatherings."

Tamsin noted the frown lines crossing his forehead beneath the brim of his hat, though he wasn't exactly frowning. "Do you know why?"

"Not specifically," Min replied. "He is fairly serious and very committed to his work—running his estate and sitting in the Lords. Sheff has said that because Droxford never expected to be the baron, he sees his responsibility as a privilege and does his best to preserve the legacy he's inherited."

"Perhaps he's just uncomfortable in social situations," Tamsin said. "I'll try to put him at ease." Smiling, she made her way toward the baron.

He was tall with broad shoulders, his clothing as dark as his expression. Thick brows crested his tumultuous gray eyes. They somehow managed to be simultaneously cool and smoldering.

His gaze met hers. The frown lines did not disperse.

"Good afternoon, Lord Droxford," Tamsin said.

In fact, the lines now deepened. "Are you here to prod me to smile?"

"No, but would that be bad?" When he did not respond except to slightly narrow his eyes at her, she continued, "I understand you don't care for social occasions."

"Typically, I do not. I was thinking of going into the house. I've correspondence that requires my attention." He shifted his focus toward the door, and Tamsin moved to block his view.

"Please don't. Min has worked very hard to prepare this luncheon, and she'll be cross if there's an empty seat at the table." Tamsin lowered her voice. "It will also give Sheff something to tease her about."

The baron's gray eyes widened slightly. "I hadn't considered that." He exhaled. "I've no wish to cause disharmony. I suppose I must stay."

Tamsin smiled. "That's the spirit. What is it about social occasions that you dislike?"

"The social part."

His answer was both dour and wry. Tamsin felt the urge to giggle. "I think you possess a sense of humor, my lord. How disarming."

He narrowed one eye at her, his expression becoming skeptical. "Are you flirting with me, Miss Penrose? You should know that I do not flirt."

"I'd heard you were not a rogue like your friends, but to answer your question, I was not flirting. I simply enjoy people who know how to laugh."

"That is not me," he said darkly. "Perhaps you haven't heard that I don't laugh. Ever."

"Never ever?"

He shook his head.

"Then you can't possibly be a rogue. They tend to laugh as well as flirt."

"That is your definition of a rogue? A man who laughs and flirts? Forgive me if I disagree. A rogue is far more dangerous than that."

Dangerous? Tamsin supposed that was true. She was just surprised to hear that from a man whose friends' behavior was, arguably, the definition of roguery. "A rogue is also someone who flouts convention and Society's rules, who perhaps gambles too much or pursues the companionship of women to the detriment of his reputation, who oversteps when it comes to young ladies and appropriate behavior.

Moreover, someone who lacks integrity and decency. Your friend Bane is a prime example of a rogue."

Droxford looked away from her, the muscles of his throat working. "I'm not sure Bane is still my friend. You are correct that he is a rogue. Some might even say a blackguard. What he did to Miss Barclay was unforgiveable."

Tamsin was surprised at the vehemence in Droxford's tone. He'd also disagreed with the notion that rogues were simply men who flirted and laughed. He clearly had an opinion on the matter. "You feel quite strongly."

"I was raised with a very distinct sense of right and wrong. Bane's behavior was decidedly wrong."

"It's settled, then," Tamsin declared. "You are most definitely not a rogue." She looked into his eyes and gave him a brilliant smile.

For the barest moment, something flashed across his face. It wasn't quite surprise, but something with a grim edge. Horror or revulsion? "I daresay you do not know me well enough to make that assessment."

His tone was cold, and his features shuttered. Yes, that was an apt description, for looking at the baron made her feel as though she regarded someone who held himself apart —and not just physically as he'd done by standing away from everyone. Did he think himself a rogue?

She had a keen and sudden desire to pull him forward into the light. Would he come?

"You can't be a rogue because my friends and I do not associate with rogues. Well, the other gentlemen notwithstanding," she said with a grimace as she glanced toward her cousin in particular. "I'm afraid we must associate with them because they are related to us. It doesn't mean we approve of their behavior. In fact, we do our best to avoid it. We even wrote down rules to keep us from being drawn in by a rogue as Pandora was by Bane." Tamsin cocked her head to the side. "Can you imagine if she'd actually married Bane? I hate that she was ruined, but she and I have agreed she's likely better off. Could there be any fate worse than marrying a rogue?"

Droxford stared at her a long moment. "No, I suppose not."

"I saw that we are seated next to one another," she said, deciding it best to direct their conversation to brighter territory rather than the topic of roguery. "I'm looking forward to deepening our acquaintance." She meant it. While she'd wanted to put him at ease, she now found she wished to go a step further and bring him cheer.

He studied her a moment. "Now I remember you from last year. And the year before. You are always irrationally cheerful."

Tamsin laughed. "Irrationally? Goodness. No one has said that to me before. I'd like to think I've a reason to be cheerful."

"And what is that?" Droxford asked, seeming genuinely curious. "Is it just that I've managed to be around you on your happiest days, or are you always like this?"

"I'm always like this, I'm afraid." She sighed. "Since I was a child. My grandfather persistently encouraged me to find joy in every single day, because each one is a gift."

"You must have had a lovely childhood," he said flatly.

"It wasn't perfect," she said, of course not mentioning her mother's abandonment. "Which was why it was important for me to generate happiness from within."

He stared at her as if she'd grown a second nose. Tamsin lifted her hand to her face. "Have I sprouted a wart?" she asked.

Before he could answer, Min announced that it was time to take their seats.

Droxford offered Tamsin his arm. "May I escort you?"

"Thank you." She placed her hand on his sleeve and felt an instant jolt of energy. It was as if a bright warmth had leapt from him to her, which seemed ridiculous since he was the opposite of bright. Nevertheless, the sensation made her want to lean into him.

The baron held her chair while she sat then took the place next to her where he was assigned. Min, who was at one end of the table, was on Droxford's other side, and Tamsin's cousin Somerton was across from him.

Footmen poured wine and brought the first course. Min looked between Droxford and Somerton. "I hear my brother is planning an excursion to Steep Holm."

"The island in the channel?" Tamsin asked.

Somerton nodded. "Yes. We're to go the day after tomorrow."

"I want to come along," Min said. "However, Sheff will likely say ladies aren't invited. I don't suppose the two of you would convince him to include us?" She smiled prettily at both gentlemen.

Tamsin noted the furrows in the baron's brow. Leaning toward him, she whispered, "Do you not want to ask Sheff?" Perhaps he was annoyed that Min wanted to go. Did he prefer to ensure it was a gentlemen-only trip?

"I have no problem speaking with him, though I can't imagine why any of you would want to go. Sheff intends to explore caves."

He hadn't kept his voice low, and Min reacted with exuberance. "Exploring caves sounds exciting!"

Droxford shrugged. "Perhaps because I grew up near caves in Dunster, I am less enthusiastic."

"I can understand that." Tamsin wondered if it was more, however. Instead of seeming uninterested, he appeared slightly agitated. Or perhaps she was making assumptions. She found herself studying him rather intently. Something about him was most alluring. Perhaps it was the fact that he didn't smile and didn't care for social gatherings. Or that he had opinions on what it meant to be a rogue. She found him fascinating.

A few minutes later, the plates were exchanged for the primary course, succulent partridge with several vegetables including parsnips and peas. Tamsin looked over at Droxford. "Since you grew up in Dunster, you must enjoy the sea."

"I do."

"I do as well," she said. "I am from St. Austell."

"I thought your accent was Cornish," he said.

"I suppose Somerton doesn't mention me." She flicked a glance toward her cousin, who met her gaze.

Somerton had heard what she said and cocked his head slightly. "We do not discuss ladies to whom we are related."

"I don't discuss ladies at all," Droxford said with a faint glower directed at Somerton, who grinned in response.

"Drox is more reserved than the rest of us," Somerton said.

"To his credit." Min lifted her wineglass in Droxford's direction.

The baron picked up his own glass, and at that precise moment, a pea hit him in the eye. He flinched, and his wine splashed across Tamsin's sleeve and onto her bodice. She gasped as some of the liquid landed on her bare flesh above the top of her gown.

"What the devil," Droxford said loudly as he rubbed at his eye.

"My apologies!" Shefford called from the other end of the table. "You were not my intended target. I really should have practiced more," he added in a lower but still discernible tone.

Min scowled at him down the length of the table. "I'm sure you meant to hit me."

"It was just a pea," Shefford said defensively.

"You hit Droxford in the eye!" Min cried.

"And caused me to spill my wine on Miss Penrose," Droxford added with clear irritation.

Tamsin mopped at her gown with her napkin. Surprisingly, the baron reached over and began to apply his own napkin, not to her sleeve, but to the skin above her bodice.

She snapped her gaze to his as another odd sensation rippled through her. His gray eyes were as storm filled as they'd been earlier, and the heat was still there. At the moment, there was nothing cold about him at all. She felt suddenly breathless as he dabbed the cloth on her bare flesh. Not just any flesh, but an area that was scandalously close to her bosom. Did he not realize?

Perhaps horrifyingly, Tamsin did not find herself jerking away.

"What are you doing, Drox?" Somerton demanded.

The baron pulled his hand away. "Forgive me. I didn't think."

Tamsin continued to dab at her gown, and a footman brought her fresh linen while taking the soiled napkin away. "It's quite all right. You were just trying to help." She smiled at him, not wanting him to feel badly.

"This is Sheff's fault," Min declared. "What a juvenile thing to do. And you've ruined Tamsin's dress."

Shefford's features pressed into a brief grimace as he regarded Tamsin. "My apologies, Miss Penrose."

"You should send one back at him," Droxford murmured to her. "Or I can."

Tamsin shot him a look of surprise, then suppressed a giggle. He *did* have a sense of humor and wasn't at all as gloomy as he seemed. "I'm afraid I wouldn't hit my target either. I'm woefully unpracticed in pea flinging," she said softly.

Droxford's lips twitched. It wasn't a smile, but it was defi-
nite amusement. Suddenly, Tamsin's chest felt incredibly
light.

"Do you want to change into one of my gowns?" Min
offered to Tamsin.

"I think I'll be all right. It's not that wet." She'd finished
dabbing at her bodice and had moved on to her sleeve.

"Ow!" Shefford exclaimed.

Tamsin swung her head about to see the earl rubbing his
forehead. He glowered toward the baron, but only briefly
before inclining his head.

"Well aimed, Droxford," Shefford said, lowering his hand
to pick up his wineglass. He offered a toast. "To the baron
who brandishes a spoon with terrifying dexterity."

Everyone lifted their glasses and toasted Droxford.

"But was a parsnip necessary?" Shefford asked in exasper-
ation. "I only used a pea."

"I simply grabbed what was most convenient," Droxford
said with a shrug.

Tamsin slid a sly smile toward the man beside her. From
what she could discern, he was not as somber as he appeared.
She looked forward to proving that theory.

∼

*W*hile pelting Shefford with a parsnip had been
most satisfying, Isaac spent the remainder of
the meal wishing he could go back in time and not accost
Miss Penrose with his napkin. He knew better than to touch
a lady inappropriately. He'd never touched a woman without
her consent.

Miss Penrose had likely changed her mind about him
and decided he was, in fact, a rogue. Good. It was better
that she knew who he was at his core and stayed away

from him. She was far too sweet to want to be in his company.

Lady Minerva stood as the meal concluded and announced there would be bowling. The guests began rising from the table and moving toward the lawn, where footmen had set up the game.

Isaac moved to hold Miss Penrose's chair. Standing, she faced him and offered her thanks.

"Droxford, I do hope you're going to take Tamsin for a short promenade so you can apologize," Somerton said as he stood. Was he teasing? Or was he angry with Isaac for inadvertently groping his cousin?

Somerton would have every right to be upset with him.

"Of course," Isaac said with a solemn nod. He'd been hoping to avoid Miss Penrose for she provoked something odd within him. Something he preferred to ignore. But he did owe her an apology. He turned to her and asked, "Will you promenade with me?"

"That would be lovely." She put her hand on his sleeve once more, and as earlier when he'd escorted her to the table, his body reacted with a flash of heat. That something he wanted to ignore was attraction. He hadn't experienced it in over a decade.

They walked from the patio to a path that wound through the formal garden. Isaac immediately launched into his apology. "I deeply regret my actions earlier," he said. "I don't know what possessed me to touch you in such an inappropriate manner. I hope you are not too angry with me."

"I'm not angry at all. It takes a great deal more than that to pique my temper." She tipped her head and looked over at him. "I am not even sure I have a temper. At least not a bad one."

He had no difficulty imagining that. "I am still horrified by my behavior. I do hope you will forgive me."

Miss Penrose put her other hand on his sleeve so that she was clasping him with both. It was somehow more intimate. And distracting. "There is nothing to forgive," she said. "You were merely trying to help, and in the moment, that seemed more important to you than propriety, which I applaud."

"Thank you." He tried not to think of how she was now closer to him with both hands on his person. "I suspected Shefford would do something to sabotage his sister's luncheon, but I didn't think he'd stoop to a food fight."

Miss Penrose paused and turned toward him. This brought them even closer together, and Isaac's breath stuttered, then came faster. "How is your eye anyway? I should have been tending to *you*. An injury is far worse than a sullied gown." She stood on her toes and looked into his left eye. "Does it pain you?"

He faced her, and she released one of her hands from his sleeve, much to his dismay. "No. It stung for a moment, but then I was more concerned with your ruined gown." His gaze flicked toward her bodice, which had dried. Though the wine had been pale, there was still a faint discoloration on the pretty golden-yellow silk. He wondered if he should plant Shefford a facer for ruining her gown.

Too late, he realized he'd been staring at her chest for far too long. And not because he'd been observing her breasts. Though, now that he looked at them, he had to admit they were enchantingly high and round. Blast, he was becoming worse than a rogue.

He jerked his gaze up to her face, then pivoted to propel them forward along the path once more. "I hope your gown isn't permanently stained."

"I'm sure it will be fine. It's seen several seasons and has survived a great many mishaps."

Isaac had little knowledge of fashion, so he couldn't have said if the gown was à la mode. "Has it?"

"Actually, I do not have occasion to wear it often. I spend most of my time at home or visiting neighbors and people in town. In St. Austell, I mean. This gown is for more formal gatherings, and I rarely attend any."

He found that interesting since he perceived her to be someone who enjoyed being social, unlike himself. Perhaps they were at odds—she wished to be more social and wasn't and he preferred to do less. Unfortunately, his position in the House of Lords required him to attend events that he otherwise wouldn't.

And yet here he was in Weston, as he was every year, with friends. It seemed he didn't dislike being with others as much as he thought. Rather, it was this specific group of people and the fact that it was a small gathering.

Miss Penrose also didn't hurt matters. Indeed, she improved them.

"Why is it you don't attend more formal events?" he asked.

She lifted a shoulder. "St. Austell is small. There isn't much of a society there. Mostly, I take care of my father's household. It's just him and me—and our retainers, of course. But we don't have a great many of those. Penrose House isn't large. I do love to spend time on the beach where I collect shells. That is a solitary endeavor, however."

"Why? Is there no one who will accompany you? I would." Had he offered to spend time with someone he'd just met? Isaac didn't quite understand what was happening here.

"How heartening to learn," she said, her eyes sparkling. Isaac was absolutely enchanted by her. He could stare at her all day. "What of the excursion to Steep Holm? By your own admission, you weren't enthused. Would you rather the ladies didn't come?"

"Not at all." He exhaled. "Honestly, *I'd* rather not go."

They'd almost completed their garden circuit. Isaac would prefer to go around again than bowl.

"Because you aren't interested in seeing the caves?" she asked.

"Actually, I don't care for boats." Had he actually admitted that out loud? What sort of spell had she cast upon him to coax forth his secrets as well as provoke him to desire her company?

"Is there a particular reason?" Her expression was so sympathetic, so caring, that for some reason he couldn't identify, he was going to reveal one of his secrets, which he'd never done.

"When I was a boy, I assisted a fisherman in Dunster where I grew up. I didn't really like being on the boat—it made me queasy—but my father insisted I work to build my character."

"And did it?" she asked with a sincerity that surprised him.

"I'm not certain, but I suppose everything we do in our youth supports that."

"Is it that the boat will make you queasy, then?" She looked at him with such care that he blurted the truth, which he'd never shared with anyone.

"The water was especially rough one day, and we capsized. I was afraid I would drown." Thinking of it now, he felt as though he couldn't draw a full breath.

Her grip on his arm tightened but not painfully. "I'm so sorry. You needn't go to Steep Holm."

"That may be, but I don't spend a great deal of time in Weston, not even the full week the other gentlemen typically stay, and Shefford is campaigning most strongly that I go."

"If he is a good friend, he'll respect your desire not to accompany them."

"I'll consider it." He couldn't help but feel encouraged by

her support. Shefford was a good friend, but Isaac suspected he'd made another friend today in Miss Penrose. "Will you go if the ladies are invited?"

"It does sound exciting, I admit." She cast him an eager smile. "I haven't been out on the sea, if you can believe that. I do wonder if I would be queasy too."

"You should go," he said, despite thinking it would have been nice to go shell collecting on the beach with her instead. "Everyone should experience being on the sea at least once."

"I'll consider it," she echoed with a teasing smile. "If we're even invited, though I won't discount Min's abilities of persuasion, even with her brother. They have an odd relationship. I know they love each other very much, but they also tease each other ruthlessly. I suppose I don't understand because I don't have siblings. Do you?"

"No, I do not have siblings either. But if I did, I would not behave the way Sheff and Lady Minerva do."

"It's easy for us to say as spectators," she said with a light laugh. She sent him a sidelong glance. "I have a question for you. If the pea hadn't hit you in the eye, would you have found Sheff's prank amusing?"

"Doubtful. I haven't ever cared for such antics."

"But your return volley was most excellent. I would have guessed you had experience with flinging food." Her eyes were alight with mischief, and Isaac was falling deeper into her entrancement.

Again, he revealed a secret, or a long-buried truth. "I may have participated in a food fight or two at Christ Church—the college I attended at Oxford where I met Sheff."

"Aha! I knew it," she crowed. "Perhaps someday you can teach me how to launch a parsnip."

He felt the urge to smile, which rarely happened. "Why? Do you plan to begin a career of pelting people with vegetables?"

She giggled. "No. I suppose I don't really need to learn." She sighed in mock disappointment as they reached the patio. "It's a shame you don't stay very long at the Grove. You are most diverting. Can I convince you stay longer? At least until the other gentlemen leave?"

She wanted him to stay? He was used to Sheff and Somerton trying to convince him to remain, and they were never successful. Miss Penrose, however, might be able to persuade him. He found he was very much looking forward to seeing her again.

But no. He couldn't want that. What would be the point? He had no interest in courtship or marriage. He was busy with Wood End and in the House of Lords. There was no time or space for a woman.

"I'll consider—"

She cut him off. "Don't say it." Then she laughed. "You really are the most sober gentleman. I shall take it as a personal challenge to coax a smile from you before you depart. I'll have to work quickly in case you leave after the soiree at the Weston Hotel."

Isaac wasn't aware of a soiree. He nearly groaned. More people. More socializing. And probably dancing, which he loathed. "When is that?"

"The day after the trip to Steep Holm."

Lady Minerva called out to them, "Tamsin, aren't you going to come and bowl?"

"Yes!" She pivoted toward Isaac once more. "Let's join them."

"You go. I've correspondence to complete."

"Do you really, or have you simply reached your limit for socializing?"

The truth was that he could have stayed and talked with Miss Penrose all day. That was not an option, however, as they would need to go join the others or else raise eyebrows for their behavior. Indeed, he was likely to sustain a great deal of teasing from his friends about this lengthy promenade. Isaac didn't do such things.

Why on earth was he doing it now, then?

"Both, I'm afraid," he said in response to her clever question. She saw him in a way others did not. It was both wonderful and terrifying.

She took her hand from his arm. "Don't be afraid," she said softly, her eyes dazzling him with a bright heat. "Be joyful. If you want to go work, go work and be glad for it. If you choose solitude to quiet your mind, or whatever the reason, do so because it makes you happy."

Giving him a brilliant smile, she turned and skipped away toward the lawn.

It took Isaac a moment to recall what he was doing or even where he was. The spell Miss Penrose had cast lingered, and he suspected it would for some time.

CHAPTER 4

*T*he following day, Tamsin gathered with her friends in the sitting room they used at the Weston Hotel. With wide windows that overlooked the ocean some half mile away, the room was decorated in pale blues with ivory accents and had a cozy fireplace that they used from time to time, even in August. They'd begun meeting here four years ago, and the hotel owner knew that for the month of August, they would occupy the space every afternoon.

They drank tea, ate scrumptious cakes, watched the ocean in the distance, and, most importantly, talked about everything. Today's conversation was, as expected, focused mostly on yesterday's luncheon, which one of their number—Pandora—had not attended.

Though Pandora had recovered somewhat from the scandal of her and Bane's compromising situation, she still preferred to avoid social gatherings. In this case, she was avoiding Bane's friends, whom she had no desire to spend time with, her brother-in-law Wellesbourne notwithstanding. He had reformed, and Pandora had embraced him as family. Wellesbourne had also done all he could to help Pandora last year after the scandal. While she wasn't yet entirely welcome in society, she wasn't given the cut direct. Though she had been, just not recently.

Tamsin understood Pandora's hesitation to expose herself to others. She'd been completely in love with Bane and had expected they would wed. Then he'd broken her heart into bits and married someone else. In Tamsin's opinion, Pandora was perfectly entitled to her bitterness. Tamsin just hoped it would continue to ease in time.

Min looked around at everyone after setting down her teacup. "I've been working on convincing Sheff to allow us to accompany them to Steep Holm tomorrow. I do think my offer of organizing an extensive picnic may have won him over. While he could simply ask the cook to prepare one, he thankfully—and unsurprisingly—hadn't thought of that."

"I don't know that I want to go," Persephone said. "But Acton does, so I will try and hope I don't become ill."

That reminded Tamsin of Droxford, not that he'd been far from her mind. She'd thought about him a great deal since yesterday. She wondered what he'd decided regarding the excursion. Would the lure of a delicious picnic persuade him to face his fears?

Not that he needed to. He'd suffered a terrible ordeal in his youth, and Tamsin couldn't blame him if he didn't want to risk repeating it.

"Pandora, will you consider coming?" Gwen asked hopefully.

Pandora shook her head. "While it sounds exciting, I am not yet ready to spend that much time with those who would still call Bane friend."

"Droxford does not, if that helps to know," Tamsin said. "He even suggested Bane is a blackguard."

Min looked at her with great curiosity. "You and he took a lengthy promenade yesterday."

"Did you?" Pandora asked, also with avid interest.

"He invited me to promenade so he could apologize again for spilling his wine on me." That mishap had already been discussed, and Pandora had heard about it after the luncheon from Persephone, as she was residing with her sister and Wellesbourne at their cottage.

"It wasn't his fault," Min said with a brief glower. "My brother was entirely to blame."

"Sheff apologized to me as well," Tamsin said, recalling his very sincere regret at ruining her gown. Though her gown wasn't, in fact, ruined because her grandmother's housekeeper was incredibly skilled at cleaning just about anything.

"I'm glad to hear it," Pandora said. "So, your promenade with Droxford wasn't eventful?"

Eventful, no. Interesting, yes. Tamsin had found the baron incredibly intriguing as well as attractive. She'd been disappointed when he said he wouldn't be staying long. "I found him charming, actually."

"Droxford?" Ellis asked. "Forgive me, but I've come to know him somewhat the past few years he's stayed at the Grove—as well as one can since he is so reserved—and charming is not a word I would use to describe him. And I mean no offense by that. He seems perfectly…fine."

"Perhaps he revealed a part of himself to Tamsin that he doesn't to anyone else," Gwen suggested. "I imagine he's looking for a wife, or will be at some point." Her inference was clear, at least to Tamsin.

"He made a point of telling me he doesn't stay in Weston long," Tamsin said. "We had a friendly promenade and nothing more. In any case, I've news to share if you want to discuss potential courtship and marriage." She paused as they all stared at her with rapt attention. "My father wrote to inform me that he has a suitor in mind for me to wed. Before you ask, I do not know who it is."

Pandora wrinkled her nose. "Why am I not surprised he left out vital information? He barely spoke to you while I was visiting."

"That's not true," Tamsin said in defense of her father. "Of course he spoke to me. He just did so privately." That he'd allowed Tamsin to have a guest for so long had been remarkable. Her father didn't generally care to be around people, particularly those he didn't know. The only people he spent any measurable time with were other scholars who shared his passions.

"Even so, he didn't seem terribly interested in what you were doing," Pandora continued. "I don't mean to disparage him. I'm just making an observation."

She wasn't wrong. Tamsin's father was dedicated to his work. He always had been. Which meant Tamsin was used to his behavior and didn't feel slighted. "It is the way things are," she said without rancor. "He works too much, and I don't mind." At least he was present. He hadn't left like her mother had.

"I do wonder who this suitor is," Pandora mused. "Beware of matchmaking parents. Look what ours tried to do to Persephone." She sent her sister a half smile.

Persephone rolled her eyes. "First they tried to marry me to Acton, and when I refused because he was a rake, they moved on to Mother's cousin's son." A shudder passed across her shoulders as she looked toward Tamsin. "I will hope your father is not trying to marry you off for his own reasons, as my parents did. Rather, that he has your best interests in mind."

"I'm sure it's the latter." Her father had no self-serving reasons to see her wed. Indeed, he liked having Tamsin at Penrose House, and he'd certainly discouraged courtship thus far. It was that last part that made Tamsin skeptical. Why was he seeking to marry her off now?

"Do you even want to wed?" Min asked. "You've never talked about it."

Tamsin cocked her head. "I hadn't given it much thought until my father's letter. I am not in a position to have a Season like all of you." She sent a sympathetic look to Pandora, who would not have a Season either after what happened last year. "I imagined I'd live in St. Austell, probably as a spinster. Or perhaps a handsome gentleman would miraculously sweep into town on a white horse and carry me away to his Cornish castle." She made the comment in jest, but since learning her father wanted her to wed, she'd begun to imagine something similar. Her ideas were too fanciful, but she enjoyed them nonetheless.

"But what about a family?" Persephone asked softly. "Now that I'm to be a mother, I didn't realize how much I would want that."

Motherhood was not something Tamsin had contemplated at all. Was that because her own mother had been such a disappointment? Tamsin had few pleasant memories of the woman who'd left when she was just eight years old. She'd read to Tamsin and occasionally sang to her, and that was about all Tamsin remembered. The rest was a blurry haze in which Tamsin felt her mother's unhappiness, but didn't recall specific memories.

"Honestly, I hadn't considered motherhood either," Tamsin said. "I realize that must sound strange. However, I was not raised to think that marriage and motherhood were my only future." And for that, Tamsin was actually grateful. But now that she *was* thinking about it, she couldn't deny that a family of her own was tempting. Perhaps she could be the mother she'd always wanted.

"What will you do if this potential suitor isn't to your

liking?" Pandora asked. "Perhaps he's a rogue." Her lips pursed briefly in distaste.

"What will you do if he *is* to your liking?" Gwen asked, waggling her dark brows, which prompted everyone to laugh.

Tamsin was hoping for that very thing. The notion of marriage and family had become very appealing. "That wouldn't be the worst thing," Tamsin said with a smile.

Min glanced toward the window. "Speaking of rogues, my brother and his merry band of scoundrels are playing Battledore and Shuttlecock on the lawn."

Tamsin diverted her attention to see four of the gentlemen were playing while the fifth stood and watched. It did not surprise her that the one not wielding a racket was Droxford. "I don't think Droxford is a rogue. Or a scoundrel." She glanced around the room. "Unless being reserved is roguish behavior?"

"Certainly not," Ellis said. "And neither is lacking charm, though now I feel badly for saying that I wouldn't describe him as charming," she added sheepishly.

Tamsin gave her an encouraging smile. "Don't feel badly. I think if you asked him to describe himself, he would likely not use the word *charming* either." Was that true? Could she have discerned that from just their single conversation, even if it had been lengthy?

"I would agree with that assessment," Min said. "Given how hard he apparently works, I doubt he has time to be a rogue." She stood abruptly. "Come, let us interrupt their game to ensure they'll include us on the excursion tomorrow."

They all rose and began to leave the sitting room. Except Pandora. Tamsin lingered to speak with her, standing before Pandora's chair. "You won't come?"

Pandora exhaled. "I suppose I should. I can't hold a grudge forever."

"I don't think you're holding a grudge. I think it's difficult for you to be around people who are—or were—close to Bane. I know how deeply you'd come to care for him and how badly he hurt you."

Pandora looked up at Tamsin. "It was all a lie, and I was such a fool. I know what people must think of me. I know you all don't look at me and see an imbecile or a pariah, but I'll wager they do." She inclined her head toward the windows.

"I doubt that. Droxford was most critical of Bane. Perhaps they all are. You could give them a chance?"

"I'll think about it." Pandora settled back in her chair. "For now, I'm fine sitting here. You go."

"You should go to Steep Holm tomorrow," Tamsin said. "I can see how much it intrigues you."

Pandora gave her a warm smile. "I'll think about that too. Thank you, Tam. You're a dear friend."

Blowing her a kiss, Tamsin hurried from the sitting room to join the others outside. When she arrived at the lawn, the game had halted, and everyone stood conversing.

Shefford was speaking, and while he primarily looked at his sister, he seemed to be addressing all the ladies. "After great consideration, I've decided you can come tomorrow. We will meet at the dock at half ten. Earlier than we are usually about, but the departure time was set by the ship's captain based on the tide."

Min smiled widely, the blaze of victory in her eyes. "I'll make sure our splendid picnic lunch is ready."

"Now, may we get back to our game?" Gwen's brother asked.

"Definitely." Shefford headed back onto the lawn.

Before joining them, Somerton stepped toward Tamsin. "You coming tomorrow?"

"I'd like to. It sounds invigorating."

"I can drive us to the dock in Grandmama's gig," he offered.

"She'll love that we're going somewhere together," Tamsin said with a smile. Inclining her head toward the lawn where the net stood, she asked, "Are you winning?"

"Yes, Price is devilishly good. We drew blades of grass to form teams, and I was initially disappointed not to be paired with Sheff, but Price is better." He waggled his brows. "Lucky me."

"Why isn't Droxford playing?"

"He will in the next set. We just have uneven numbers. I suppose we'll need to recruit another rogue." He sniggered.

Tamsin gave his arm a light, playful shove. "How about you find someone who isn't a rogue? What you need is another Droxford."

Somerton eyed the baron. "How do you know he *isn't* a rogue?" He winked at her before dashing toward the lawn just as Shefford called his name with impatience.

Was Somerton teasing her, or was the baron hiding a secret roguish personality that the ladies didn't see? She cast a surreptitious glance toward Droxford, only to find him staring straight at her.

Again, she wondered how a man who behaved so coolly and was regarded as reticent could look at her with such heat. Tamsin felt his perusal in the deepest part of her belly. In perhaps an area that wasn't her belly at all.

She moved toward him as if pulled by some invisible force. She noted that he was also walking in her direction. Were they somehow magnetized?

"Good afternoon, Miss Penrose."

"Good afternoon, my lord. Have you decided whether you will go on tomorrow's excursion?"

He clasped his hands behind his back, facing the lawn as the Battledore and Shuttlecock match resumed. "I plan to remain at the Grove. I've work to do, and that is a better use of my time. And you?"

"I'm going along." However, disappointment dampened her enthusiasm a little. His dedication to his work above all else brought her father to mind. Though she understood, she couldn't deny that his lack of attention—or affection—had been disheartening at times. "Is it the work that's keeping you behind or what happened in your youth?" She laughed softly. "I'm being terribly intrusive. You must tell me to mind my own business, if you like."

"Your questions don't bother me." He fixed his gaze on hers. "You are unlike anyone I've ever met, Miss Penrose."

Tamsin's insides fluttered, like a bird's wings as it tried to take flight. "I shall take that as a compliment."

"Good, because that's precisely how I meant it."

The heat his stare had stirred within her flared anew. She wanted to touch his sleeve again. Or perhaps some other part of him. His chest was rather broad, and she imagined he was quite muscular. Was he staring at her mouth?

She suddenly wondered what it would be like to kiss him. Wonderful, she suspected. Too bad she would likely never find out.

"Tamsin!" Min called, interrupting Tamsin's increasingly wicked thoughts.

Looking toward the hotel where Min's voice had come from, Tamsin realized her friends had gone back inside. She'd hadn't noticed at all, for she'd been completely enraptured by Droxford.

"I wish I could see you tomorrow," she said. "Then it would be three days in a row. But I understand why you aren't coming. I shall look forward to seeing you at the soiree here instead."

He didn't respond as she turned and walked toward the hotel. Min saw her coming and went inside. At the door, Tamsin turned her head to see the baron once more.

Again, he watched her, his attention entirely on her person. She felt her face flush, and wondered what his interest could mean.

Nothing, because they would part in a few days, and at some point, her mystery suitor would arrive—a point she'd forgotten to mention to the others.

Pivoting on her heel, she went into the hotel and planned to reveal that missing detail. Best to focus on that than the shocking sensations Droxford aroused.

She could only hope the potential groom her father had chosen provoked a similar reaction. How delightful that would be.

CHAPTER 5

*A*gainst his better judgment, Isaac decided to join everyone on the excursion to Steep Holm. Shefford, who'd continued to try to persuade him to attend, was very pleased. Isaac said he was going in order to stop him from yammering on about it. In reality, he was going because of Miss Penrose. However, he wasn't admitting that to anyone, not even himself, really.

He'd thought of her far too much since the luncheon the other day and seeing her at the hotel yesterday had been an unexpected boon. She'd looked so fresh and bright, her cheeks rosy, her lips curled into her nearly ever-present smile. He'd been unable to keep his eyes from her, hoping she would take time to speak with him. And when she did…he'd been foolish enough to say he wasn't coming today. But that had been before she'd told him she wished he would be here, that doing so meant they would see one another three days in a row.

After that, he'd changed his mind despite knowing he should stay away from her. It was only one day, and he'd be leaving soon.

Isaac and Shefford had ridden to the dock in Isaac's coach, along with Lady Minerva and Miss Dangerfield. Stepping down, Isaac tipped his head up to look at the frustratingly blue sky. Not a rain cloud in sight, and while it was breezy, the wind wasn't troublesome enough to prevent their journey. Pity, for he'd rather hoped a surprise storm might roll in.

He was willing to suffer a great deal of anxiety just to spend time with Miss Penrose. What on earth was wrong with him? He ought to turn back to the Grove right now, citing some work he needed to finish.

Except there she was, standing next to her cousin, Somerton, along with their appointed chaperones, the Duke and Duchess of Wellesbourne. Dressed in a rather plain grayish-green walking dress, wisps of her honey-lightened brown hair fluttering against her temples beneath a straw bonnet, she fed something within him. Something that had lain dormant and was hungry for her curiosity and smiling provocation.

Isaac moved with the others to greet the rest of their party. Pulling his gaze from Miss Penrose, he eyed the boat sitting a little farther along the dock. The vessel looked solid, and it was much larger than the fishing boat he'd spent time on as a boy.

Then his gaze moved to the water, the grayish blue waves moving like a living, breathing—sinister—thing. Deciding to come seemed a poor idea indeed.

Miss Penrose approached him, her pretty features arranged in her signature smile. Her presence immediately soothed his anxiety, at least a little. "Good morning, my lord. I'm surprised, and delighted, to see you. The sea looks rather favorable, does it not?"

He glanced toward the water again, and a wave of unease washed over him, in spite of her calming presence. A wave like those cresting past the dock. Soon they would be on the boat bobbing atop them, completely at the mercy of the impetuous sea.

Isaac shuddered. And hoped Miss Penrose didn't notice.

She moved close to him and whispered, "Can I tell you a secret?"

Her scent of lilies and violets distracted him. He was grateful and fully turned his back to the sea. He fixed on Miss Penrose, allowing himself to be completely consumed by her. This reaction she provoked him in was nearly an obsession. One he hadn't felt in some time. Because he didn't allow himself to. Somehow, Miss Penrose had stolen past his defenses and elicited a sustained desire. Such thoughts brought Mary to mind, but he pushed them away.

"What is your secret?" He kept his voice low like hers and tried not to think of how they shared their secrets with one another.

She pressed her lips together, hesitating a moment. "I've decided I don't want to go on the boat."

He didn't believe her. She'd said just yesterday that she was inclined to go. "What changed your mind?"

"What changed *your* mind about coming today?" she asked, arching a brow at him.

She had him there. "You convinced me."

"Did I? Well, I'm sorry to have troubled you, because now I've changed my mind about going." She met his gaze with clear eyes, but he saw the hint of mischief behind them. "I'd prefer to collect shells on the beach."

"You could do that on Steep Holm," he countered, wondering if he could provoke her to say why she was really changing her mind. But did it matter?

Yes. She was choosing something he wanted. He needed to know if that was why she was doing it.

"I could," she allowed. "But Somerton informed me on the

way here that if the sea is rough around the island, we may not even be able to go ashore."

Isaac grimaced faintly. To suffer a horrible trip in a bobbing boat just to have to turn around and come back was about the worst thing he could imagine. "I somehow missed that detail."

She raised her voice. "Pardon me, everyone, but I'm afraid I've changed my mind about going. I'm going to remain here and have my own picnic nearby."

"You can't stay by yourself," Lady Minerva said, her brow creasing.

"I'll stay with her," Isaac said without thinking.

"You would need a chaperone," the duchess said, sounding almost wistful. "I would offer to stay, but then who will chaperone on the boat?"

"Actually, I don't mind staying also," Miss Dangerfield put in. "But I am not a chaperone either." As Lady Minerva's companion, she was a friend who accompanied her everywhere. She did not, however, possess the requirements of a chaperone. Though she was apparently the eldest of the female set, she was neither a spinster nor a widow. And she was certainly not married. "Should we send for Mrs. Ogilvie?"

Chaperone requirements were laughable to Isaac. The only thing that made Wellesbourne and his wife acceptable chaperones was the fact that they were wed. And, in Isaac's experience, Mrs. Ogilvie nodded off often enough during her "duties" as to be completely ineffectual.

Miss Price cocked her head. "Why do we need a chaperone at all? Evan is my brother, and Min and Sheff are siblings. Seems as though those connections are proper and acceptable, particularly if Miss Dangerfield and Miss Penrose aren't coming."

"I can't argue with that logic," the duchess said. "I'm

staying too, then." She looked to her husband and smiled. "You go ahead. I insist."

Wellesbourne kissed his wife's temple. "You are the best of women." He spoke softly, but Isaac heard. It was also impossible to miss the love the two of them shared. It would give some optimistic person hope that they could find the same. But not Isaac.

Shefford looked toward Isaac. "You can come along, then, since Miss Penrose will not be alone."

Panic tore through Isaac. He'd been so close to not having to set foot on that boat. Now there was no reason for him to stay.

"We need our own picnic," Miss Penrose said. "We'll take one of the baskets. Is it heavy? Lord Droxford, if you truly don't mind staying behind, you can carry it for us."

Isaac saw through her ruse. She was absolutely working to keep him off that boat. Because she knew what had happened to him and that he was anxious. No one had ever done anything like that for him.

That wasn't entirely true. He glanced toward Shefford, who'd stepped in and helped Isaac when he'd needed it most, when he hadn't a clue where to turn when Mary had become pregnant. And now Miss Penrose was behaving in the same manner—coming to his rescue.

"That would be helpful," Miss Dangerfield added. "But I don't want to keep you from the excursion."

"I would be honored to remain and help with your picnic," Isaac said, willing his muscles to relax and his pulse to slow.

Miss Penrose grinned at him. "Brilliant."

How was she not put off by him? His moodiness generally kept people from engaging with him, particularly women. Although, there were some who sought to catch his eye, for a brooding baron with a fortune was still a baron. With a fortune.

Miss Penrose was not a title or fortune hunter, however. He would stake his bees, of which he was most fond, on that. Neither would she want to marry him if she came to know him well, for she would see that he was truly a rogue, which she—and her friends—had vowed to avoid.

"Both baskets are already on the boat," Somerton said. "Do you want to fetch one?" he asked Isaac.

Sweat broke out along the back of Isaac's neck as a new surge of panic came over him.

Miss Penrose once again spoke up. "Pardon me, Lord Droxford, but would you mind if we took your coach to our picnic? You could go arrange that with your coachman."

Shefford started toward the boat. "I'll grab the basket."

As Isaac made his way to his coach, he wondered at the lengths Miss Penrose might have gone to in order to prevent him from having to get on the boat. There was no need for him to arrange things with his coachman, at least not in that moment.

Even so, he explained the change of plans to Davis, who nodded. Shefford came toward them with the basket from the boat and handed it to the coachman. Looking to Isaac, Shefford asked, "You sure you don't mind staying?"

"Not at all," Isaac said. "I shall look forward to hearing about the trip later."

Shefford narrowed his gaze. "Is this perhaps an elaborate plan to avoid going so you can return to the Grove and work? Or, perhaps you're going to leave entirely. Have we bored you already?"

Isaac nearly scowled at him. "Of course not. And I'm not returning to the Grove. I'm having a picnic with several ladies. Tell me which of us will have the better time."

"You make an intriguing argument. We shall compare

notes later." Shefford flashed a grin, then took himself back to the others.

Those going on the excursion filed onto the boat. Isaac couldn't even look at them once they were on board. How would he have ever endured the trip?

Isaac helped the duchess into his coach, then Miss Dangerfield, and finally Miss Penrose. He held her hand slightly longer than necessary. "Thank you," he said softly.

To her credit, she said nothing. Though, her gaze burned into his and, along with her small smile, conveyed a distinct message: she'd been glad to help.

This growing attraction could be trouble. He held to a strict code under which he stayed clear of romantic entanglements, and Miss Penrose was threatening his resolve. Climbing into the coach, he swept those thoughts away in favor of thinking of what he'd narrowly avoided. With Miss Penrose's help.

Settling in beside her, he closed his eyes briefly and allowed the tension to flow out of him. As the coach moved away from the dock, he imagined darkness and agitations slithering away as if they were beasts. This was what he'd done in his youth, when he'd had to learn to control his emotions lest he further infuriate his father, who'd expected Isaac to be unfailingly obedient and respectful. He hadn't been interested in Isaac's fears, worries, or disappointments.

"Life is a disappointment," Isaac's father would say.

And yet, when his father stepped into the pulpit on Sundays, he would preach optimism and kindness, saying that they must help one another and be grateful for what they'd been given. It was as if he became a different person. There had been the rector, and there had been Isaac's father.

"I must say, I am quite relieved not to be on that boat," the duchess said. "I just got over feeling queasy last week." She glanced toward Isaac. "My apologies, Lord Droxford. I didn't mean to speak of such things in your presence."

Wellesbourne had shared that they were expecting a child. Isaac assumed she was referring to that. He merely inclined his head.

"I wasn't terribly enthusiastic about it either," Miss Dangerfield said. She sat beside the duchess on the forward-facing seat. "But Min was so looking forward to it."

"You pretended to be eager too," the duchess said with a nod. "Pandora will be sorry I didn't go. She was looking forward to hearing all about it."

"It's too bad she wouldn't come," Miss Penrose noted. "But I understand why."

Because she preferred to avoid Bane's friends, or former friends if that was what they were. Isaac wondered how Bane felt about ruining a young woman. Did he even think of Miss Barclay at all?

Isaac shifted uncomfortably as his mind turned to Mary. He tried not to think of her, and sometimes, more often than he liked, really, he failed.

His thigh brushed Miss Penrose as he moved, and she turned her head toward him. He'd felt a blast of heat from the brief connection. Had she experienced the same? He moved away from her as much as space would allow.

They arrived at the location Isaac had selected for the picnic. They would be on a nice patch of grass with a view of the direction the boat would take to Steep Holm. He didn't particularly care to watch their progress, but reasoned the others might.

After exiting the coach, he helped the ladies down, one by one. His coachman handed him the picnic basket.

"Thank you. I imagine we'll be a few hours." They likely wouldn't even want a picnic lunch for some time as it was still midmorning. Indeed, the entire outing seemed almost absurd, as if it were an excuse to avoid something, which it was. Isaac inclined his head toward the basket. "Davis, take something for yourself."

Like most of the retainers at Wood End, the coachman had been in Isaac's employ since Isaac had inherited the barony four years ago. He was a hardworking fellow in his late thirties. "Thank you, my lord." Davis selected something wrapped in paper and tucked it into his pocket before moving to attend the horses.

Carrying the basket, Isaac followed the ladies to where Miss Dangerfield was spreading out a blanket. He waited until they were all seated before setting the basket on a corner. Then he stood nearby wondering what he ought to do. It felt awkward to be picnicking with three young ladies, even if one of them was actually a chaperone. He realized he *could* return to the Grove, even though he'd told Shefford he wouldn't. After Davis deposited him at the Grove, Isaac could send him back to fetch the ladies.

But he wouldn't abandon Miss Penrose. Not after she'd gone to such lengths to rescue him.

More accurately, he didn't want to leave her, even though he knew he should.

"Are you going to sit?" Miss Penrose asked. She patted the blanket beside her and smiled up at him.

Isaac sat down in the unoccupied quadrant of the blanket. How he wished it was just him and Miss Penrose.

Miss Dangerfield sent him a small, appreciative smile. "It was most kind of you to stay with us."

The duchess nodded. "Indeed, though I do wonder what we'll do for the duration of their excursion."

"I plan to walk along the beach shortly," Miss Penrose stated. "You are all welcome to join me."

"I think I'll stay," the duchess replied. "It's a marvelous day, and this is a picturesque view." She lifted her hand to her mouth as she yawned. "And perhaps I'm a little tired." She gave them a sheepish look.

Miss Dangerfield reached over and touched the duchess's skirt, giving her a sympathetic glance. "I'll stay with you."

The duchess smiled. "I'm such a dullard now that I'm carrying. I'm tired and, honestly, I am not the most charming person in the mornings. But at least I am feeling better than I was." She speared Isaac with a stare of abject apology. "Forgive me, I can't seem to keep myself from speaking of delicate matters."

"That is the consequence of choosing to stay behind with us," Miss Dangerfield said with a bright laugh, and the other ladies joined in.

"It is no consequence for me," Isaac said. "I daresay the other gentlemen should be jealous."

Miss Penrose arched a playful brow at him. "Careful, we may decide you're a rogue after all."

"You've decided I'm not?" Isaac's brain faltered. Was he...*flirting*?

"I have," Miss Penrose declared.

"She's convinced us as well," Miss Dangerfield said with a nod.

Before Isaac could chase that knowledge—that Miss Penrose had spoken of him to her friends, Miss Dangerfield added, "Though, I'd already concluded that you weren't after seeing you interact with the others at the Grove. You don't behave inappropriately. You seem, in fact, above reproach."

If they knew the truth, they would shun him—and rightfully so. His transgressions exceeded Bane's, whom they *had* turned their backs on. Isaac was uncomfortable with their assessment of him, but they couldn't know the truth about him nor would they ever. He would simply have to let them, including Miss Penrose, believe what they wished. Though they couldn't be more wrong about him.

He was a rogue, and he had an abandoned family to prove it.

"Will you be attending the soiree at the Weston Hotel tomorrow?" the duchess asked him.

Pulling himself from his gloomy thoughts, he replied, "I'm considering it." He heard a stifled giggle and glanced toward Miss Penrose. She met his gaze with a knowing look, and he recalled their conversation from the luncheon. The shared moment filled him with a surprising warmth.

He'd forgotten what it felt like to share such things with another person. It was as if they had their own secret.

"I'm a bit parched," the duchess said. "Shall we have lemonade?"

Miss Penrose lifted the basket to the center of the blanket, demonstrating they hadn't needed his help at all. Would anyone notice? Would they deduce how Miss Penrose had aided him in avoiding the trip?

She set out four cups while Isaac plucked the bottle from the picnic basket. As he poured the lemonade into the ladies' cups, he felt strangely domestic. It was the presence of so many women, he reasoned. Growing up, his household had contained one woman, Mrs. Wilkes. She'd served in the roles of housekeeper, maid, and cook but hadn't lived at the rectory. She lived in Dunster and came to work during the day. Except on Sundays, per his father's edict.

"There's the boat," Miss Dangerfield said, pointing out to the water.

Isaac cast a few glances in that direction but then busied himself exchanging the lemonade for the ale and pouring it into his cup.

The duchess twitched her shoulder. "Can't say I regret staying."

"I hear the beach calling," Miss Penrose said. "Today is the day I will find the elusive intact cockleshell."

"Would you like assistance?" Isaac asked.

"I would, thank you. Perhaps you will bring me luck at last. I have found any number of cockleshell pieces, but not one that is whole."

Isaac rose and helped Miss Penrose to her feet. She asked her friends if they were certain they didn't wish to join them. They confirmed they were content to stay on the blanket.

"This way, we get the entire contents of the basket to ourselves," the duchess said with a devilish grin. "Did I mention I'm hungry much of the time? There I go again, revealing too much." She shooed them away. "Away with you so I can unburden myself to Ellis without feeling as though I'm being improper."

Miss Penrose curled her hand around Isaac's elbow and pulled him from the blanket. He didn't at all hesitate. Rather, he relished her touch and the impending time alone with her.

Flirting and now this. He was treading on dangerous ground.

They followed the path down to the sand. When they were a fair distance from the others, Isaac said what he'd been longing to say since the dock. "You wanted to go to Steep Holm. Don't lie and tell me you didn't. You were *eager* to go."

She exhaled. "You've caught me." Catching her lip between her teeth, she turned her head toward him. "But I thought it was more important to save you from having to make the trip. You looked so anxious."

He wasn't sure he liked that she saw that in him. Had anyone else? "That was exceedingly observant of you. And thoughtful." *So* thoughtful.

"It was the right thing to do, then? I confess I was nervous that my attempt would be foiled—either because you really *did* want to go, or someone would make it so you had to."

"That nearly happened."

Miss Penrose laughed as she bent to look at a shell. "I had to think fast, so I suggested we needed you to carry the basket."

"Which clearly you did not as evidenced by you hauling it to the center of the blanket," he said drily.

Her eyes rounded briefly, and her lips parted in realization. "I did, didn't I?" She giggled. "Hopefully, Persephone and Min didn't notice. I'm not sure it matters if they did. They likely won't think anything of it." She gave him an earnest look. "Your secret is safe with me."

He didn't doubt it. "I appreciate that. And your efforts. I was certain I was going to have to fetch the basket from the boat."

She pivoted toward him as they walked. "I know—it was a near disaster! Sending you to arrange our transportation was even more feeble than saying we needed you to carry the basket, but it was all I could come up with. If it had been windier, I would have loosed my bonnet as a distraction. I envisioned you chasing after it." Her eyes gleamed with mirth.

Isaac felt a surge of brightness.

She narrowed one eye at him. "The corner of your mouth...it's lifting. You are very nearly smiling. Yes, that is a *half* smile."

"It's a smirk," he clarified. "That's what my friends call it—the Droxford Smirk."

"You have an expression named after you and it's not a glower? Or a brood?" she asked with a laugh. "Is *brood* even a noun? My father would hate to hear me abusing the English language."

"I say it is now, and if your father is a decent man, he would agree." If he had the poor character to quarrel with his daughter, Isaac would not think well of him. Isaac stopped and faced her, growing serious, for that was what he did best.

"What you did for me…I am very grateful. I didn't realize how much the trip would affect me until I stepped onto that dock today. I thought I could do it."

"I understand," she replied softly. "Perhaps one day you will be able to get onto a boat. But it didn't have to be today. Nor does it have to be with a crowd of people."

"We were hardly a crowd," he said, feeling another splash of light being this close to her. Alone.

"I suppose not." She flashed a brief smile. "There you go smirking again."

"It seems you are very good at provoking smirks."

While they'd walked, he noted that her gaze often scanned the sand. He realized he wasn't providing assistance in searching for the shell. He'd been far too distracted by her.

"Oh!" she exclaimed, taking her hand from his arm and dashing toward the water where the wave was receding. She picked something up.

When Isaac reached her side, he looked at the item in her palm. It was indeed a cockle, but it wasn't quite intact. "That's close," he observed.

"Yes, but I have several like this already," she said with a sigh. She dropped the shell back onto the wet sand. "Perhaps I should break them and paste them together to make a complete shell."

"I could do that for you," he offered before he realized she was joking. Of course she was. She wanted a whole cockleshell.

She smiled at him. "That is very sweet of you."

Sweet was not a word he'd ever heard used to describe himself. Isaac couldn't bring himself to correct her assessment.

"How long have you been collecting shells?" he asked.

"Since I was a child." She seemed to hesitate. "My mother left us when I was eight," she said softly. "After that, I stole into her room to see if she'd left anything behind. I found a pair of shells in a drawer. I kept them and eventually added to the collection."

Her mother left? Isaac's insides twisted. He would never have guessed she'd suffered such sadness. "Why did she leave?" He realized he was being as curious as she'd been with him.

Miss Penrose continued to scan the beach as they walked. "She wasn't happy. Apparently, she thought an actor from a passing theatre troupe would make her so."

"And did it?"

Her gaze flicked to his but only briefly. "I don't know. We never saw her again after she left, and she died about a year later. The actor sent us a letter. My father burned it, but I always thought it was kind of him to tell us."

"How do you not carry that with you?" The question was a bare whisper. He hadn't meant to ask it, but he had to know. His mother's death weighed heavily on him, and she hadn't abandoned him, not on purpose, anyway. While he *had* abandoned Mary and their child. What did she think of him now? Had she told their son about his father and how he'd left them? Did his son suffer for not having Isaac in his life?

Miss Penrose's shoulders lifted gently. "My grandfather told me I could be morose, as my father was, or I could choose to find joy every day. I didn't want to be sad." Now her gaze met his and held it. "That sounds overly simplistic, and perhaps it is, but that is what I do. I choose happiness and optimism."

That sounded so hard. And so unbelievably admirable. Isaac wanted nothing more than to remain with her, to borrow some of her joy.

Too late, he realized a wave was rushing toward them.

The water hit their ankles as he swept her into his arms and hurried away from the water.

When they were on much drier sand, he slowly lowered her to the ground. But he didn't release her. Her hands around his neck made this feel like an embrace. He wanted to just stand there to savor her proximity and the intimacy of the moment.

Their gazes locked and held, and he felt an inexorable pull to kiss her. Her lips parted, as if she were inviting him to do so. His body quivered with anticipation.

Could he really kiss her and then leave Weston without regret? Of course he couldn't.

But the truth was that he would have regret either way.

CHAPTER 6

*A*s Droxford carried her across the sand, Tamsin clasped her hands around his neck. She'd been too focused on him instead of the ocean. But here he was rescuing her. Like a hero in a fairy tale. Tamsin had never felt so safe, so *protected*.

When he stopped, she was aware of his hands clasped around her waist. Their chests nearly touched. She could feel the brush of his hair against her fingertips where they touched his nape, just above his collar. Staring into his eyes, Tamsin imagined this was what it felt like just before a kiss.

Would he kiss her?

She knew in that moment that she wanted him to.

But then his hands were gone from her waist, and he took a step backward. "My apologies for overstepping, Miss Penrose. It seemed necessary with the wave rushing in." He glanced down at her skirt. "I deeply regret that you may have ruined another gown in my presence."

Tamsin looked at the hem of her skirt and waved her hand. "This won't be ruined, and neither was my yellow gown. Mrs. Bilson had no trouble removing the stain. She is my grandmother's housekeeper and cook."

"Still, I think my prediction that I may bring you luck was woefully inaccurate. I seem to deliver the opposite."

"That's absurd," she said, shaking some of the water from her skirt. "Neither the pea incident nor the wave was your fault. On the contrary, you saved me from the wave as I may have been drenched. You are, in fact, a hero."

He snorted. "Your characterization of me as a hero is amusing. Let us consider that you saved me from the boat trip and now I've saved you from an errant wave. We are friends who look out for one another."

"I like that." She looked down at the water droplets on his boots. "It's not fair that men can dress in a way in which a small wave doesn't dampen their clothing. Your boots are wet and nothing more. I, on the other hand, need to wring out my stockings."

"Did the water make it over the top of your half boots?" he asked with concern. "You should go back to the blanket and dry them out. I won't accompany you for propriety's sake."

Because seeing her bare feet would be scandalous. The idea made Tamsin want to giggle again. What on earth could be so imprudent about seeing a lady's bare feet? They weren't even a particularly attractive body part, at least in her estimation.

"That is for the best, I suppose. Will you continue the hunt for the cockleshell?" she asked.

"It is my primary objective," he said crisply. "Shall I accompany you to the path?"

"No, it isn't far. You needn't stay away too long." She turned but not entirely, pausing to say, "Thank you for plucking me out of the water."

"Thank you for preventing me from being on it in a boat."

Tamsin turned and hurried toward the path. The charged moment on the beach repeated in her mind. What a fool she'd been to think he would kiss her. Why would he? And why would she want him to? She was practically betrothed.

Or could be, anyway.

She now knew she wanted that—a husband. Whether it was the mystery man her father had written about or someone else. Droxford? Was he even looking for a bride? He had to be—he was a baron with a duty to provide an heir.

When she reached the blanket, she immediately flopped down and lifted the hem of her skirt to remove her boots.

"What happened?" Persephone asked.

"A wave caught us by surprise. I just want to wring out my stockings. They are wet and becoming cold."

"You should go home before you catch a chill," Ellis said with a slight frown.

Tamsin paused in removing her first boot. "Do you think so? It's a warm day."

Persephone shook her head. "You'll be fine. Just air them out for a bit. Where is Lord Droxford?"

"He's looking for my cockleshell." Tamsin set one boot aside and lifted her skirt high enough to unfasten her garter. She then rolled her stocking down and waved it around. It wasn't really wet enough to require wringing.

"I hope he's going to stay away while you practically disrobe." Ellis laughed softly. "You're lucky Mrs. Lawler isn't around to see this. She'd likely say you are ruined since the baron is within shouting distance." She rolled her eyes.

Mrs. Lawler was the busybody who'd seen Pandora and Bane kissing and then told every person she knew, as well as plenty she didn't.

"She absolutely would," Persephone said darkly. "Let's not speak of her. I do hope we won't see her at the soiree tomorrow night. I've nearly convinced Pandora to come, at least for a quarter hour. If we encounter that harpy, Pandora will want to leave immediately."

"Pandora should give *her* the cut direct," Tamsin said as she removed her second stocking. She laid the two of them out on the blanket and hoped the sun would sufficiently dry them before Droxford returned. How would he know it was safe to approach? They hadn't discussed that. Ah well, Mrs. Lawler wasn't here to cause problems, and anyway, nothing about this was at all improper.

Ellis picked up her lemonade. "We all should."

"I plan to steer clear of her," Persephone said. "Tamsin should too if something is stirring between her and the baron."

"Is it?" Ellis asked. Both she and Persephone looked at Tamsin with interest.

"Why would you think that?" Tamsin reached down to shake the hems of her garments in the hope they would dry faster.

Persephone arched a dark blonde brow. "Because you took a promenade through the garden at the Grove yesterday, and now he's off finding a shell that you covet."

Tamsin didn't meet their gazes. If they knew that she'd imagined him kissing her just a short while ago, they'd… what would they do? Would they encourage her growing interest in the baron? "We are friends. Nothing more. As you know, I'm to consider marriage to someone else."

Checking her stockings, Tamsin found them to be only slightly damp. She pulled them back on in case Droxford returned soon.

Persephone gave her a pointed look. "Well, if you were romantically interested in Droxford, I would advise you not to let your father's plans for a suitor deter you. He can't force you to wed anyone, though my parents did try to negotiate a marriage contract without my consent. I'm sure you know that story from Pandora."

Indeed, Pandora had shared that outrageous tale when she'd stayed with Tamsin. "Did you not feel even a slight duty to at least consider your parents' choice?"

Persephone laughed. "Not at all. For one, I'd already met my cousin Harold, and I knew I would never be interested in marrying him. Furthermore, they'd already tried to persuade me to marry Acton. My mother had set up a meeting where they fully expected we would agree to wed."

Ellis sipped her lemonade and set her cup securely on the blanket-covered ground. She looked to Tamsin. "I will hope that your father supports your decision, whatever it is."

Persephone cocked her head to the side. "On second thought, I can't imagine Tamsin with Droxford. She's far too cheerful for a man such as him. I'm afraid it would be a mismatch."

"Apparently, he *can* smile and even laugh," Ellis noted. "Shefford says he's seen it, that the baron was quite different when they met at Oxford."

Tamsin was now incredibly curious. If she asked him about that period, would he tell her?

"I do think it's time for some sustenance," Persephone said, leaning toward the picnic basket.

Tamsin finished putting her boots back on, and though they and the stockings were drier, they were still damp. And her feet would become damp again in no time.

Perhaps she ought to return to her grandmother's. Except then she wouldn't know if Droxford had found a cockleshell.

In the end, she opted to stay. Unfortunately, he returned empty-handed and in a decidedly aloof mood.

Yes, they would likely be a mismatch. While he seemed to lose some of his broodiness when in her presence, they were still quite different in temperament. It was for the best that Tamsin thought of him as just a friend. She ought to be thinking of the man her father wanted her to marry. A man who could very well be the fairy-tale hero she now knew she wanted.

~

Following a morning ride the next day with Shefford and Price, Isaac had broken his fast and bathed. Now, as he made his way downstairs, he reflected on how this year's trip to Weston had become extraordinary. He'd all but decided to leave tomorrow after attending tonight's soiree at the hotel, but after his walk on the beach with Miss Penrose yesterday, he nearly reconsidered that decision.

For a fleeting moment after he'd swept her into his arms to remove her from the water, he'd lost himself completely. Desire had crashed into him as surely as that wave, and he'd nearly kissed her. When was the last time he'd kissed a woman? More than a decade ago, for that was not one of the activities he paid for at the Rogue's Den, and his companion there knew not to engage him in it.

Thankfully, he'd regained his senses and moved away from Miss Penrose before he'd surrendered to behavior that would only lead to trouble. He would not be ruled by his roguish tendencies. That way led to ruin.

Shefford and Price were already in the billiards room when Isaac arrived. Shefford was drinking ale, and Price was throwing darts.

Isaac helped himself to an ale and sat down near Shefford.

"Either of you going to the soiree tonight?" Price asked. "My mother is insisting I attend." He made a disgruntled face as he launched a dart at the board.

Shefford sniggered. "You'd go anyway. I've never known

you to miss a chance to dance with and charm the ladies. I'm going."

Price took aim with another dart. "While that is true, Weston is not London or even Bath."

"I've decided to attend," Isaac said, bracing himself for the inevitable surprise that would come.

Shefford turned toward him. "You missed the boat trip yesterday, and now you're going to the soiree?" He narrowed his eyes. "What's going on?"

"Nothing's going on. I'm here. There's a soiree. I decided to attend." Isaac shrugged.

"No, no, it's not that simple." Shefford speared him with an inquisitive stare. "Is it because of Miss Penrose?"

Isaac nearly choked on his ale. After swallowing, he managed, "No. Why would you think that?"

Price responded. "Because you stayed behind yesterday after she changed her mind about going. Seemed to me you wanted to spend time with her."

That wasn't it at all, but Isaac didn't want to reveal the truth of the matter. In the back of his mind, a voice said he hadn't remained with the ladies *just* to avoid the boat. While that had been his primary motivation, the chance to hunt seashells with Miss Penrose had been a wonderful benefit. He said nothing to the others.

"She appeared to practically invite you to stay behind—all that nonsense with the basket carrying and the coach," Shefford said with a chuckle. "When I thought about it later, I deduced the two of you had arranged it, particularly when you said you hadn't concocted the scheme in order to return to the Grove."

"We did not arrange anything." Isaac drank more ale and contemplated going somewhere else.

"You walked off together at the luncheon the other day." Shefford studied Isaac. "And now you're going to a soiree without me dragging you. It seems plausible that something might be sparking between the two of you."

Isaac tried not to scowl. "Nothing is 'sparking.'" If he were honest, it was flaring into a steady heat. At least for him. He'd no idea what Miss Penrose was thinking or feeling, nor did he want to find out. It didn't signify as he was not looking for courtship, and certainly not marriage.

Price turned from the board with a teasing smile. "When the duchess and Miss Dangerfield also opted to remain yesterday, did that ruin your plans?" This was what they did —provoke each other over nonsensical, unimportant, often far-fetched things. They did not typically taunt Isaac about women, but Price, with whom Isaac had spent little time before this week, didn't know that.

Tone dripping with sarcasm, Isaac responded, "Fine, you've caught me. Miss Penrose and I *did* hatch an elaborate scheme where we would be left alone while the rest of you took a boat to Steep Holm. That sounds exactly like something I would do."

Shefford exhaled. "It does not. Particularly after what Bane did last year, and your clear disapproval of his actions." He held up a hand. "Before you launch into another diatribe about his improper behavior, let me assure you that I agree. He behaved poorly."

"So, there's nothing between you and Miss Penrose?" Price asked.

"No," Isaac said firmly.

"I suppose I will owe Somerton five pounds," Shefford said with a sigh.

Isaac stared at him. "You made a wager with her cousin that we were becoming attached?" He should not have been surprised.

Shefford lifted a hand with a shrug. "We've wagered on worse."

"Somerton told you it was a bad bet," Price said with a laugh. "He said Droxford may never wed and certainly not soon."

"Somerton is correct," Isaac said. But *if* he were to marry, would he be romantically interested in Miss Penrose? Her behavior yesterday at the dock, seeing his agitation and doing whatever she could to keep it from worsening, made her a singular woman. And he was most definitely attracted to her. Indeed, his fixation on her was a distraction he couldn't afford and didn't want.

But the truth was that he didn't wish to wed. At least not now and, as Somerton had said, perhaps not ever.

As if conjured by their conversation, the viscount strolled into the billiards room. "I've arrived! What did I miss?"

Isaac glanced toward Shefford before smirking at Somerton. "Shefford owes you five pounds. There is nothing between your cousin and me beyond friendship."

"Told you," Somerton said to Shefford, also smirking. "Tamsin is my cousin, and while I spend most of my time here, I do see her and my grandmother. I would surely know if she had any romantic inclinations."

Shifting in his chair, Isaac felt a pang of disappointment. Why should that bother him? Did he want her to have romantic feelings for him? That would be pointless since he had no interest in forming any kind of lasting attachment with her.

"Go on and gloat." Shefford dug five pounds from his pocket and thrust the notes toward Somerton.

"Thank you very much," Somerton said as if they'd just concluded a successful business arrangement. Which it had been for Somerton, anyway. After tucking the notes into his coat, he turned toward Isaac. "If you were to become romantically interested in Tamsin, I would caution you. She is about as opposite to your sensibilities as one could be. I can only foresee her eternal cheer and positivity driving you mad."

For some reason, that made Isaac even grumpier. He set his ale down and stood. "I'm going for a walk. Alone."

"We wouldn't want to interrupt your brooding time," Shefford called after him.

Isaac didn't turn, but waved his hand as he left the room. Fetching his hat and gloves, he walked outside, where it was a bit overcast with a gentle breeze.

His mood had taken an absolute turn toward surly. Between his friends teasing him about Miss Penrose and learning from Somerton that she was not at all interested in him, Isaac wondered if he should depart for Wood End today.

But no, he couldn't. He had found the shell Miss Penrose had been looking for, despite telling her he hadn't, but hadn't wanted to give it to her in front of the duchess and Miss Dangerfield. He'd planned to give it to her at the soiree tonight. That would be the end of their association. Then he would leave tomorrow and return to his normal life.

Yes, normal. Where he managed his estate and did baron things, both of which he'd never anticipated.

Miss Penrose had made him forget what normal even was. She was exemplary in every way, and if he didn't find a way to stop thinking about her, he would be in serious trouble.

Already, he'd nearly fumbled by almost kissing her. Thankfully, he still had a rein on himself and was able to keep his inner rogue at bay.

Tomorrow, this would be a moot issue. He'd be on his way to Wood End, and Miss Penrose would be nothing more than a pleasant memory. Why did that trigger a sense of loss?

Blast, he was being incredibly maudlin, even for him. Kicking a rock on the path before him, Isaac looked about.

He'd been walking without much thought for direction or destination.

Perhaps a quarter mile ahead, he glimpsed a roof. It appeared to be a cottage on a rise. He could make out smoke curling from a chimney.

He would walk as far as that, without going close enough to be intrusive, then return to the Grove. The narrow track led toward a lane, but there was also a less-traveled path veering to the left. Opting for the less-used direction, he strode through low grass and soon saw the rear of the cottage. It was larger than he'd anticipated and a substantial, ordered, very pretty garden was laid out along the back.

The flowers were simply stupendous, and Isaac wished he had something similar, but larger, at Wood End. The bees would love it. He had an urge to take a closer look so he could note the flowers in use.

Stealing closer, he saw many bees buzzing about. They seemed to be quite plentiful. And now he wondered if the cottage owner kept any bees. It would be a perfect opportunity to do so.

"Who's there?" a feminine voice called.

Blast, he'd moved too close. He waved. "The Baron Droxford. I was just admiring your garden," he called.

"Come have a look, then," she responded.

He hadn't realized she was older, in her sixties at least. Her voice hadn't betrayed her age. Indeed, her age was a bit of a mystery, for while her hair was gray and her skin slack, she possessed an exuberant air he typically saw in someone far younger.

Hoping she would be able to tell him about her garden, Isaac strode toward her. She stood next to a rosebush with a pair of pruning shears in her hand.

"Pardon my intrusion," Isaac said.

She chuckled. "You forget that we've met, my boy. I'm Somerton's grandmother."

Isaac *had* met her on a previous visit to Weston. He just hadn't recognized her, nor had he realized this was her cottage. He'd made her acquaintance at the hotel, if he recalled correctly.

"Of course, it's a pleasure to see you again, Mrs. Dewhurst." At least he remembered her name.

He suddenly realized that if this was her cottage, then this was where Miss Penrose would be. Unless she wasn't at home. How had he managed to find himself here of all places?

"My garden attracted you?" she asked. "Are you a bee, Lord Droxford?" she asked with a chuckle.

"No, but I do keep them at my estate. I'm quite fascinated by them, in fact. Your garden is abundant with bees. I should very much like to know what flowers you keep."

"I'd be delighted to give you a tour." She set her shears on a low stool sitting nearby then guided him through the network of paths laid out among her extensive flower beds.

Isaac tried to catalog everything in his brain, but wasn't sure he'd recall it all. "Would it be too much trouble to ask you to write a list of your flowers?"

"Not at all. Why don't you come inside for tea? You can see my granddaughter. I know you've met."

Had Miss Penrose talked about him to her? "That would be lovely, thank you."

He followed her onto a small patio and then into the house, entering through a rear door that led to what appeared to be the drawing room. It was furnished with two distinct seating areas but still felt cozy with a floral-patterned wall covering and a thick, yellow and green carpet.

"Tamsin, we've a guest," Mrs. Dewhurst stated.

Was Miss Penrose here?

BECAUSE THE BARON BROODS   77

A head popped up from a chaise on the other side of the room. She'd been blocked from their view by other furniture. Standing, she held a book which she closed. Dressed in an ivory gown with sprigged flowers, her hair plaited atop her head in a simple but charming style, she was even prettier than she had been in his mind. And she'd occupied a great deal of it lately.

"Lord Droxford!" she exclaimed, coming forward. "What brings you to Beachside?"

"Is that the name of your cottage?" he asked Mrs. Dewhurst.

"Yes," Miss Penrose's grandmother responded before looking to her granddaughter. "The baron saw my garden and was compelled to speak with me about it."

"I was fortunate you were outside," he said.

"You like gardens?" Miss Penrose asked.

"Bees, actually. Your grandmother's garden supports a great many. I should like to duplicate that at Wood End. We keep bees there, and I'd like to attract more of them."

"I'm just going to write a list of the flowers I keep," Mrs. Dewhurst said. "I'll have tea sent in before I go to my writing desk. You'll both excuse me for a bit?" she asked, then bustled off without waiting for an answer.

"You have won an admirer for life," Miss Penrose said with a smile. "Anyone who shows interest in my grandmother's garden is exceptionally well regarded by her."

"Lucky me," he said. "She took me on a tour, and I was amazed to learn that she designed the garden herself. Her knowledge is astonishing. Perhaps I should just invite her to Wood End and ask her to lay out a new garden."

Miss Penrose laughed lightly. "She would probably do so with glee. Where is your estate?"

"Hampshire. I have just over eight hundred acres."

"That's quite large."

He shrugged. "Not as large as some. Somerton's estate has over a thousand."

"Does it?" She blinked. "I confess I've never paid attention to such things. My father's property in St. Austell is *not* large, but it is sufficient."

Isaac hoped he didn't sound pompous. "Actually, eight hundred acres *is* large, particularly when one is raised at a rectory in a small seaside village."

"I imagine that was an adjustment for you. Somerton has told me that you hadn't expected to inherit the title. I understand that means others in your family passed away, and I'm sorry for that."

"It was a surprising—and grievous—series of events, to be sure. I'd just become a barrister when I had to completely change my plans. It was jarring, but I found the challenge invigorating."

"You like being the baron, then?"

"I do. I very much like working on and managing the estate. Not that I do everything. I employ a very accomplished and reliable steward."

"And you keep bees," she noted. Suddenly, the book fell from her hand, landing on the carpet.

Isaac bent to retrieve it, and she did the same. They met as they crouched together, their hands colliding as they both reached for the book.

He did not pull his hand away, nor did she. Nor did they rush to straighten. Instead, time seemed to lengthen and still as they looked at one another, their hands touching. Again, Isaac contemplated kissing her, which was shocking since he hadn't kissed anyone in over a decade. What about Miss Penrose had captivated him completely? For he was truly enthralled by her.

She blinked, and he withdrew his hand. Picking up the

book, she rose. Isaac did the same, sorry the moment between them was over.

"Forgive me, shall we sit?" She led him to a small round table at the edge of the seating area where she'd been reading, as if they hadn't just shared a charged encounter. Or perhaps it had only felt that way to him. That would be unsurprising given his nature. Of course, he would think like a rogue and want to kiss her. It was precisely why he should be staying away from her, and yet here he was in her presence again.

Settling into one of the three chairs at the table, she added, "Mrs. Bilson, Grandmama's housekeeper and cook, will bring tea in a moment. I hope you like almond cakes, for she makes the very best."

Isaac took the chair to her right. "I do like almond cakes. Is she the one responsible for saving your gown from the wine disaster? I do hope your garments were not damaged by the wave yesterday."

"Yes, Mrs. Bilson can remove any stain from anything. And there was absolutely no harm done to my clothing, though the interior of my boots did not appreciate the saltwater dousing. They are still drying in the kitchen."

The housekeeper entered carrying a tray, which she set on the table. After exchanging pleasantries, she offered to pour.

"I understand you make the best almond cakes in England," Isaac said to Mrs. Bilson.

She blushed faintly as she finished preparing two cups. "Tamsin thinks so. I hope she hasn't set you up for disappointment."

"I'm sure she has not."

Mrs. Bilson looked to Miss Penrose. "You'll make your grandmother's cup when she returns?"

"I will, thank you."

Inclining her head and giving them a smile, the house-keeper departed.

Miss Penrose took a cake and placed it on the plate before her before looking at him. "Did you come to Beachside on purpose to see my grandmother's garden?"

"No. I went for a walk and happened upon it. I didn't even realize who the cottage and garden belonged to until your grandmother told me. I'm afraid I didn't recognize her," he said with regret as he helped himself to an almond cake. Taking a bite, he could confirm it was, in fact, among the best he'd tasted. He would not tell Mrs. Corwin, the cook at Wood End.

"I thought perhaps Somerton had told you about it—the garden, I mean. Well, what a happy coincidence that you are here."

A *happy* coincidence. But she would likely say that about everyone who happened by. She was, by her very nature, positive and charming and it had nothing to do with him specifically.

She sipped from her teacup. "Do you dance? I hoped I might look forward to you asking me tonight at the soiree."

Grimacing, he admitted, "I don't care for dancing. Nor am I good at it." But in that moment, he wished he did and was. It seemed unlikely he could improve his lackluster skill enough before that evening. "We could promenade in the garden, if you like?" Then he could give her the shell and tell her he'd enjoyed making her acquaintance.

"I would like that, thank you."

"Here we are," Mrs. Dewhurst announced as she sailed into the drawing room with a piece of parchment. "A list of flowers for you, my lord." She set the paper on the table, then took the remaining chair.

Miss Penrose moved to pour her grandmother's tea.

"Droxford and I have decided you should go to his estate and design his new garden."

Mrs. Dewhurst's lively blue eyes lit with interest. "Have you? I can't say I wouldn't enjoy that." She plucked up her teacup and smiled broadly at Isaac. "Just tell me when, and I'll be there."

It seemed tonight might not be the last he'd see of Miss Penrose. Assuming she accompanied her grandmother to Wood End to design his new bee garden. And why would she? It was his understanding that Miss Penrose only visited Weston for the month of August. The rest of the year, she resided in distant Cornwall. Far enough away to be untouchable.

Isaac didn't know whether to be greatly relieved or massively disappointed.

CHAPTER 7

"*Y*our gown is simply glorious," Grandmama said as they stepped out of the coach at the Weston Hotel that evening. She'd insisted on Tamsin having a new gown for the soiree. Tamsin hadn't argued since her wardrobe was rather wanting, not that it mattered. She had almost no occasion to wear evening clothes at home in St. Austell.

Looking down at the luminous blue-green silk, Tamsin felt grander than she ever had. She also wore an aquamarine pendant that belonged to her grandmother, along with matching combs in her hair. "I feel like a princess," she said softly.

"You look like one." Grandmama beamed as she took Tamsin's gloved hand, giving it a squeeze. "I'm sure Lord Droxford will think so too. I very much enjoyed his visit this afternoon, and I am pleased he will take you for a promenade. It's not a dance, but it is promising." She gave Tamsin an enthusiastic grin.

Tamsin nearly tripped. Was her grandmother hoping they might make a match? They were still awaiting a response from Tamsin's father about her potential suitor. "Grandmama, I don't think a promenade with the baron promises anything. Besides, what about my father's mystery bridegroom?"

Grandmama waved her hand as if she were batting away an annoying insect. "Bah. Never mind that nonsense. And you never know what could happen. Perhaps Droxford will take one look at you tonight and decide he must have you as his wife."

Tamsin could not deny that she liked the baron or that she was attracted to him. But marriage? She thought of what her friends had said about him, that his disposition was so different from hers.

There was no reason for her to consider a future with Droxford. They weren't even courting. However, there was a gentleman out there who was interested in marrying her, and he would arrive in Weston at some point. Tamsin needed to put her energy toward that, not the baron.

They walked into the hotel and made their way to the parlor, the largest room on the ground floor. Much of the furniture had been moved out, but there were chairs along the walls.

"Do you want to sit, Grandmama?"

"Not yet. I'd like to speak with a few people. Oh, there is Mrs. Price. I enjoyed meeting her last year." She referred to Gwen's mother, a tall, dark-haired woman with a simple but elegant sense of style. She wore a burgundy gown that complemented her almost olive complexion.

They went to greet Mrs. Price. Gwen was standing with her and smiled upon seeing Tamsin. "Your gown is splendid. That's a beautiful color on you. It matches your eyes nearly perfectly."

"That is why my grandmother chose it," Tamsin said. "Are the others here yet?"

"Min and Ellis are." Gwen, who wore a dark golden-yellow gown and a matching feather in her hair, inclined her head toward the other side of the room where they stood speaking with a local couple.

Tamsin noted the arrival of Lord Droxford. He walked over the threshold into the parlor, and the room contracted. He looked very handsome in a black coat and breeches. His waistcoat was gray but shot with silver thread, and his cravat was simple but pristinely arranged. She imagined he didn't like a fussy neckcloth, nor would that suit him.

His gaze traveled around the room until it met hers. He didn't move, but his eyes held hers, seeming to promise...something.

Tamsin experienced a wave of heat and a flutter of antici-pation in her belly. She wished they could dance. Perhaps she could change his mind.

"What are you looking at?" Gwen's gaze moved to the doorway. "Droxford?" She pivoted toward Tamsin. "He looks most pleasing this evening."

"He does indeed," Tamsin murmured. He still hadn't looked away from her.

Another gentleman stepped behind the baron. Tall, with brown hair that had gone gray at the temples, he said some-thing to Droxford. The baron moved out of the way so the other man could move into the parlor.

As the older man stepped into the light from the chande-lier overhead, Tamsin recognized him. He was a friend of her father's, a scholar from Gloucester. What was he doing here?

As Droxford had done, the man, Mr. Octavius Brimble, looked about the room until his focus settled on Tamsin. He walked directly toward her. "Good evening, Miss Penrose. I am pleased to find you here."

Tamsin dipped a brief curtsey to the man she'd known most of her life. He visited once each year and stayed a week, or sometimes a fortnight, during which he and her father shut themselves in the study to discuss…whatever interested them. Though her father was even more unreachable during that week, Tamsin had always been glad her father had a friend.

"Mr. Brimble, I'm surprised to see you in Weston."

"Are you? I thought your father had written to inform you that I would be arriving here to convey you to St. Austell."

A horrible sinking feeling pulled on Tamsin's insides. "Why is that?"

Mr. Brimble's brow furrowed in a vexed expression. "I am keen to arrive in St. Austell with due haste as I need to be at Oxford by the start of October for a conference. We will need time for the banns to be read."

Tamsin was glad Gwen was near, for she instinctively gripped her friend's arm. Gwen, bless her, put her hand over Tamsin's and held her tightly.

"I was, ah, not aware that you were the gentleman coming to Weston," Tamsin said, her dreams of a fairy-tale hero turning to ash. "Or that a betrothal had been finalized," she added faintly.

Mr. Brimble's thin lips pursed into a near pout. "Your father wrote to me that this would be acceptable. Indeed, he seemed quite eager for us to wed."

Tamsin couldn't believe this man was her father's choice, his friend whom she'd known since she was a child. She could not, under any circumstance, consider him as a husband.

However, she said nothing as she couldn't seem to put words together. Her thoughts somersaulted over themselves trying to make some sense of what was happening. Had her father really thought they would make a good match?

The hotel's owner announced that the dancing would

begin. Mr. Brimble held out his hand to Tamsin. "Shall we dance?"

It would be rude to decline, and Tamsin hadn't ever been rude. Not once. She released Gwen, who seemed reluctant to let go, and hesitantly placed her hand in his, grateful they were both wearing gloves.

He led her to the middle of the floor, where they joined the line that was forming. Soon, the music started, and Tamsin was able to focus on the dance instead of the disaster brewing before her. She did not want to cause a scene. Hopefully, she could keep Mr. Brimble at bay and inform him tomorrow that she would not be going with him to St. Austell, nor would she be marrying him.

Tamsin took a deep breath. This was not a calamity. It was a misunderstanding. Her father, for some reason, had thought Mr. Brimble would be a satisfactory husband to her. She just needed to smile and endure this dance. Then she would explain to Mr. Brimble that she was not aware he was her potential suitor. And then she would let him down easily, for she could not marry him. He was her father's friend, and she knew him entirely in that capacity.

She saw that her grandmother was frowning slightly, her forehead puckered into delicate pleats. Then Tamsin's gaze fell on Droxford. He stood near the doorway to the terrace. Scowling didn't adequately describe the dark expression thundering about his features. It was as if he were...seething. But it was more than that. He was looking at Mr. Brimble as if he wanted to do some sort of violence.

Was he...jealous? No. That couldn't be. Still, her heart tripped at the notion of the baron having those kinds of feelings for her. Of *anyone* feeling that way about her.

The dance seemed to last longer than usual, and Tamsin was relieved when it finally concluded. Her grandmother stood at the edge of the dancing area, her gaze and posture expectant.

Grandmama's gaze fixed on Mr. Brimble in an assessing and almost suspicious manner. "I don't believe we've met. I'm Miss Penrose's grandmother."

Mr. Brimble bowed. "Pleased to make your acquaintance. Forgive me for not meeting you earlier. Miss Penrose did not mention you were here."

Tamsin took her hand from the man's arm and stopped herself from pursing her lips at him. How dare he insinuate that she was to blame for not introducing him to her grandmother? The music had started, and he'd immediately steered her onto the dance floor.

Grandmama's eyes narrowed toward Mr. Brimble. "I should think you would have sought out my granddaughter's chaperone as soon as you arrived." Her tone dripped frost.

Tamsin moved to stand beside her. "Grandmama, this is Papa's friend—the one he wrote to me about, Mr. Octavius Brimble."

Grandmama's eyes rounded briefly. "We did not know when you would arrive or who you were, actually. My son-in-law's letter lacked certain pertinent information."

Mr. Brimble blinked, appearing nonplussed. "Well, I am here, and I am Miss Penrose's intended. We will depart for St. Austell tomorrow."

Before Tamsin could speak and inform him they were not actually engaged, Grandmama gave him a tight smile. "I'm afraid that won't be possible. She's not due to return to Cornwall for many days yet." She turned toward Tamsin, and now her gaze softened, but her chin was firm. "You promised Lord Droxford a promenade, dear." Glancing briefly over her shoulder toward Mr. Brimble, she murmured, "Please excuse us." Then she took Tamsin's arm and guided her to the doorway where Droxford had been standing during the dance.

Where did he go?

"Outside," Grandmama said, as if she'd heard Tamsin's thought. "I saw the baron leave this way when the dance ended. Goodness, Tamsin, I am so sorry you were swept up by Mr. Brimble. How dare he show up here at the soiree without calling on you first. And he thinks you're already betrothed? This is beyond the pale. Not to mention his age. He is far too old for you."

"He's a friend of Papa's. I've known him my entire life."

Grandmama blanched. "Well, this is not a matter to be discussed or settled here. I'm afraid it will have to wait until morning."

Tamsin wished she could glower as well as Droxford. "He was surprised I was not aware of our betrothal. He informed me that he wishes to wed quickly because he's due in Oxford by October." Tamsin clutched at her grandmother's arm. "I can't marry him." It wasn't just that Brimble wasn't what she'd hoped. He wasn't someone she would consider at all.

"Don't fret, my dear," her grandmother said soothingly. "You will not have to marry Mr. Brimble. Now, put him from your mind and go promenade with Lord Droxford. He looked nearly murderous while you were dancing with that nincompoop. You must explain who the man is, and why the baron mustn't be jealous."

There was that word again.

"He wasn't jealous, Grandmama." Tamsin couldn't believe it.

"I have seen jealous men, and if Lord Droxford wasn't ready to pummel that man for daring to dance with you, I will strip all the flowers out of my garden."

That was a *very* strong statement. Still, Tamsin was not inclined to agree.

Patting her grandmother's hand briefly, Tamsin turned and walked toward where Droxford stood slightly away from the hotel. The gardens were well lit, with numerous lanterns at intervals, and there were a few other people outside with them. Tamsin paused and looked back at her grandmother who remained outside the door. She nodded toward Tamsin and made a hand motion for Tamsin to keep going.

Droxford stood in shadow, and Tamsin had to move quite close to see his face. While he'd been glaring at Mr. Brimble before, his features were now impassive.

Tamsin felt nervous in a way she hadn't in his presence. It was as if her stomach were made of jelly. "Good evening, Lord Droxford. Are you enjoying the soiree?"

"No."

The single word was frigid and did not encourage further conversation. It was also quite honest, for he didn't look as if he were having a remotely good time.

"I can't say I am either," Tamsin confessed. "I was surprised by the arrival of my father's friend, Mr. Octavius Brimble. I believe you saw us dancing?"

"That man is your father's friend?"

"They are academic colleagues. I think their shared interest is military history."

"I didn't realize." He seemed relieved. His features lost their rigidity, and his shoulders relaxed.

"He is also, regrettably, the man my father hopes I will marry." Tamsin couldn't suppress the shudder that ran through her.

Droxford's gaze hardened once more. "Your father wishes to betroth you to that man?"

"He sent a letter the other day saying a potential suitor would be arriving in Weston. However, he didn't say when, nor did he identify the man. Mr. Brimble solved the mystery with his arrival tonight and his pronouncement that he is my 'intended' and will take me to St. Austell, where we will wed with haste." Again, a tremor of dismay wobbled her frame.

"Are you cold?" Droxford asked.

"No." The evening was quite warm. She just didn't care to think about traveling with Mr. Brimble.

"Are you considering marriage to him?" The question was cool, his expression again unreadable, but there was an underlying heat. Some volatile emotion…

Jealousy?

That word again! Tamsin pushed it from her mind, for it was her own imagination. He wasn't interested in her in that way. They were friends.

"I am not," she said plainly. Though she refused to believe he could be jealous, he was perhaps *something*. "Were you concerned for me?"

"As your friend, of course. I am sorry your father has sought to plan your marriage without consulting you."

Tamsin wondered what she was going to do about that. Her father would likely be disappointed she didn't want to marry Mr. Brimble. But would he be difficult about it? Would he try to insist? The better question was why he'd thought his *friend* would be a good match for his *daughter*. It was unconscionable to Tamsin.

She didn't want to think about any of that right now. She wanted to try to enjoy this soiree to which she'd been so looking forward.

"I do appreciate your concern," she said. "May we take our promenade now? I would like to do something that will help me regain my cheer."

"Certainly, but I should warn you that relying on me to provide anything cheerful is probably a mistake." His tone was so wry, his delivery so sardonic, that Tamsin couldn't help but laugh.

"You've already done it. You are nowhere near as sullen as you think."

"I'm not sure I would describe myself as sullen. However, I'm sure others have."

Again, he spoke drily, and Tamsin's mood continued to improve. He offered his arm, and she placed her hand on his sleeve. He was warm and solid and familiar. He made her feel safe, she realized.

They walked a few steps along the path before he said, "I wanted to speak with you. I will be returning home to Wood End tomorrow." His gaze was directed straight ahead.

Tamsin stared at his profile, feeling unaccountably sad that she wouldn't be seeing it tomorrow. Or the day after. She said the first thing that came to her mind. "You can't leave. I haven't seen you smile yet. And that smirk doesn't count."

He flicked a glance in her direction. "While that is a marginally compelling argument, I'm afraid it will not convince me to stay. I'm ready to return home."

"I won't pretend I'm not disappointed," she said. "I have very much enjoyed your company the past few days."

"I have too." He looked over at her. "Your company, I mean. My company gets rather dull. And yet, I continue to choose it above all others." The corner of his mouth lifted, and it was slightly more than a smirk.

"That's it! A half smile," she crowed. "I shall claim that as victory. Particularly since you showed me another one yesterday. Two halves do make a whole." She could paste them together—in her mind anyway—like the parts of a shell.

"Then I can leave without feeling as though I've disappointed you. Except you say you are disappointed." He paused, stopping with her near a fragrant rosebush. "Does that half smile improve things even a little?"

"It does," she said softly.

They were near the center of the garden, but between lanterns so that they were in one of the more shadowed areas. Still, she could make out his features, and the intense set of his jaw and the dark cast of his gaze.

She hated that their time together was at an end. Until next year. Although, by next year, she expected she might be wed, even if it wasn't to Mr. Brimble.

"I have something for you," he said, his voice low and rough as he pulled something from his coat. It was small and wrapped in paper.

Tamsin took her hand from his arm and accepted the item. "A gift?"

"Something you've been searching for," he said.

Holding her breath, Tamsin carefully unfolded the paper and revealed a perfect cockleshell nearly the size of her palm. It was magnificent.

And it was the first shell in her collection that she hadn't collected since the ones she'd found in her mother's room. Her father had never accompanied her. He'd always been too busy. That made this shell very special.

She raised her gaze to his. "Thank you. Wherever did you find it?"

"Ironically, not far from where I lifted you out of the water yesterday. I saw it after you returned to the picnic."

"But you said you didn't find anything."

His gaze was again a cool smolder. "I didn't want to give it you in front of the others. I preferred for us to be alone."

Alone. The rogue rule "Never be alone with a rogue" floated through her mind. But she ignored it.

"I love it." Clasping the shell in her hand, she stared into his eyes. Something was happening. Something electric and entirely between them.

The magnet returned, drawing her to move closer so they

nearly touched. Now he would kiss her. She could feel it in her bones. Her lashes fluttered, and her lips parted. She pressed her hand gently to the front of his coat. His hand brushed her waist, and her body quickened with a heady sensation with which she had little experience—desire. His head dipped, and she closed her eyes.

"Miss Penrose?" Tamsin turned her head toward the sound of Mr. Brimble's voice. She saw him just outside the hotel, his gaze scanning the garden until it landed on her.

"Blast," she muttered.

"I'll take you back inside," Droxford offered. "I won't leave you to him."

"Thank you," she said, relieved.

Thoroughly frustrated that Mr. Brimble had interrupted them, Tamsin clasped the baron's arm. He escorted her toward the hotel, but Mr. Brimble was coming toward them. He was nowhere near as tall as the baron, and his frame was much lighter, despite the slight paunch he sported.

"Pardon me," Mr. Brimble said a trifle too loudly, perhaps to catch their attention. As if they could miss him since he was walking directly into their path. "I should like to walk with my betrothed."

Tamsin didn't bother hiding her vexation. "I am not your betrothed. I am going into the hotel. Please excuse us."

Droxford propelled them forward. Mr. Brimble stepped aside at the last moment, but he grabbed Tamsin's elbow, halting their progress.

"You *will* be my betrothed, and I must insist you remain here with me."

Gasping, Tamsin pulled her arm from his grip. "Don't touch me without permission. You may not insist anything."

As he rounded on Mr. Brimble, Droxford's countenance looked darker and more forbidding than Tamsin had ever seen it. His lip curled as he addressed her father's friend.

"Touch her again, and you will be flat on your back with a swelling eye. Or jaw. I haven't decided which."

"See here, you can't threaten me. Nor can you make demands about my intended."

Droxford snarled. Like a beast. And to Tamsin, he was magnificent. "I am certain I heard her say she is *not* your intended."

Mr. Brimble sniffed. "This is simply a misunderstanding. If Miss Penrose would allow me a few moments of her time, we can sort this out." He reached for Tamsin, his hand grazing her arm.

Only grazing because he was very quickly knocked backward by Droxford's fist, which he'd sent into the man's midsection. Tamsin, who'd let go of the baron as he'd moved, gasped again and slapped her hand to her mouth.

Beside her, Droxford was stiff and unyielding, his face a mask of fury. She moved closer to him and put her hands on his arm. "Thank you," she whispered. "I'm all right now. We should go inside."

He turned his head toward her, his features softening slightly as he found her gaze.

"What have I just witnessed?" a shrill voice demanded.

Tamsin pivoted to see the busybody Mrs. Lawler approaching, her mouth open and her face pale. As bad as the altercation with Mr. Brimble had been, this was surely going to be worse.

Mrs. Lawler looked toward Tamsin and Droxford. "I saw everything that happened—your intimate tête-à-tête and Lord Droxford punching this man. I can only surmise that the two of you are on the verge of some important announcement." She blinked, her expression expectant.

It was so much worse. It was as bad as what had happened between Pandora and Bane. No, not that bad, because he'd used her cruelly and cast her aside. But Mrs.

Lawler's presence here would be just as damaging. She'd seen Tamsin and Droxford talking in the garden—almost kissing. Her choice of words indicated she'd seen precisely what was happening, and even if she was wrong, that was the story she would tell.

And now there were other witnesses as people filtered out of the hotel, likely because they'd heard the commotion of the baron and Mr. Brimble arguing. Had they seen Droxford hit him? Conclusions would be drawn, and right or wrong, the verdict would be that she and Droxford were somehow attached.

Though Tamsin tried to find the bright side in this moment, she utterly failed. This was verging on disaster.

"Indeed we are," Droxford said, his baritone filling the garden. "Miss Penrose has just agreed to become my wife."

Tamsin swung her head to gape at him. His wife? Surely, she'd heard him wrong.

Mrs. Lawler appeared surprised too, but she quickly rearranged her features. "Then congratulations are in order." She looked to Tamsin, smiling, "You must be thrilled to become the wife of a baron."

In that moment, Tamsin didn't know what she was.

CHAPTER 8

*J*saac clenched his jaw as if he could keep the words he'd already uttered from spilling forth. What had he been thinking?

That they were cornered. That this busybody woman was going to tell everyone that Isaac had hit someone in defense of Miss Penrose. Not to mention what she thought she saw before that—a tête-à-tête.

It hadn't been any such thing. They were two friends bidding one another farewell. While thinking about kissing. Probably that had only been him. If Brimble hadn't interrupted them, what would Mrs. Lawler have seen?

It didn't matter. They were already betrothed. Isaac could have kissed Miss Penrose senseless, and nothing would be different. Except that Isaac might be in a better mood.

Isaac noted that Miss Penrose did not respond to Mrs. Lawler. What was she to say to the woman? The busybody had butted her nose into this situation as she'd one with Bane and Miss Barclay a year ago. She could have walked away from what she'd seen then and preserved Miss

Barclay's reputation, and she could have done the same tonight.

However, it wasn't just her, he realized. Others had come from the hotel, and now there were at least ten people gawking at Brimble sprawled on the patio bricks. Isaac ought to help him up, but he could *not* bring himself to do so. The blackguard had put his hands on Miss Penrose and meant to cart her away under the falsehood that she was his betrothed.

Mrs. Lawler blinked several times as she looked from Isaac to Miss Penrose and then cast a pitying glance toward Brimble who'd managed to push himself up to a sitting position. "As pleased as I am for your betrothal, Lord Droxford, I thought I heard this gentleman say Miss Penrose was *his* intended."

"You misheard him," Miss Penrose replied hastily.

"But why would Lord Droxford have hit him if not because of a quarrel over you?" Mrs. Lawler asked, sounding genuinely curious, though there could be nothing genuine about her.

"It was a misunderstanding," Brimble grumbled as he got to his feet. "I offer my sincere congratulations to Miss Penrose and his lordship."

Isaac speared Mrs. Lawler with his most damning glower. "Since you've secured the latest on-dit, perhaps you can go inside and do what you do best."

"What is that?" Mrs. Lawler asked.

"Spread gossip," Isaac responded coldly.

Mrs. Lawler sucked in a quiet breath as she managed to appear completely offended. "That is not what I do best," she hissed.

"You may be right," Miss Penrose said, surprising Isaac with her interjection. "I do believe that would be spying." She turned briskly and grabbed Isaac's arm before marching away from the unpleasant scene.

"Where are we going?" he asked evenly.

She stopped on one of the garden paths. "I don't know. I just needed to get away from that horrid woman."

"I understand." Isaac wanted to get away from her too, but then he was having a hard time not leaving the garden entirely. He'd just changed the course of a young woman's life without her consent—*again.*

Releasing his arm, she turned to face him. "Is your hand all right?" She took the hand he'd used to hit Brimble between hers and held it between them, stroking the back with one of her thumbs.

Her touch was incredibly distracting, and his body was completely at odds with his head, which was telling him to put distance between himself and this woman. But why? If they were to be married, it wouldn't matter if they stood at twenty paces or if he took her in his arms.

"It's fine. Brimble's middle is rather soft."

She stared at him in silence for a bare moment, then giggled. Letting go of his hand, she brought one of hers to her mouth and fell quiet. "I'm sorry this happened," she mumbled behind her fingers. Eyes wide, she appeared quite apprehensive. "But we don't really have to get married."

"She will tell everyone we are betrothed," Isaac said, fighting to keep calm in the face of his life completely changing in ways he didn't want. Never mind her future being ripped out from under her.

"Yes, but interest will wane. You're leaving tomorrow, and I'll be departing for Cornwall in another ten days or so. People will forget this happened."

While Isaac appreciated her optimism, he didn't think she could be more wrong. "You assume the gossip won't spread outside Weston. What happened last year traveled all the way to London. I am not surprised Bane hasn't shown his face there—everyone is aware of what he did to Miss

Barclay." And Isaac was *not* Bane. He would marry the woman he'd ruined or was perceived to have ruined. Or almost ruined.

This was an absolute calamity. He shouldn't marry her, regardless of what had happened. He was precisely the sort of man she didn't want, and now he had forced her into marriage.

"No one is going to care about a nobody from Cornwall," she said with a gentle shrug.

"Perhaps not, but they will most certainly comment on my behavior. While I am not heir to a dukedom as Bane is, I *am* a baron and I have built a not insubstantial place for myself in the House of Lords. My not marrying a woman to whom I was believed—publicly—to be betrothed would reflect poorly on me and could affect my work." He couldn't help scowling. This was a disaster.

Miss Penrose blanched, and he wished he'd thought to speak more gently. He schooled his features to stop scowling at least. "I hadn't thought of that," she said quietly, her features strained with tension. "I don't want anyone to think poorly of you."

"They won't, because I am not Bane. I will not allow your reputation to be damaged by what happened. I should not have behaved as I did." He'd nearly kissed her and then he'd resorted to violence to protect her. He'd practically screamed his interest in her, and now he would pay the price for his lack of self-control. Just as he had more than a decade earlier. "We will wed."

She stared at him. "I could just cry off in a fortnight or so. Then you can walk away free of blame. Your reputation will be fine."

"And yours will be ruined."

"Not in St. Austell it won't. No one will care. I can continue as I always have."

With no hope for marriage. But perhaps that had always been her plan. "It won't upset you to become a spinster?"

"I always considered that would be a possibility, if not a likelihood."

Isaac envisioned a future where she was alone. Would she still be as cheerful as she was now? Or would loneliness and despair overtake her as it had his father? "While your optimism is admirable, I think you are being shortsighted. This will affect you adversely, even where everyone knows you. You've seen what your friend, Miss Barclay, has gone through. Do you really want that for yourself? Please don't make me insist upon the marriage, but it must happen."

Deep furrows lined her brow. "I don't wish to be a burden. Do you even want to wed?"

He didn't want to answer that truthfully, for then she would know this was not his choice and she would continue to insist they needn't marry. Which led him to the obvious conclusion: she didn't want to marry him. "You are not a burden. While this may not be what either of us would have chosen, we must make the best of it."

"You don't have to," she whispered.

"Yes, I do. Let me do the right thing for you. Allow me to protect you from Mrs. Lawler's gossip. You deserve that."

She stared at him a long moment, and he had no idea what was going on behind her inscrutable gaze. "All right."

He took a deep breath and set his mind to what needed to happen next. Planning and execution were comforting activities as well as being the things he was best at. "I will depart for Wood End tomorrow and ready things for you there. I have some things to manage before I can come to St. Austell, but I will write to your father as well as to the rector to instruct him to read the banns. We will wed three weeks hence, probably closer to four weeks with the banns on three consecutive Sundays." He could purchase a license and wed her sooner, but he needed the time at Wood End. He also reasoned that reading the banns, then wedding in due course would make it appear as if this had been planned and wasn't a rush to avoid a scandal. "Is there a particular day you wish to have the ceremony?"

She blinked before answering, and he wondered what was going on in her mind. Probably as many things as were whirling in his. "The Tuesday after that third Sunday is acceptable."

"Then we are agreed."

"I suppose we are." Her expression was resigned.

Isaac pushed aside the horrid sensation that he was ruining another woman, albeit in a different way. With his thoughtless actions, he'd decided her future for her, and now she was stuck. If anyone was a burden, it was him. He'd ignored the warnings in his head and continued to put himself in her presence. Everything that had happened tonight was his fault. "Let's go inside and tell everyone, namely your grandmother."

He offered her his arm, and this time when she put her hand on his sleeve, he didn't feel a warmth or a desire to pull her closer. He tensed, knowing she likely felt as though she was marching to her doom.

~

*T*amsin felt as if she were walking through wet sand. Up to her knees. That reminded her of the cockleshell, which she'd thrust into her pocket amidst the drama. Droxford giving her the shell now felt like another lifetime. She supposed it was—her life before she'd become betrothed.

She still couldn't quite believe this was happening, even while she understood why he'd done it. He'd leapt to

Tamsin's aid, saving her from certain ruin—or so he believed.

He'd said this wasn't a choice either of them would have made, which made her think he didn't really want to marry her. But why would he? This had been a forced betrothal, a matter of propriety, a desperate attempt to save Tamsin's reputation. And, it seemed, his own. This wasn't the fairy-tale marriage she'd so recently become enamored with.

Tamsin didn't like the sense of uneasiness settling over her. This was dangerous territory where sadness lurked and threatened to drag her down.

It could be worse. She could be marrying Brimble. Drox-ford had asked her to let him protect her and told her she deserved that. His words had entranced her. He was doing this for her, to keep her safe from ruin.

A calming warmth pushed away her unease. This might not have been what they had chosen, but they *would* make the best of it, just as he'd said.

She glanced over at Droxford as they walked into the hotel. His expression was stoic, his attention fixed straight ahead. But he often looked like that, she reasoned. She mustn't read too much into his expression.

Tamsin scanned the parlor. "My grandmother is over near the hearth." She stood with Persephone and…was that Pandora? Her back was to them, but Tamsin was certain it was her.

Had Pandora seen Mrs. Lawler? Had she yet heard the news? Tamsin wished she'd told the harpy to keep their betrothal to herself for a while so that Tamsin could tell her grandmother first.

Grandmama saw them approach and immediately moved toward them. "Are you all right?" she asked, looking at Tamsin. It seemed she'd heard what had happened.

"I'm quite well," Tamsin said, not wanting to worry her

grandmother. She also should have asked Droxford if they could pretend this was a happy occasion. Well, Tamsin would do that anyway, in part because she was determined to make it so. They were committed, so why not try to find the joy in it?

"I'm glad to hear it." Grandmama looked visibly relieved. "Mr. Brimble has left. He was clutching his middle." She transferred her attention to the baron. "Thank you for protecting my granddaughter."

Droxford said nothing, but inclined his head. His features were still impassive, his eyes stormy. He appeared every bit the brooding baron.

Persephone and Pandora moved to join them. Tamsin wanted to hug Pandora. This situation was likely summoning bad memories of Bane to the surface.

"I'm so sorry, Pandora," Tamsin said. "I hope you didn't have to see Mrs. Lawler."

"She kept her back to that vile woman," Persephone responded.

Pandora glanced toward her sister. "Only because you told me she was coming, for which I am grateful." She looked at Tamsin with deep sympathy. "I'm so sorry this happened to you."

Tamsin brought forth a smile. "It is not a tragedy. Lord Droxford has sprung to my defense, and now we will be married." No one said anything for a long moment, and Tamsin hated the discomfort. "Did you not hear me? This is a happy occasion!"

Grandmama gave Tamsin and Droxford an encouraging smile. "Indeed it is. My marriage to Tamsin's grandfather was arranged, and we were very happy together. I loved him deeply."

"We will wed in St. Austell," Droxford said, his tone clipped. "I'll be leaving for Wood End first thing tomorrow."

Tamsin had noted he was quite thorough in his mental preparations. "We will wed after the banns are read. I do hope everyone will come."

Grandmama patted Tamsin's arm. "You know I will. We'll leave for St. Austell in a few days."

"We'll all be there," Pandora said to Tamsin.

"Please excuse me, then," Droxford said.

Tamsin realized she was still clutching his arm and released him with alacrity. "I wish you safe travels."

He inclined his head. "I wish you the same." How formal they'd become.

Sliding her hand into her pocket, Tamsin stroked the cockleshell and yearned for the way they'd been before. Marriage would be much easier if they were at least friends, wouldn't it?

"You are a good man," Grandmama said to the baron. "I'm proud to welcome you as my grandson-in-law."

Droxford gave her a succinct nod. "Good evening to all of you." He bowed, then took his leave.

The next time she saw him, they would be wed. Or nearly so.

Just a week ago, she hadn't seriously considered marriage. She'd never had to. Then her father's letter had arrived, and she'd surprisingly warmed to the idea. How she'd hoped her father's chosen suitor was the groom she'd dreamed of! Alas, he hadn't been, and now she was betrothed to the man she'd come to know and like. A man who'd made her feel special, even as he told her he would not have chosen marriage. She realized suddenly that he'd never actually answered her question as to whether he wanted to wed.

She felt confident she knew the answer, and it was no.

"Do you want to leave?" Grandmama asked softly, drawing Tamsin from the tumble of thoughts running rampant through her mind.

"I think so, yes."

Persephone touched Tamsin's arm. "We'll call on you tomorrow."

"I would like that." Tamsin smiled at her friends—she didn't want them to worry either—and turned to go with her grandmother.

They were silent until they were settled in Tamsin's grandmother's coach. They sat together on the forward-facing seat. Grandmama didn't wait for the coach to move before she angled her upper body toward Tamsin.

"My sweet Tamsin, I can't tell if you're upset, because you are always so cheerful."

"I'm just surprised by the events of the evening. I didn't expect to meet my father's intended suitor, and I certainly didn't think I'd become betrothed." She laughed softly, but Grandmama was still watching her with a stern, concerned expression.

"You don't have to pretend to be happy with me," Grandmama said softly. "Though, you could do much worse than Lord Droxford. He strikes me as a man of integrity."

Tamsin would agree. She'd already decided he wasn't a rogue. "We were enjoying a lovely walk." She placed her hand over her pocket and felt the faint ridges of the cockleshell through her gown. "Then Mr. Brimble came outside and insisted I walk with him. He tried to grab me, and Droxford warned him not to, but he did it a second time, and that was when Droxford hit him in the belly."

"Good for Droxford. You see, I told you he was jealous."

"Do jealous men resort to violence?" Tamsin asked.

"They do if they think the woman that they care about is under attack. I believe he did." Grandmama's lips pursed. "And this is when Mrs. Loose-Lips interrupted?"

Tamsin giggled at her grandmother's nickname for the woman. "Yes."

Grandmama relaxed against the squab. "You're going to be the wife of a baron. How proud your grandfather would be. I do wonder what your father will say, particularly when he learns his choice of suitor was felled by your betrothed."

"Should we bother writing to him or just arrive in St. Austell to inform him of the news?" Tamsin asked.

"I expect Brimble will write to him immediately, so we should do the same."

"I'll do that when we get home."

Would he be angry? Disappointed? Tamsin wasn't sure, in large part because she didn't really know why he'd wanted her to wed in the first place. When she arrived at Penrose House, she would learn the truth of things.

Hopefully, her father would be happy for her. Though, Tamsin wasn't sure that happiness was an emotion she'd ever seen him feel. Perhaps this would be the thing that provoked it in him. Yes, that sounded right to Tamsin. He would be thrilled that his daughter was marrying—and a hardworking baron to boot. Indeed, she could see them having much in common, at least with regard to their work ethic.

Grandmama patted Tamsin's knee. "I hope Lord Droxford realizes how fortunate he is. Probably, since he seems to already hold affection for you, if his jealousy is any indication. By the time I visit you to plan his new garden, you'll be smitten as can be. Mark my words."

Tamsin wasn't sure she agreed, but it was certainly something to aspire to. In the meantime, she looked forward to getting to know the man who made her heart race, who swept her into his arms, who gave her cockleshells, and who told her she deserved to be protected. Could there be any greater hero than that?

CHAPTER 9

*T*hough Tamsin had clung to her optimism regarding her impending marriage, she'd awakened in the middle of the night from a dream in which Droxford had banished her to Cornwall while he carried on very publicly with a mistress in London. While unsettling, the dream was preposterous. Tamsin couldn't imagine Droxford swanning about London with a mistress on his arm.

She wondered how early he'd left that morning and what the others at the Grove had said to him, if anything. Had he even seen them? She was particularly curious if Min or Ellis had encountered him, and if so, what had transpired. Tamsin would find out shortly when they arrived. Persephone had sent a note earlier that she'd invited the others to join her and Pandora in visiting Tamsin today, which Tamsin didn't at all mind.

The sound of people in the entry hall signaled someone's arrival. Tamsin waited in the drawing room, and a moment later, Persephone and Pandora entered.

"You don't have to go through with this," Pandora said without preamble as she made her way toward Tamsin.

Persephone cast her sister an impatient look from the corner of her eye. "Good afternoon, Tamsin."

Pandora moved to sit on a dark-gold settee. "I'm sure Tamsin is unconcerned with pleasantries. We are her dearest friends, and she is in a crisis."

"It isn't really a *crisis*," Tamsin said. She hated to cause anyone trouble or upset. And in this case, she desperately wanted to protect Pandora from the memories of last year. However, it was precisely because of last year that this was likely a crisis in Pandora's eyes.

"Don't tell me you're being ridiculously optimistic about this too?" Pandora asked.

Persephone glared at Pandora as she sat down beside her. "Should she become cynical like you?"

Tamsin took the chair near the settee. "I can't help being optimistic, just as I know this entire mess has surely aroused all of Pandora's worst memories."

"Thank you," Pandora murmured. "I just hate that this happened to you. Mrs. Lawler is a menace."

"My grandmother has a new name for her," Tamsin said. "Mrs. Loose-Lips."

Pandora laughed with delight, and the tension eased. When she sobered, she apologized to Tamsin. "I will not be cynical. Not about you and Droxford."

"Thank you. Truly, this is not the worst thing." Before Tamsin could say more, the others arrived.

Min and Ellis sat on the settee opposite Pandora and Persephone, while Gwen, whom they'd fetched from the hotel on their way, took the chair at the other end of the seating arrangement.

"Please tell me we haven't missed anything," Min said.

"Not at all," Persephone assured her.

Tamsin turned toward Min. "Did Droxford leave this morning?"

Min gave her a sympathetic smile. "Yes, he departed early. We didn't see him—not last night or today."

"He didn't call on you this morning?" Gwen asked.

Tamsin shook her head. "I didn't expect him to. He'd already planned to return home today. He told me before… what happened in the garden."

"Yes, please tell us exactly what happened," Pandora urged. "Unless you'd prefer not to."

"I don't mind telling you," Tamsin said. "Ironically, Droxford was behaving in a most gentlemanly fashion."

"Because he is not a rogue," Persephone said. "And he is doing the responsible thing by marrying you."

Tamsin nodded. "Yes. He takes full responsibility, particularly because of the way he reacted to Mr. Brimble."

"Please explain this Mr. Brimble person," Ellis said, and everyone looked at Tamsin expectantly.

Tamsin told them how he was a friend of her father's and had come to escort her to St. Austell for their wedding, that he believed them to be betrothed already.

"Did your father tell him that, or did he leap to his own conclusion?" Persephone asked crossly. "I cannot abide meddling parents." That made sense because of the way her parents had interfered in her life.

"I don't know," Tamsin replied, going on to detail what happened next, with Brimble insisting they were betrothed and trying to grab her and Droxford warning him not to touch her again.

"But he did?" Gwen asked, her eyes widening slightly.

Tamsin nodded. "That's when Droxford hit him."

Min smiled. "You have to agree that it's very romantic, the way he defended you."

That made Tamsin think of what he'd said, how she deserved protection. "I don't know if it's romantic, but it's certainly thoughtful."

"What happened next?" Gwen asked. "Had the baron planned to propose before Brimble made a nuisance of himself?"

"No. Droxford saw the certain scandal with Mrs. Loose-Lips—because she was clear about what she thought she was seeing—and immediately announced our betrothal."

Pandora sniggered. "Mrs. Loose-Lips is perfect."

"Credit my grandmother," Tamsin said with a grin.

"What did she think she was seeing?" Min asked.

"I believe she said a tête-à-tête, and then she witnessed Droxford hitting Brimble. She drew her own conclusions—that they were fighting over me." Tamsin rolled her eyes.

"Weren't they, though?" Persephone asked.

Tamsin hadn't really considered that. "I don't think so. Droxford merely prevented the man from overstepping. Brimble was behaving most obnoxiously."

"Sounds as though he deserved it," Ellis observed.

"I still don't think you have to go through with the betrothal," Pandora said, her brow furrowed. "I can't see this being a problem for you in sleepy St. Austell."

Tamsin didn't tell her that she was repeating Tamsin's own initial reaction, and she didn't disagree with Pandora's assessment. Pandora had been to St. Austell. She knew how remote it was.

"You could say that you don't suit after all," Min suggested. "If that's what you want. Do you want to avoid the marriage?"

Droxford's insistence that they wed came back to Tamsin, along with this plea that she let him do the right thing. How could she deny him that? And as she'd told her grandmother, there were worse things than marrying a baron.

"You're taking too long to answer," Pandora said. "You must cry off."

"No, I mustn't. Honestly, I'd begun to look forward to

getting married after my father sent that letter about a suitor. Droxford and I get on rather well, at least as friends, and I've every reason to believe we can have a pleasant marriage."

Persephone arched a brow. "I will hope it's more than pleasant."

"Aren't you worried you may be too different?" Gwen asked, her brow also pleated. Indeed, they were all regarding her with grave concern. "He's so dour, and you are so cheerful."

Tamsin actually hadn't spent much time dwelling on that since last night, but now she would. Or at least consider it. "We do have different temperaments," she said slowly. "But sometimes that's for the best, isn't it? Each person balances the other."

"What a wonderfully optimistic attitude." Persephone winked at Tamsin. "Not that I'm surprised."

"I hate to think of you being trapped in a marriage without love," Gwen said. "You at least deserve affection."

"I think we have that," Tamsin said. "Last night, before Brimble interrupted us, Droxford gave me a whole cockleshell."

Min's nostrils flared. "Did he know you've been looking for that?" At Tamsin's nod, she added, "That is a very special gift."

"I did think he might kiss me just after that, but that's when Brimble came along."

Gwen's eyes rounded. "Oh! Perhaps we must all share your optimism, then."

"You have time to change your mind," Pandora put in. "If you want. Just know that we will support you no matter what."

Everyone joined in with their agreement.

"I'm still concerned their personalities are too different—he is *so* broody," Min said.

"We will find our way," Tamsin said with a bright smile. They simply had to.

Gwen looked to Tamsin. "I don't suppose you're staying in Weston until the end of August?"

Tamsin shook her head. "Grandmama and I think it's best if we remove to St. Austell in a few days to prepare for the wedding."

"Is it wrong of me to be selfishly disappointed that once again our wonderful summer time together has been irreparably interrupted?" Ellis asked.

"You are being kind by saying interrupted," Pandora said sardonically. "I would say ruined. Next year, we must find a way to guard our August from Mrs. Loose-Lips. And from rogues."

"Droxford isn't a rogue, though," Tamsin pointed out. Of that, she was absolutely certain. A rogue would not have made her feel utterly safe and protected or important and valued.

Tamsin's friends stayed awhile longer and made plans to join her in St. Austell a few days before the ceremony. She sensed they weren't entirely convinced this marriage was the right choice, but Tamsin didn't want to defend it to them. Droxford had persuaded her that they needed to wed. Aside from avoiding scandal and another disastrous match organized by her father, Tamsin wanted to be married. She was eager for the chance to have the family she didn't, to be the mother she'd lacked. And she saw the possibility for happiness.

She couldn't turn away from that chance.

~

*T*amsin had to awaken her grandmother when they arrived in St. Austell. "We're nearly to Penrose House, Grandmama."

Lifting her head from the small pillow she'd tucked between her head and the side of the coach, Grandmama blinked her eyes open. "Already?"

Hiding a smile, Tamsin nodded. It had been a long day of travel, and unlike her grandmother, Tamsin found it difficult to sleep in a moving coach. Particularly in Cornwall, where the roads were not as well developed.

A few minutes later, they arrived at Penrose House and stepped out of the coach. The day was quite fine, with a clear blue sky and a brilliant sun warming the late afternoon. A seabird squawked as it flew overhead, as if welcoming Tamsin home.

The door opened before they reached it, and Mrs. Treen, the housekeeper, smiled widely upon seeing them. At sixty, with white hair and a round frame, she was the closest thing to a mother Tamsin had known. "Welcome home, Tamsin."

Tamsin embraced the woman, then turned toward her grandmother. "You remember my grandmother, Mrs. Dewhurst."

"Of course I do," Mrs. Treen said with a touch of reverence. "I'm sorry it has been so long since we've seen you."

Thinking back, Tamsin realized her grandmother—and grandfather when he'd been alive—hadn't visited Penrose House since Tamsin was ten, the year after her mother had died. Following that, Tamsin had always visited them in Weston. Because her father and grandparents did not get on well.

"I'm sorry too," Grandmama said. "I have always been grateful for your presence here, Mrs. Treen. It has given me immense comfort over the years."

Mrs. Treen blushed. "Tamsin means a great deal to me, to all of us here at Penrose House. We love her like our own."

Grandmama smiled brightly. "I could not ask for more."

"Look at my lack of hospitality!" Mrs. Treen declared. "Come inside immediately."

She held the door wide, and Tamsin gestured for her grandmother to precede her. Once they were in the entrance hall, they removed their hats, and Mrs. Treen eagerly accepted them. "I'll fetch some lemonade and cakes. Unless you'd prefer to retreat directly to your rooms." She looked to Tamsin with a pleated brow. "Though, I'm afraid your father requested you attend him in his study as soon as you arrived."

Grandmama looked aghast. "He can't even be bothered to leave his hermitage to greet her?"

Tamsin stifled a laugh at Grandmama's use of the word *hermitage* to describe her father's study. It wasn't wrong.

"He's in the middle of a project," Mrs. Treen said somewhat lamely, as if she didn't want to say it.

"Isn't he always?" Grandmama sniffed.

"Don't fret, Grandmama," Tamsin reassured her. "You rest in the sitting room, and I'll be along shortly." She couldn't imagine her father would spare much time to speak with her if he was busy with something. Still, he would want to congratulate her on her marriage and ask about her betrothed.

"I'll be waiting," Grandmama said.

As Tamsin walked to her father's study, apprehension ticked up her spine. In her letter to him, she'd shared her betrothal to the Baron Droxford before apologizing for not making a match with Brimble. He had not responded, but then she'd told him not to for they would shortly be traveling to Cornwall.

Why was she worried? Or course he would be happy for

her, even though she wasn't marrying his friend.

The door to his study was closed, as usual, and Tamsin knocked softly as required. "Papa, it's me." Announcing oneself was also a necessity.

She realized the stark difference between living at her grandmother's cottage and residing here at Penrose House. Here, there were strict rules and expectations, particularly surrounding her father. She'd followed those because it had not only been easiest but seemed to make him happy, which in turn, made her happy. She dearly hoped that her happiness —her upcoming marriage—would make him happy.

"Come in."

Tamsin opened the door and slipped inside, closing it behind her. The study was dark and masculine, with oak bookcases lining the walls and heavy amber drapes on the windows. Besides the desk at which her father practically lived, there was a large table where he laid things out that he was researching. There were no seating areas, just the chair at his desk, another near the hearth where he liked to read at night, and two other wooden ones he moved about the room as necessary. Again, she was struck by how different it felt to be at Penrose House after being at her grandmother's.

"It's good to see you, Papa," Tamsin said cheerfully.

Of average height, with graying brown hair and hazel eyes, Charles Penrose looked up toward Tamsin, his gold-rimmed spectacles perched on the middle of his nose. Removing them, he set the glasses atop his desk. Rather, on the open book that was there.

"You look well. I trust your journey wasn't too taxing."

Tamsin relaxed. If he had time to make pleasant chitchat, he likely wasn't angry with her.

"It was quite tolerable, even for Grandmama."

Papa's nose wrinkled, but he said nothing about his mother-in-law. Perhaps there was another reason for his reaction. He fixed Tamsin with a perturbed stare, and she perhaps had her answer. "I was most upset to receive your letter."

Tamsin's pulse quickened with a spike of anxiety. He *was* angry. "You were upset to learn I am betrothed to Lord Droxford? Surely that is happy news, Papa."

"Not when I'd expected you to marry Octavius. I told you I'd chosen a husband for you."

Staring at her father, Tamsin pushed through her surprise at his reaction. He truly wasn't happy for her, and he'd absolutely expected her to marry his friend—not just to consider him, but to wed him. "You also neglected to tell me who that was, Papa. I've known Mr. Brimble my whole life. He's your friend. He's not…a suitor. Not for me, anyway."

Papa pursed his lips. "He was a perfectly acceptable suitor. Plenty of young ladies marry older men."

"I suppose they do," Tamsin said evenly. "However, it happens I am going to marry a younger man. Furthermore, Mr. Brimble did not behave as a gentleman ought. He was presumptuous about our betrothal, which was not finalized, and was much too forward."

"From his letter, I gather that he was only trying to settle the betrothal with you, and you did not allow him the courtesy."

"I wasn't rude." Tamsin was growing frustrated. "I wish you wouldn't take his version as the absolute truth. He tried to grab me without my consent. Surely that doesn't recommend him."

Papa's eyes rounded briefly. "I did not realize." He coughed. "Well, I'm sure it was all a misunderstanding. Brimble is a good man. He would have made you a fine husband."

Had he heard her correctly? Tamsin was suddenly struck with a barrage of memories where she either hadn't felt listened to by him or he hadn't even bothered to listen. All her hurts, both physical and otherwise, had been tended to by Mrs. Treen. How many times had she tried to speak to him at dinner only for his attention to be directed on a book he'd brought to the table. He'd distractedly respond to her, but had he actually heard what she'd said? She recalled one instance in particular when she'd excitedly told him about finding a rock that looked like a shell—it was the most peculiar thing. He hadn't even spared a glance for her or the curiosity.

Tamsin's frustration mounted. "Aren't you pleased to hear I'm marrying a baron? His estate has eight hundred acres. And he's very involved in the Lords." She'd thought that would impress him.

"I was not pleased to learn he won't be coming until the day before the wedding. What sort of groom risks waiting to arrive until the last minute? One who's fallen into the parson's trap and doesn't really wish to wed."

"That isn't true," she argued, hating this conflict between them. But was it worse than his usual silence? "Droxford is merely busy." In truth, she was bothered by this news. She would write to him immediately and ask him about it.

"Why did you decide to marry him?" her father asked, pulling her focus back to their discussion.

She was *not* going to explain the truth of the matter. It didn't signify, especially to her father who had never cared to ask her things before. He hadn't even been interested in her marrying before a few weeks ago!

"I'm marrying him because he's a good man, and we'll be happy together." Tamsin was glad she didn't have to convince Grandmama. After her friends' skepticism and now her father's near hostility, it was nice to have at least one person who was happy for her.

Her father grunted in response.

"Papa, I must ask why you thought Brimble was a good choice for me. I don't see that we have much in common."

"You seemed to enjoy his visits. He's a good friend, a highly intelligent man. You do such a fine job taking care of me. I thought you would be delighted to do the same for him." Papa said all this in a rather matter-of-fact manner, as if it were obvious. "I must say, I can't see you as a baron's wife. Are you truly ready to take on London Society? You don't know the first thing, and I certainly can't guide you."

His lack of faith in her stole every last bit of her optimism. It was one thing not to like her choice of husband but to question her abilities was just...cold. But then he'd been cold her entire life. Or at least since her mother had gone. Though, she didn't really remember him being anything other than focused on his work. She'd just chosen to believe he cared about more than that, that he cared about *her*. It seemed as though that had all been an illusion created by her need to find joy and not feel disappointment or despair. Years of pushing that away crashed down on her as she saw the truth. She was alone here and had always been.

"I'm sorry you think that, Papa. After the way I've managed your household, from a very young age, I might add, and taken care of you, I would have thought you would have more faith in me. Why did you decide I should wed in the first place? You've never even hinted that you wanted me to marry. Indeed, you've discouraged me from attending assemblies or doing anything else that might foster meeting eligible gentlemen."

He coughed and picked up his glasses without looking at her. "It's always been in the back of my mind. And when Brimble suggested he was interested in marrying you, I thought it would be a fine match, as I just explained."

"So, it was Brimble's idea?" Tamsin asked.

"He suggested it, and I agreed the match had merit. Little

did I know you had set your sights on a lofty baron." Now he glanced in her direction. "I never took you for a social climber, Tamsin."

Gasping, Tamsin felt a rare flash of anger. "I am not, and I can't imagine why you would think that of me. I became acquainted with Droxford in Weston, and we decided we would suit." She didn't like lying to her father, but she couldn't bear him doubting her marriage, not when he wasn't even in favor of it. "I would have thought you would talk to me about marriage. You didn't even ask if I wanted to wed." He'd never asked her about anything. It wasn't that she hadn't known that, but she was finally acknowledging his treatment of her.

And it hurt.

"You must be tired after your travels," he said gruffly. "I'll see you at dinner."

How many times had she waited for that, only for her to end up bringing his dinner here after he'd failed to come? "I hope so."

Did she? Or would she prefer to dine with just her grand-mother? Grandmama would certainly be happy if her father didn't show up. And perhaps for the first time, Tamsin would like that too.

Soon enough, she would leave Penrose House for good. She was going to start a new life with a husband who wanted to protect her and put her first.

She wouldn't be lonely as she'd been here, since Droxford had already proven to be a wonderful companion whether he was keeping her company at a luncheon or hunting for shells on the beach. They may not have chosen this path, but they'd committed to it, and she had the chance to build a real marriage with Droxford.

Finding her optimism settled the upset she'd had with her father. She just needed to cling to that, as she'd always done.

CHAPTER 10

As Isaac approached the door to Penrose House, he was filled with the anxiety he'd been ignoring the past few weeks. He could no longer avoid thinking of the fact that he was about to be wed—tomorrow—that his life was going to change and not in ways he wanted.

During the journey, he *had* considered the benefits of having a wife, namely one with Miss Penrose's affable nature. She would be an excellent hostess and would provide a warm counterpoint to his aloofness. Indeed, she would be most helpful to him in London.

At night, in the darkness and privacy of his bedchamber, he'd also thought about the other benefits of having a wife. But the idea of letting Tamsin that close filled him with dread. Because he'd ended up ruining the one other person who'd been intimate with him like that. And if Tamsin knew the truth of that, who he really was, she'd never want to come near him.

She'd been clear about not wanting to marry a rogue, and here he was, forcing her to do just that. He had not changed or reformed as Wellesbourne had done.

Perhaps he should have let her cry off.

He and Miss Penrose had exchanged two letters each, but the missives had been bereft of anything that might indicate how either of them were feeling about their upcoming nuptials. She'd asked about his arrival date, and he hadn't been able to tell if that troubled her. Granted, he hadn't asked. He deemed it better to save their conversations about the marriage for when they were together in person. That moment was upon them.

Isaac knocked on the door, and a few moments later was greeted by a white-haired housekeeper with rosy cheeks and dark brown eyes that creased at the edges. She looked to be a cheerful woman who smiled often. Since this was where Tamsin lived, Isaac expected nothing else.

The housekeeper's eyes rounded. "You're here at last!" Her lilting Cornish-accented tone carried happiness as well as a tinge of relief.

"I am Droxford. I regret my late arrival." He'd hoped to arrive earlier in the day, but there had been rain yesterday, and it had slowed their progress.

The housekeeper gestured for him to move inside as she opened the door wide. "I am Mrs. Treen. Tamsin will be delighted you're here."

Isaac removed his hat and gloves, and the housekeeper offered to take them as she closed the door. He delivered the items to her and looked about the dark-paneled entry hall. "Is Miss Penrose available to greet me?" he asked.

"Certainly. However, Mr. Penrose has determined that you must see him first. I'm to show you to his study upon your arrival. If you'll follow me?"

Isaac wanted to insist he see Miss Penrose first, but he didn't wish to trouble the housekeeper. Her employer had set her a specific task, and he wouldn't ask her to go against that.

Tension bunched his shoulders as he anticipated the

coming interview. Penrose had responded to his letter regarding the wedding plans with irritation. His response had said that Isaac should have asked permission to wed her, and that she'd already been nearly betrothed to someone else. Isaac hadn't bothered replying.

Following Mrs. Treen through the house, Isaac determined the structure to be at least a hundred years old. It was in good condition, but some of the walls could use new paper and paint. The furniture, while nice, was somewhat out of fashion. The only reason Isaac knew that was because of comments his aunt had made about the furnishings at Wood End. She tried to keep things elegant and fashionable as well as comfortable, but her husband had not always been in favor of spending money on such things. Isaac hadn't replaced a single piece of furniture since taking up residence four years ago.

Would Miss Penrose wish to update things? He had to think she'd want to put her mark on the home she would manage. Had she been allowed to do that here?

The study was in the rear corner of the ground floor. Mrs. Treen stopped before a dark wood door. She hesitated before knocking, and her jaw seemed to tense.

Isaac heard footfalls before the door opened to reveal Tamsin's father. He was several inches shorter than Isaac and possessed a thin, rather tired-looking face.

Mrs. Treen dipped her head slightly. "Begging your pardon for disturbing you, Mr. Penrose, but you asked to see Lord Droxford as soon as he arrived."

Penrose's gaze fixed on Isaac. "This him? Must be. Come in." He turned away, and Isaac exchanged a look with Mrs. Treen.

"Go on," she whispered. "I'll let Tamsin know you're here." She gave Isaac an encouraging smile as he moved into the study.

The door closed behind him with a swift snap. Isaac glanced back, surprised that they'd been shut inside. Was this to be a sensitive interview?

Penrose had moved to the other side of his desk. Was that because he felt most comfortable there? He was clearly in the midst of something, given the books and papers spread across the desk. Or did he want a barrier between them for some reason?

"It's past time you arrived," Penrose said gruffly. The downward pitch of the man's brown brows and the irritated twist of his lips, along with his dark tone, gave the impression he was annoyed—just as his letter had sounded.

Already inclined to find fault with the man based on his letter, Isaac worked to summon a pleasant expression. Or at least a placid one. "I am glad to make your acquaintance. I regret I was not able to arrive sooner."

Penrose's frown deepened. "I must say I am disappointed in the lateness of your arrival."

Isaac tried not to scowl. "My letter indicated I had a great deal of business to attend at my estate."

"Don't you have an adequate steward to manage things for you?"

Isaac's ire stirred. He'd spent much of his youth explaining himself, or, more accurately defending himself, to his father, and he wasn't going to do the same with this man he'd just met. Even if he was to be Isaac's father-in-law. "I have an excellent steward. However, my presence was required. If you are concerned that your daughter is less important to me than my estate, rest assured that I will place her welfare above all else."

Penrose stared at him a moment before letting out a soft harrumph. "I am glad to hear that. If you truly mean what you say, you will allow Tamsin to return here in November and to remain through January. She will want to spend Yuletide with those she knows best. She will also need to return in June and stay through August. Through July, anyway, before removing to Weston in August with her grandmother." He said the last with a bit of distaste, as if he didn't care for that arrangement.

Was that what she wanted? She hadn't mentioned anything in the letters she'd sent Isaac, but perhaps she was waiting to discuss this with him in person. He decided the matter would need to be settled with his bride, not her father. "Your daughter and I have not discussed where we will spend Yuletide."

"She is likely too nervous to broach the subject," Penrose said. "Which is why I wanted to mention it to you. She may not convey how important it is to her that she spend that time here for fear you won't understand."

Isaac didn't like that she felt she couldn't talk to him about such things. But why wouldn't she feel that way? They'd become betrothed to avoid a scandal and had spent no time together since. There was a great deal they hadn't discussed and should.

Did Isaac care if she preferred to spend half the year in Cornwall? Neither of them wanted to marry, so perhaps this was an acceptable solution. "If spending that much time here will make Miss Penrose happy, how can I refuse?"

"Miss Penrose?" her father asked. "Is that how you address your soon-to-be wife?"

Isaac hadn't ever called her Tamsin or even thought of her by her given name. He supposed he ought to start, at least with the latter. "Until we are wed, yes."

"Very proper of you," Penrose muttered. "I'm pleased you value my daughter's happiness. I am not, however, pleased with how you behaved in Weston. You should have asked for my permission to wed my daughter."

Irritation pricked at Isaac once more. "You said as much

in your letter. However, she is of an age that doesn't require your permission. I understood your disapproval when I received your letter."

Penrose gave him a particularly sour look. "Since you did not respond, I wasn't sure if you did. Your treatment of my friend was abominable. Did you send him an apology as I suggested?"

"I did not," Isaac said firmly. "The man touched your daughter—rather roughly—without her consent. Surely, she explained all this to you?"

"She did, and I said it was likely a misunderstanding," Penrose said defensively. "Brimble was only trying to settle the betrothal with Tamsin."

Isaac tried to cling to his patience. "I daresay Brimble's account was one-sided. Your *friend* tried to grab her, and I warned him against doing so again. Recklessly, he tried a second time, and I was forced to ensure he was not able to make a third attempt."

"That does not sound like Brimble."

How could this man take the side of his friend over that of his own daughter, who probably couldn't fabricate a lie if she was forced to? How did the man not possess a need to protect her and keep her safe that rivaled Isaac's?

"Nevertheless, that is what happened," Isaac said coolly, relieved that he would be taking Tamsin away from her selfish father.

Penrose harrumphed, and Isaac had to muster every bit of self-control not to tell the man that he was being a horrible father. Instead, he said, "I gather you'd hoped the two of them would suit, but they did not. As it happened, I got there first." That characterization was laughable, but it was also necessary.

"And do you suit?"

"Apparently." What else could Isaac say?

"I confess I wonder if your betrothal wasn't entirely due to the presence of some woman who seemed keen to start a scandal. Brimble informed me of what happened." Penrose's gaze had turned accusatory.

Again, Isaac fought to keep a tight rein on his patience. "Not entirely, no. While that was not how Miss Penrose and I would have chosen to announce our engagement, that is, regrettably, what occurred. If not for Brimble's unacceptable behavior, the entire event would not have happened as it did." He took a deep breath as he ignored his own unacceptable behavior—he never should have been in that garden, and yet now he considered that if he hadn't been, what would Brimble have done? "I would appreciate if you could stop focusing on the past instead of the bright future that awaits your daughter." Isaac didn't add *as a lady of the peerage*, though he was certainly thinking it. What father would not be happy about that?

Penrose's jaw clenched. "Tamsin is my greatest concern. You permitting her to spend the holiday season here as well as the summer will make her happy. She has been moping about since arriving home. She will miss everyone here at Penrose House."

Isaac had difficulty imagining Tamsin moping, but what if she was dreading their marriage? He didn't want her to be unhappy. There was still time for them to cancel the wedding. He'd resigned himself to the marriage, in name only at least. There was simply no other way.

If he didn't marry her, he would be branded a rogue, which he actually deserved. But Tamsin would be ruined, and she did *not* deserve that. Furthermore, she'd be stuck here with her father who didn't value her and would likely try to marry her off to someone unsuitable again.

At least as Lady Droxford, Isaac could give Tamsin a fulfilling life as mistress of her own house and of a grand estate. She would preside over his house in London, and he could see her reveling in that as she infused joy into a space where there wasn't any.

All that was fine. Excellent, even. But it was still a marriage in name only. He could not be intimate with Tamsin because he would need to tell her the truth so she could fully consent. Which brought him back to why he was going through with this marriage without being honest with her first: because if she knew he was a rogue, she wouldn't marry him, and she'd be ruined. And at the mercy of her father. He was right back where he'd started in that garden three weeks ago—in an impossible situation.

A knock made him and Penrose look toward the door. Before Isaac pivoted, he caught the flash of irritation in Penrose's gaze. He seemed easy to annoy.

"Come," Penrose said brusquely.

The door cracked open a scant few inches. "Papa? I heard Lord Droxford had arrived."

Isaac couldn't see her face. She kept the door nearly closed as she spoke. But just the sound of her voice made his pulse quicken. Time apart had not lessened his desire for her, solidifying that this was indeed an obsession. As much as Mary had been, if not more. And look how that had turned out. He shook away a sense of foreboding.

"He's here," Penrose answered. "Come in, girl. Better yet, take him with you, as I've work to do."

Tamsin pushed the door wider, and at last Isaac saw her. Dressed in a simple, soft rose-colored gown, her brown hair piled into a neat style, she looked even lovelier than he remembered.

Her lips curved into a wide, room-brightening smile. "Droxford, how pleasing to see you."

"Off with you both," Penrose said impatiently.

Isaac looked back toward her father. "Thank you for the

opportunity to become acquainted. I am certain we will spend more time together at dinner and of course tomorrow." On their wedding day. He ignored the persistent ripple of anxiety running through him.

Tamsin gestured with her head for him to join her. "Let us go now."

He didn't need to be prompted twice to leave her father's company. When he was outside the study, she quickly closed the door.

"I take it your father prefers his door closed," Isaac said sardonically as he glanced back at the study.

"Always. I hated having to knock just then. He doesn't like to be disturbed unless it's an urgent matter."

He arched a brow. "This was not?"

"Well, it was urgent to *me*," she said smiling. "But not to him." She waved her hand toward the closed door. "Never mind him now. I'm glad you're here."

"I'm sorry I am arriving so late," he blurted.

"You said in your letter that you had a great many things to see to." She shrugged. "I'm sure you left as soon as you could. Come this way." Without touching him, she led him through the gallery that cut through the ground floor until they arrived in a cozy sitting room.

"I hope you weren't concerned," he said, thinking that arriving the eve before the ceremony was perhaps rogue behavior, which she and her friends disdained.

"I was surprised when my father informed me, but you explained it in your response to me after I asked you about it." She smiled at him. "I understand you're a busy baron."

He was glad to hear she wasn't upset. "Thank you."

They regarded each other in silence for a moment. Was she, like he, trying to determine what to say? When had things become awkward between them?

What a foolish thing to wonder. Their friendship had

fractured the moment he'd punched that idiot Brimble.

Isaac spoke first. "I realize we haven't had much time— any time—to talk since…that night at the hotel. I should have called on you before I left the next day so that we could discuss a few things."

"It's all right," she said, magnanimous as ever. "You were already planning to leave, so I wasn't expecting you."

"Everything happened so quickly, and things were tense that evening." Isaac didn't want to prevaricate any longer. He needed to get to the heart of things. "You indicated you wanted to cry off. I shouldn't have discounted your wishes. Do you still want to do that?"

She stared at him, then blinked, her throat moving as she swallowed. "Er, no. I am ready to get married tomorrow. Unless *you* want to cry off? I confess I did wonder if you delayed your journey because you were having second thoughts."

Isaac hated that she wasn't entirely wrong. "I do not wish to cry off. I am a man of my word." He was also a man who hadn't told her the truth. "What if I told you that I am, in fact, a rogue? That I've done things of which I am not proud. Things that would likely make you want to run as far away from me as possible. But please don't ask me what those things are. They are in the past."

It took her a moment to respond, and Isaac feared she was going to change her mind. Feared? He should want her to.

"The fact that you are worried and that you say those things are in the past tells me everything I need to know," she said quietly. "If you ever were a rogue, you are clearly reformed. I am not running anywhere."

They were getting married. He'd given her the chance to cry off, and she hadn't taken it. Relief washed through him, which proved he hadn't reformed at all.

"Do you still wish to leave tomorrow after the breakfast?" he asked, trying to divert his thoughts. Though they'd agreed to that in their correspondence, Isaac wanted to make sure she hadn't changed her mind, particularly since, according to her father, she was having a hard time leaving.

When she didn't answer immediately, Isaac took that to mean she was at least torn on the matter. "Why don't we stay for a day or two," he suggested. "Or three, even. We needn't rush off. Then, you can return for Yuletide and Epiphany."

Her brow gently pleated. "Will you be coming back with me?"

Now, *he* hesitated before answering. "If you want me to, though I may not come for as long as you wish to stay."

"How long—"

Before she could finish, Mrs. Treen walked into the sitting room and gave them an apologetic smile. "Pardon me for interrupting, but Ellie needs to see Tamsin for some final adjustments to her wedding costume."

Tamsin looked to Isaac. "Ellie is our upstairs maid who also helps me from time to time."

Isaac knew she didn't have a lady's maid because she'd said so in one of her letters. She'd indicated that her housekeeper had said she would need one. Then she'd asked if he'd agreed.

What did he know of what a lady needed? He'd had trouble adjusting to a valet himself. But he'd asked his housekeeper, and she'd been delighted to train a maid for the new lady.

Though he hadn't said everything he needed to, Isaac recognized it would all have to wait. They'd settled the most important matter anyway—that they would indeed be getting married tomorrow.

"I'll take my leave so you can attend to your wedding garments," he said. "I'll see you tonight when I return for dinner." They were to dine here at Penrose House with their friends.

"Until then." Tamsin picked up her skirts and departed, leaving him with the housekeeper.

After Tamsin had gone, Mrs. Treen said, "I confess I was concerned when Tamsin became betrothed so suddenly." She regarded him with unabashed interest, as if she were taking his measure. "But you'll make sure she's all right, won't you?"

"I will."

Mrs. Treen gave him a firm nod. "Good. She looks like the happiest, most cheerful person you'll ever know—and she is, truly. However, there is more to her than that, my lord, and I hope you see that she needs a kind and loving husband who will be her staunchest ally, someone on whom she can depend, no matter what." She started toward the gallery which would lead to the entrance hall. "Your hat and gloves are by the door."

As Isaac followed Mrs. Treen, he considered her words carefully. Of course there was more to Tamsin than her joyful disposition. Just as there was more to him than his brooding seriousness. Not that he let anyone see past that. Would she show him the other side of herself, and if she did, would he let down his guard in return?

He hadn't given any thought to how they were different, and he really should have. Perhaps he was doing her a disservice by shackling himself to her. She was definitely at the poorer end of the arrangement if one considered their personalities.

But he'd given her the chance to cry off, and she'd refused. Their future together, however it progressed, was assured.

Whatever happened, he had no doubt she would be an excellent wife and lady of the manor. He would find a way to ensure her happiness—it was the least he could do.

CHAPTER 11

The sapphire ring on Tamsin's left hand felt foreign beneath her glove as they rode from the church to Penrose House in a barouche. Her husband sat beside her, looking impeccably handsome in a dark blue suit of clothing and gleaming black Hessians.

The ceremony had been lovely, particularly with all their friends present. Tamsin's grandmother had cried happy tears and said she hoped to visit them at Wood End soon.

Before the ceremony, her father had asked if she was certain about marrying Isaac, saying it wasn't too late to change her mind.

Tamsin had tried to put their conversation yesterday behind her so she could be happy on her wedding day, but his continued pressure about not marrying Isaac had reignited her frustration with him. It had also made her glad that she was getting married to a man who cared about her.

"Was your father pleased to hear that we're staying for a few days?" Isaac asked as the barouche moved through St. Austell. There were some people about, waving to them as they passed. Tamsin smiled and waved back.

"Actually, I didn't speak to him about that." She sent Isaac a sideways look as she waved at someone. "I'd prefer to leave after the breakfast, as we originally planned. If you don't mind."

"I don't mind at all. I just thought you wanted to stay awhile before leaving the only home you've ever known. I understand you're going to miss everyone, and it's been difficult for you to contemplate leaving."

Tamsin angled herself toward him as they left the town behind. While she was going to miss everyone, she wouldn't have characterized her upcoming departure as "difficult." "Why do you think that?"

He lifted a shoulder. "Your father told me yesterday. He wants to ensure your happiness. He cares that you are content. As do I, which is why I am more than amenable to your desire to return for Yuletide and Epiphany as well as next summer."

When Isaac had suggested yesterday that she come home for the holidays, she'd worried it was because he'd preferred to be apart, but that was not the case. He really did just care about *her* and what she might want. She felt incredibly lucky to have that after realizing how little her father thought of her. "It is not my desire to return for those periods," she said. "I did wonder why you mentioned that yesterday. Did my father tell you that too?"

"He did."

Her father didn't want her to marry, and he wanted her home for months at a time. Pursing her lips, Tamsin felt another rare burst of anger, again toward her father. Why was he aggravating her this way? He'd told Isaac she was having trouble leaving and that she wanted to return for the holidays. Neither of those things were true. "I don't know what my father was about telling you any of that, but I expected to spend Yuletide and Epiphany in my new home."

She paused, looking over at him with trepidation. "Isn't that what your wife should do?"

"Yes, but I want you to be happy and choose where you'd like to be."

Tamsin's anger at her father mellowed in the face of Isaac's concern. She was so glad to have his support. Any doubts she had about their marriage were drifting away. "My choice is to be with you," she said eagerly. "I made it when I agreed we should wed, and I confirmed it a short while ago in the church."

"Then that is settled." His throat was working, his jaw clenched. He didn't appear "settled."

"Is there something else?" Tamsin asked.

He took a moment to respond. "I would prefer a marriage in name only. At least for a while, as we grow used to one another," he added.

"I see." Tamsin wasn't surprised, though hearing him say it stung. She was just glad he wasn't talking about a permanent situation.

"We should have discussed this yesterday," he said, his brow deeply furrowed and his eyes hooded. "I'm sorry."

Because it was too late now. They were wed. Which meant there was no use being upset about it. Tamsin summoned a smile. "I am patient. Of course, we must get to know one another."

"I'm glad you agree." He appeared relieved. "At Wood End, we will share an apartment but have separate bedchambers. I have also ensured that we have separate bedchambers on the way to Wood End."

While this made sense, she didn't like the way they were now. Wouldn't it be better if they were at least friends? "I should like to return to our earlier friendship."

He looked at her, his eyes clearer than she'd seen them

since he arrived. "I would like the same thing. I enjoyed our conversations."

Ironically, they fell silent as they drove out of St. Austell toward Penrose House. It was perhaps easier said than done to return to how they'd been before.

At last, he looked over at her. "Why did your father tell me you wanted to spend so much time here if that wasn't true?"

"I'm not sure what he was doing." Tamsin planned to speak with him before they left. His behavior just didn't make sense. She was also vexed with him and didn't want to leave things like that between them. "I suspect *he* is the one who wants me to return. And rather than me having difficulty leaving, he is struggling. We've only been apart for a month at a time, when I spend August with my grandmother. He's going to miss me terribly." Again, she wondered if it was because her mother had left him, and now Tamsin was going.

"I gather your father spends a great deal of time in his study," Isaac said. "I was surprised when he left the dining room last night before the final course in order to return to his work. Is that typical?"

She nodded. "Sometimes he doesn't even take dinner in the dining room."

Isaac frowned slightly. "You dine alone?"

"Occasionally, but if Papa is working, I usually eat in the kitchen."

One of his dark brows arched. "I must ask why your father would miss you if he chooses to spend most of his time closeted in his study."

Tamsin couldn't fault Isaac's logic. Nor could she deny that she made excuses for her father and did her best to explain away why he ignored her. "I suppose we have a unique relationship."

The barouche hit a bump, and Tamsin lurched forward

off the seat. Isaac's arms came around her, and he hauled her backward.

She turned in his arms and looked up into his smoldering gray eyes. Everything around them seemed to fall away so that it was just the two of them locked in this moment.

After some time, she said, "This reminds me of the day on the beach."

His gaze seemed to focus on her mouth. Would he kiss her finally?

Then he settled her on the seat beside him. Of course, he wouldn't kiss her. He desired a marriage in name only. At least for now.

"We have arrived," he announced.

Tamsin whipped her head about to confirm what he said. She hadn't even noticed they were close to Penrose House. She'd been too engrossed in his embrace.

When the barouche came to a stop, Isaac climbed down. Offering his hand, he helped her to the ground. "We will leave after breakfast. I will dispatch a note to the inn for my valet to pack my things."

She let go of his hand reluctantly. His touch, even with their gloves, sparked a pleasing warmth. The attraction she'd felt for him in Weston hadn't dissipated. In fact, it suddenly felt stronger. Was that because he'd all but told her he didn't feel the same and now she wanted even more eagerly what she couldn't have?

Or was she looking for things that weren't there? For so long, she'd imagined her father cared for her, that he truly had her best interests at heart. When, in fact, he'd been utterly detached from her.

She needed to be careful she didn't make the same mistakes with Isaac. She could be optimistic, but it might behoove her to be a trifle guarded.

~

*T*he wedding breakfast was merry and busy, with many people from the surrounding area stopping in to offer their congratulations. Isaac wasn't remotely surprised to see the number of people who wanted to wish Tamsin well.

She greeted everyone with her usual cheer, and her laughter filled every area she occupied. Isaac was glad to see her enjoying herself. Still, he detected a faint line between her brows. Just one. A lingering reaction from their conversation in the barouche, when he'd told her he preferred a marriage in name only, at least for now.

He'd realized that he needed to explicitly communicate that he didn't want intimacy, and he couldn't feel badly that he'd been honest about that, at least. He wasn't a good man. He was a rogue who'd already ruined one woman.

Even worse, he couldn't stop thinking of Tamsin in his arms, and then she'd fallen into them in the barouche. Now he was right back where he'd been with her in Weston, obsessing about when he would see her next. Whether he could kiss her…

But wanting to kiss his wife did not mean he would follow through with it. He hadn't kissed anyone in more than a decade. The thought of it filled him with a mix of apprehension and anticipation. He couldn't avoid it forever. Unless she decided she didn't want a real marriage either.

Except that wasn't his impression. She'd seemed disappointed by what he'd said, then said she could be patient, which meant she expected this was a temporary arrangement. What if it wasn't? What if Isaac was never ready to open himself up again?

Mrs. Dewhurst approached him, and Isaac relaxed a little. He genuinely liked his new grandmother-in-law.

"I would ask why you're standing over here by yourself," she said. "However, I gathered you do not care for social events, even when the purpose is to celebrate your own marriage."

"Guilty, I'm afraid. I am glad to see Tamsin having a good time."

"She always does," Mrs. Dewhurst said, her attention moving to Tamsin, who stood speaking with her cousin—who Isaac now realized was also his cousin by marriage—and the Prices.

"Does she take after her mother?" Isaac asked, thinking she definitely hadn't inherited her good humor from her father. Penrose had been skulking in the corner of the drawing room like a trapped animal for more than a quarter of an hour.

Mrs. Dewhurst visibly stiffened, and her jaw worked. Too late, Isaac realized he'd brought up the woman's daughter, who'd abandoned her daughter and husband. It was possible, if not likely, that Mrs. Dewhurst had a great many feelings about that, and he'd dredged all of them to the surface.

"No, Tamsin does not resemble her mother in any way, save some physical attributes," Mrs. Dewhurst said brusquely. "My daughter was a selfish person. Tamsin gets her optimism and pleasant nature from me and her grandfather. If I'm honest, it's primarily her grandfather. He was the kindest, biggest-hearted person I ever knew. Except for Tamsin." Her features softened as she looked toward her granddaughter once more.

"My apologies," Isaac said. "I didn't mean to bring up a disturbing subject."

Mrs. Dewhurst gave him a feeble smile. "My daughter's defection will probably always break my heart. I rarely think of her. It's easier that way."

Isaac understood that more than the woman could know.

His gaze moved to Tamsin's father, still lurking in the corner of the drawing room. His eyes were wide and darted about the room as if he were searching for an escape. He seemed ill-equipped for social occasions. On that, at least, Isaac could commiserate with the man.

However, he was not interested in commiseration. He wanted to know why he'd lied about Tamsin. It had troubled her, with good reason, and Isaac didn't want her to be upset.

Having finished his glass of wine, Isaac set the empty glass on a table. "Please excuse me, Grandmama." She'd bade him call her that after the ceremony.

"Of course," she replied with a warm smile.

He made his way to his father-in-law. "Penrose, I'd like a word. Might we remove to your study?"

A profound look of relief passed over the older man's features. "Certainly." He led Isaac back to the corner of the house to his study. Once inside, his body relaxed, his shoulders dipping, and his brow flattening.

Isaac closed the door.

Penrose arched a brow at him. "Is that necessary?"

"I understood you prefer the door closed."

"I do, actually, but this is your interview, not mine," Penrose said. "What is it you wish to speak with me about?"

"Your daughter. I do not understand your machinations regarding her departing Penrose House and returning for the holidays and the summer." Isaac hadn't even told her about that part. "You made it sound as if she wanted to spend nearly half the year here, but that isn't true. You also indicated she was having trouble leaving, but that is not the case either. Furthermore, it's evident to me that when she *is* here, you pay little to no attention to her. Why then, do you care if she leaves or whether she visits?"

Though Isaac suspected he knew the answer already, he wanted to hear the man say it.

Penrose's jaw worked, and his hands flexed. "I pay atten-tion to Tamsin, it's just that…my work is very important to me. It's all I have." His gaze met Isaac's, and there was a hint of desperation. "Surely a man who works as hard as you do understands that."

Isaac was definitely not going to commiserate with him about that. "Your work is not all you have—you have Tamsin. Why do you spend so much of your time ignoring her?" It reminded Isaac too much of his father, though he would have taken neglect over harsh expectations and unreasonable demands. His father had expected Isaac to be an automaton at a young age, and when he wasn't, the man could be quite cruel.

"I don't ignore her," he snapped. "She just…reminds me of her mother. I would never turn my back on Tamsin the way her mother did to us." Penrose scrubbed his hand over his face. "You are right—I have more than my work. I have—I *had*—Tamsin."

Penrose sank into a wooden chair next to his desk. Resting his elbows on his thighs, he stared ahead, his gaze unfocused. "I was a terrible husband. My work has always been the most important thing to me, and my wife knew that. She gave up on me. But Tamsin never did." He looked up at Isaac, unshed tears in his eyes. "She should have gone to live with her grandmother. It would have been better for her. But I couldn't let her go, not after losing her mother."

"Even though she was a constant reminder of what you'd lost?" Isaac could see her father's complicated emotions and pitied him for them. To feel such things could break a man, which was why Isaac preferred to eschew them. He began to comprehend why Penrose submersed himself in his work, especially if he had a penchant for doing so anyway. Isaac saw far too much of himself, and he didn't like it. He buried the notion.

"Yes," Penrose replied. "Though Tamsin reminded me every day of her mother, who chose to abandon us, I couldn't let Tamsin go too, even if that may have been what was best for her." He took a deep breath and wiped his hand over his eyes. "I won't do that now. I want her to be happy, and she thinks she can have that with you. She deserves that."

Isaac's gut twisted. Of course she would think they could be happy. She was a naturally optimistic person. And he'd immediately told her he wanted a marriage in name only.

Penrose stood and fixed Isaac with a beseeching stare. "Do your best to be a good husband to her. And, when the time comes, a loving father to your children. I want that so badly for her."

How could Isaac promise any of those things when he'd just told Tamsin their marriage would be something completely different? "I will do my best to ensure she's happy." That was not a lie, for he would do that. It was the least—and right now, best—he could offer her.

"Thank you. Please know you are both welcome here any time. I will even endeavor to spend more time in your company when you visit." He grimaced. "That will be easier for me—just the two of you. Last night and today are too many people for me to manage."

"I completely understand," Isaac said. "I too dislike large social events unless I have a clear goal, such as speaking to someone about business. I do not care to socialize for the sake of socializing."

Penrose's eyes lit with appreciation. "We are of a like mind, then." He smiled, and Isaac realized it was the first time he'd seen the man do so, even during the wedding cere-mony earlier. But then, Isaac hadn't smiled either.

For the first time, he was angry at himself for not smiling, for not *trying* to smile. Tamsin deserved a husband who at least smiled at her on her wedding day, especially now that

Isaac knew the kind of father she'd grown up with. While Penrose was a far sight better than Isaac's own father, he was still lacking in many ways.

At least he was trying to make up for it now. Isaac's father had never done that.

"Apparently, we are." Isaac straightened. "Tamsin and I will be leaving after the breakfast as we originally planned."

Penrose nodded, but there was a sadness lurking in his expression. "You go with my blessing."

"Thank you." Isaac glanced back at the door. "I suppose we should return to the infernal gathering."

Another smile lifted Penrose's lips. "Allow me a moment to collect myself. I'll be along directly."

Isaac turned. Before he opened the door, he looked back at Penrose. "Give yourself some grace. You've raised an extraordinary young woman. You may not have been as present as you should have been, but you did not abandon her. She seems to feel loved and secure, and that is the best we can hope for our children, isn't it?" Isaac had never felt those things. His father had made him feel like a burden and that he would never be good enough. Because, though he was his father's sole remaining family member, he couldn't ever compensate for the loss of his mother and brother. His presence hadn't been enough for his father to love him. Furthermore, Isaac had abandoned his own child. He didn't deserve a second chance with another.

Emotion began to overwhelm him. This was why Isaac hated feeling things and tried not to. When he'd revealed himself with Mary, it had all gone to hell. So, he didn't think about loving anyone. Or having children.

Having a family.

The thing he'd always craved, but had walked away from.

"That is indeed all we can hope for," Penrose said. "Thank you, Droxford. I'm pleased to welcome you to the family."

Opening the door, Isaac left the study. He purposely didn't close the door behind him. He didn't want Penrose to think he could hide or sulk. But perhaps he wouldn't want to. Perhaps he had realized that he needed to spend the last bit of time that he could with his daughter before she left to start her new life.

CHAPTER 12

"*A*nd here we are!" Gwen said as she guided Tamsin into the sitting room where Pandora, Persephone, Min, and Ellis were seated, waiting. "You didn't think we could pass up one last opportunity to be together before we go our separate ways."

"Especially after our Weston holiday was cut short *again* this year," Min exclaimed.

Tamsin was delighted to have her friends gathered, even if it would only be for a short time, as the wedding breakfast was winding down.

"We've a gift for you," Persephone said. "The same one I received when I wed Acton."

Pandora gave Tamsin a wrapped parcel.

"Thank you," Tamsin said, sitting on the edge of a chair and placing the package in her lap. "Truly, having you all here is the best gift I could ever receive."

Gwen sat down too. "Open it!"

Laughing, Tamsin, unwrapped the package to reveal a framed piece of embroidery. "The Rogue Rules." She read them quickly, smiling, before turning it around and showing everyone. "Pandora, did you make this?"

Nodding, Pandora glanced at Persephone. "Just like the one I made for Persey. Well, not just like it. Tamsin, yours has shells in the corners."

It did indeed, including a cockleshell. Tamsin hugged it to her chest and felt the slight weight of the cockleshell in her pocket, where she'd carried it during the wedding ceremony. "I love it."

"Even if your husband isn't really a rogue?" Min asked with a chuckle.

"We all need reminders," Pandora said.

"I can't argue with that, but you are right that Isaac isn't a rogue. At least, not so far as I can tell." Was he a rogue for declaring their marriage would be in name only? Better to communicate such things than not, Tamsin reasoned.

"Your father is the real rogue," Pandora said with a knowing look.

"Why is that?" Gwen asked.

"Because he ignores her and puts his work above all else. And he sought to betroth her to one of his friends." Pandora made a face.

Tamsin wasn't sure "rogue" was the right description for her father, but he was something unpleasant. However, she didn't want to dwell on that while she was with her friends for the last time for a long while. "He told me I could cry off, that no one here would judge me. He also shares your concerns about whether Isaac and I are a suitable match. But none of that matters now, since we are wed." Tamsin gave them a smile that was perhaps overbright. She was really struggling with her optimism today. And it was her wedding day!

Min reached over and touched Tamsin's arm. "Goodness, we did not mean to cast aspersions on your marriage. After what transpired in Weston, we just wanted to make sure you were confident in your decision. Because we care about you."

Only Tamsin *wasn't* confident, not since her husband had informed her their marriage would be in name only.

Temporarily, she reminded herself. She changed the topic to when they would next be together. Most of them would be in London in the spring, except Pandora. At least, Tamsin expected she would be in London. Perhaps she ought to confirm that with Isaac.

They talked for a while longer before Tamsin said she needed to prepare to leave. She hugged everyone but saved Persephone for last. "Can you stay a moment?" Tamsin asked. "I have a few questions."

Persephone's brow rose slightly, and her eyes lit with understanding. "Of course." She turned to look at Pandora who stood near the door. "I'll meet you in the drawing room."

Nodding, Pandora left, but not before blowing a kiss to Tamsin.

"I should have asked if you had questions about tonight," Persephone said. "Forgive me."

"Actually, it isn't about tonight, as I don't believe anything will be happening beyond me sleeping at an inn." Tamsin gathered her courage to share what she must. She needed someone's advice, and Persephone was the only person who could help her at the moment. "You know this marriage wasn't on purpose. We had to wed."

"Yes, but I thought doing so was amenable to you both." Persephone's lips parted, and her eyes rounded. "Droxford hasn't expressed regret, has he?"

"No, but he has stated that he prefers a marriage in name only. At least for now." Tamsin shook her head.

"I take it that means no physical intimacy?"

Tamsin nodded. "I think so. I didn't ask for details. I wouldn't know what to say. We haven't even kissed."

Persephone's brow puckered. "Perhaps you should ask him about the future, whether he hopes intimacy will come. Without it, there will be no children, and I would think he has a duty to produce an heir."

Tamsin hadn't considered children, at least not in terms of the conversation they'd had earlier. She supposed she was still thinking things through. "I feel…attracted to him. I'd like to have physical intimacy. A kiss at least would be nice," she added with a feeble laugh, thinking that she'd gone long periods of time in her life with little to no physical connection. Mrs. Treen hugged her from time to time, but Tamsin couldn't remember the last time her father had done so.

"I wish I had better advice for you, but I think you must give this time. Everything happened so quickly, and you are both in an unbreakable union you didn't anticipate. I hope you aren't regretting it." She looked at Tamsin with deep concern.

"I am not. We were friends before, and we're going to work on being that again. Perhaps from there we can find our way to a real marriage. If he even wants that."

Persephone's nose wrinkled. "He should. A lifetime without an intimate relationship with your spouse sounds horrendous. And I can't see Droxford as the type to keep a mistress. Though, perhaps you should also ask him if that's his intent." Her gaze filled with sympathy. "Better for you to know what to expect."

"I agree. So, you…enjoy the intimacies of marriage with Wellesbourne?" Tamsin asked.

"Oh, yes," Persephone replied with a grin. "That's the best part of it all."

Tamsin had hoped she wouldn't say that.

"You must write to me if you need anything," Persephone said insistently. "I am here to help—whatever you require."

"Thank you. I appreciate that more than I can say." Tamsin hugged her tightly.

They left the sitting room together, and when Persephone headed toward the drawing room to join the others, Tamsin instead went to her father's study. She needed to settle things with him before she departed.

The door was wide open when she arrived. Tamsin stopped short, finding that extremely odd. Perhaps he wasn't inside. In fact, he likely wasn't since there were still a few guests in the drawing room. Still, the door was always closed, even when he wasn't there. *Especially* when he wasn't there.

She stepped to the threshold and peered inside. Her father sat to the right of the door in a wooden chair. She would not have seen him if she hadn't moved closer to look.

Tamsin's father jumped to his feet. "Tamsin, I was just going to come find you." His gaze dipped to the embroidery in her hand, which she'd almost forgotten she was carrying. "What do you have there?"

"A gift from my friends. Pandora made it."

He nodded vaguely. "It's nice to see Miss Barclay again."

Tamsin appreciated him saying that. As she searched for the words to tell him she would be leaving shortly, he said, "I understand you and Droxford are leaving for Hampshire this afternoon. I'm glad." He didn't meet her gaze as he shuffled toward his desk.

"Papa, I need to know why you suggested to my husband that I am having trouble leaving and that I wanted to spend the holidays here. Is it because you don't want me to leave?"

Turning toward her, he blew out a breath. "You have caught me out, just as Droxford did earlier."

Isaac had spoken with him? He'd taken up her side, just as she'd known he would. Because he cared for her. He'd proven that the moment he'd insisted they'd wed. And he'd shown her many times over during their acquaintance.

"He asked me the same questions," her father continued. "I will tell you more directly." His eyes met hers, and she was taken aback by the emotion—the sadness—in them. "I don't want you to go. The reason I endorsed Brimble's suit was because he didn't mind if you spent half the year here. I asked if he would allow you to spend November through January here and then June and July, plus August in Weston."

Tamsin stared at him. "You negotiated where I would live?"

He blanched. "I am not proud of my selfishness. I couldn't bear you leaving. But I also knew you'd want to have a family of your own someday. I'd already done too much to prevent that. Brimble seemed a good answer to our problems."

"To your problem. I didn't have one." Tamsin winced at the flash of pain in her father's eyes. Her anger fled, and she was disappointed in herself for harboring it in the first place.

"You're right. It wasn't your problem. I'm sorry for…everything."

Tamsin hadn't known how much she needed to hear him say such things to her. "Thank you, Papa. You arranging a suitor made me realize I do want to marry. I would like to have my own family, to be the mother I didn't have."

He made an odd sound like a hiccup that he tried to hold in. "You deserve that, which is what I told your husband. I wish I could give you advice, but the truth is that I don't know if I ever learned how to be married or a father. I'm afraid I wasn't a very good husband to your mother, and I was not the best father to you."

"I know you love me, Papa."

His eyes glowed with a fleeting warmth. "I do. Despite that, I've been selfish. I should have sent you to live with your grandmother after your mother left. That would have been best for you."

"Why would you think that?"

"Forgive me for speaking frankly, but you are an adult and a married woman now, and it's time I was honest. Your mother's infidelity and abandonment devastated me. I was so angry and so hurt, in large part because of how she treated you. What mother leaves her child?"

Tamsin worked to ignore the pang of sadness that gripped her. "I don't know."

He looked at her with naked remorse. "I drove her away from us. And instead of ensuring you were cared for, I continued as I had always done, immersing myself in my work, perhaps even more than I had before in order to bury my own pain."

"You don't know that you drove her away," Tamsin argued, not wanting him to bear the brunt of that. "We will never know."

There was silence for a moment before he said, almost wistfully, "You remind me so much of her—in appearance if not in demeanor. Though, when I first met her, she was so full of joy. Like you."

Tamsin didn't remember those qualities about her, at least not to the extent her father was describing. "I recall she was occasionally happy, but not always."

"That was how she became," he said sadly. "Until she decided she could be happier somewhere else. And then she died." Papa looked away and sniffed.

Her mother had taken ill and died in a matter of weeks. Tamsin hadn't been able to see her or even write to her. "I hope she died happier." That was what Tamsin had chosen to believe. The truth, she'd long ago decided, didn't matter.

"I hope so too." A sad smile curved his mouth. "I loved her

so, and I love her still, if you can believe that. I love you too, Tamsin."

The words seared into Tamsin's heart. She'd known he did—she'd just told him that, and he'd affirmed it—but hearing him say the words filled her with an indescribable joy. She couldn't remember the last time he'd said them.

He went on, "I hope you can forgive me for my selfishness. I am a foolish old man."

Overwhelmed with emotion, she went to him and touched his sleeve. "I understand why you did all that, Papa. And I am not angry. I know how hard it must be to say this, especially to encourage me to go and leave you."

He smiled at her and brushed a kiss on her forehead. Tamsin couldn't remember the last time he'd done that. Her heart lodged in her throat.

"I hope you will be very happy with Droxford," her father said. "I confess I have been impressed by him. I am confident your marriage will be more successful than mine. I will pray every day that it is."

"Oh, Papa, thank you." Tamsin set the embroidery on his desk and hugged him tightly.

"Good heavens, this is a shocking display," Grandmama said from behind Tamsin.

Stepping back from her father and turning, Tamsin wiped at her eyes, for a trace of moisture was leaking out. "Papa has been telling me how happy he is for me." Those hadn't been his exact words, but overall, that was what Tamsin believed he meant.

Surprise flashed in Grandmama's eyes then she narrowed them slightly toward Tamsin's father. "I'm glad to hear it." She returned her attention to Tamsin, smiling. "The last guests are going to leave, and you need to say farewell."

"Of course." Tamsin picked up the embroidered Rogue

Rules and started toward the door. Looking back at her father, she asked if he was coming.

"I'll be along directly."

Nodding, Tamsin stepped from the study. But she lingered outside the door for her grandmother.

Except Grandmama didn't immediately follow her. Tamsin's father was speaking.

"I owe you an apology for always being so distant," he said.

"I appreciate that. I apologize for blaming you for my daughter leaving." Grandmama sounded a bit weary.

"You had every right," Papa said. "She deserved better than I gave her. I regret that more than you can know, especially since I continued my selfish behavior after she left when Tamsin needed me most."

"I should have insisted you let me take her," Grandmama said flatly. "But you convinced me that the two of you needed each other."

"I definitely needed her, though I had a terrible way of showing it. I'm trying to make things right now. I want her to go and be happy. That's all I could hope for."

"Then we are in agreement. At last." Grandmama laughed, and Tamsin could hear the irony in it.

Papa laughed too, and Tamsin had to clap a hand over her mouth lest they hear her giggle along with them.

Before Tamsin could hurry toward the drawing room, her grandmother walked out of the study. Face flushing, Tamsin started moving. "I didn't mean to eavesdrop," she said as her grandmother walked alongside her.

"I don't mind, dear." Grandmama patted Tamsin's arm. "It's good that you heard that. Your father and I have been at odds for a long time. We will never be close, but I'm gladder than I can say to see that he's supporting you in this way. It's about time."

"Should I have gone to live with you?" Tamsin asked, allowing a pain she'd long buried to surface. She'd always been so happy to be with her grandparents and later her grandmother after Grandpapa had died. Leaving them at the end of a visit had always been difficult, but she knew her father needed her more than they did.

Grandmama stopped just outside the drawing room and drew Tamsin to face her. "Do not look backward, my darling girl. You have been happy, and that is all that matters. And you are embarking on a future that looks even brighter. Droxford is a good man, and you'll have a wonderful, happy marriage—with many children." Her eyes twinkled with joy. "I just know it."

Tamsin wished she felt as certain. She wanted to. Indeed, that she couldn't was disturbing. Her usual optimism had been shaken by her father, even though they'd resolved matters. She could no longer ignore his selfishness and the ways it had shaped her. She'd sought joy because it hadn't been easy to come by, not after the loss of her mother and not with the way her father had treated her.

She was also troubled by the observation by her friends and her father that she and Isaac were not a good match. Even Isaac seemed to think so if he preferred a marriage in name only. He'd said, "for now," but she'd seen the hesitation in his eyes, heard the uncertainty in his voice. What if they weren't really meant to be together? What if this was another instance of her looking so hard for happiness that she'd lied to herself as she'd done for so long with her father? Perhaps her friends were right to be worried.

The fairy tale Tamsin had spun when she'd first heard of a possible marriage completely crumbled. Not that it had ever taken full shape. She'd tried to make the best of a situation that was perhaps beyond her control. But hadn't she been doing that her entire life?

Now she would do it with her marriage. Because here was no turning back. Making the best of it was all she had.

"I love you, Grandmama."

"I love you, my beautiful girl. Now let us find your husband so you can be on your way!"

Taking her grandmother's arm, Tamsin walked into the drawing room and did what she must. She summoned a smile and looked for joy wherever she could find it.

CHAPTER 13

"My goodness, this is much larger than I expected," Tamsin said with awe as Isaac helped her from the coach into the midafternoon sunlight. "It's beautiful."

Isaac couldn't deny a sense of pride as he watched her survey the facade of Wood End. The part she was looking at featured a steep, gabled roofline as well as timbered beams and a bricked front entrance. Why he should feel proud of something he'd merely had the fortune to inherit he didn't know, but there it was. He took his duty as baron very seriously. Indeed, it was the thing that had given his life a distinct purpose. Without it, he would likely have been a successful barrister, perhaps even rising to a position within the government as Price had done, but this was something more. Something that was entirely in his care. It was no wonder he worked so hard to ensure it didn't falter.

"When was it built?" she asked as he escorted her to the door, which was being held open by Blunt, the butler.

"The original house was erected in 1603—the year Queen Elizabeth died. It has been expanded twice, most recently about thirty years ago when my grandfather added the ball-room." Isaac glanced over at her. "Which I never use."

She laughed softly. "Why doesn't that surprise me? Perhaps we'll change that. *If* you're amenable. Did you spend much time here as a child?" she asked.

"Not until my uncle, the baron, invited me to stay just before he sent me to Oxford to study. He thought it was terrible my father hadn't brought me round."

"Why didn't he?"

Isaac shrugged. "My father didn't like to speak of his family, let alone see them. He said they were too hedonistic, that they would not understand his simple life. He chose to mostly ignore them. Even so, he eagerly accepted my uncle's offer to send me to Oxford. But he did so because he expected I would follow his path into the church."

"But you did not."

He shook his head. "Much to my father's annoyance, I was admitted to the Inns of Court and became a barrister instead."

They'd arrived at the door, and Isaac inclined his head toward Blunt, a man of middling height with a stout midsec-tion and impossibly slender legs. He possessed a serious, dedicated nature, and Isaac had found him indispensable since the moment he'd arrived.

The butler bowed to Tamsin. "Welcome to Wood End, Lady Droxford. It is my esteemed privilege to be the first to congratulate you and his lordship." Blunt extended his bow to Isaac.

"Thank you, Blunt," Tamsin said warmly. She'd asked Isaac to tell her the names of all the retainers. Except, Isaac couldn't recall *every* name. The scullery maid was Janet or Judith, and the footmen were Arthur or Alfred and Matthew or Melvin. He'd given her the names he could remember—Blunt; the housekeeper, Mrs. Jennings; the cook, Mrs.

Corwin; and his valet, Milner. And, of course, the steward, Edwin Seales.

Blunt's usually stoic features flickered with unease, immediately putting Isaac on alert. "Ah, before we go inside, I must inform you of a sudden *temporary* change to the household."

"Is all well?" Isaac asked.

"Mrs. Jennings has gone to care for her sister, who has suffered a fall. She feels terrible that she is not here to greet her ladyship." Blunt gave Tamsin an apologetic look. "However, she has arranged for Sophia, Lady Droxford, to come and provide guidance in her absence. She hopes to only be gone a fortnight."

While Isaac was surprised by this turn of events, he was glad Mrs. Jennings went to help her sister and had requested his aunt's presence. "Aunt Sophia is here already?"

Blunt nodded. "She arrived yesterday, my lord."

Tamsin turned to Isaac. "Is she not the Dowager Lady Droxford? I want to be sure I address her correctly."

"She is not a dowager because I, as the current title holder, am not a direct descendant of her husband. She is Sophia, Lady Droxford. Though, I daresay she will ask you to call her Aunt Sophia. You will find her quite friendly."

"Wonderful," Tamsin said with a smile.

They moved into the entrance hall, where all the household retainers had gathered. They stood in a line, as they'd done the day Isaac had arrived after inheriting the title. His Aunt Sophia was there today as she'd been on that day too. Except, this time, she was not draped in black crepe, but a pretty violet.

Isaac also felt different than he had on that day, which had been one of the most uncomfortable of his life. How was he to know how to be a baron?

He could ask himself a similar question today—how was he to know how to be a husband?

Sophia moved toward them, her gaze landing on Isaac before moving warmly to Tamsin. "Welcome to Wood End, Lady Droxford."

"Thank you. I'm so pleased to make your acquaintance," Tamsin said. "Thank you for coming in our time of apparent need."

"I am more than happy to help." Smiling, she took Tamsin's hands in her own. "I know precisely how you must be feeling. You're a new wife with much to learn before you. I'm so pleased I could be here to guide you."

"Honestly, I am too," Tamsin said before Sophia released her hands.

"You must call me Aunt Sophia as my nephew does." She pivoted. "Now, it is time for you to meet everyone."

Isaac watched as Tamsin greeted the retainers, spending time speaking to each of them. She charmed them all, just as Isaac had expected, spending extra time with the maid who'd been promoted to serve as her lady's maid. While they spoke, Aunt Sophia made her way back to Isaac.

"I hope you don't mind that I'm here. I can imagine you must want time with your new bride. I will make myself scarce. Indeed, I can dine in my chambers." She gave him a knowing smile.

Except she didn't know. She likely assumed their marriage was as close and loving as hers had been with his uncle, or so she'd told him. Isaac had barely seen them together, having met his uncle only a handful of times.

"I don't mind at all," Isaac replied. "I'm grateful for your presence, and I know Tamsin is too. Please don't concern yourself with leaving us alone. I will be quite busy catching up on work since I've been traveling."

Surprise dashed across her expression. "I did notice that

you'd rearranged the baron's suite. I checked it earlier to ensure all was ready. Won't you miss the bathing and dressing room?"

While Isaac had appreciated having a well-appointed space for his toilet, it was more important that he and Tamsin have separate bedrooms. "No."

"I also learned that you've designated the baron's chamber—the one your uncle and I shared—as your wife's." Her brow gently furrowed. "Is that wise? I wonder if your bride might not feel more comfortable in the smaller chamber. It was, after all, the lady's chamber before we converted it. And the furnishings are much more feminine."

Isaac had wanted to give Tamsin the larger and more finely appointed of the two rooms. Hers had the more comfortable bed, and the furnishings were complementary. The smaller bedchamber had been assembled with a mismatch of furniture from various rooms in the house. They were things that appealed to Isaac for one reason or another without concern for how it looked. He hadn't thought that the decor appeared feminine.

"I hadn't considered that," Isaac replied. He would see what Tamsin said about the apartment.

"You could add a bathing and dressing chamber if you cared to," Aunt Sophia suggested. "You could use some of the sitting room and just make that smaller. It would be an undertaking, but quite worth it. Or, perhaps you and Lady Droxford will decide to share a bedchamber as your uncle and I did. It didn't take us long to realize we were well suited." She gave him a small smile before moving to join Tamsin and her maid.

Isaac, of course, could not explain that he'd never planned to get married and now found himself in an impossible situation. He'd been feeling better about things after telling Tamsin of his expectations and the return to their friendship.

However, now he feared he'd consigned them both to a life-time of awkwardness, at best, or even disappointment.

As the retainers dispersed, Blunt asked if dinner at half six would be acceptable. Isaac looked to Tamsin and after a brief pause during which she clearly realized she should answer, she said yes.

"You'll become accustomed to your new duties," Aunt Sophia said with a light chuckle. "Do you want to tour the ground floor now, or would you prefer to go straight to your apartment?"

"I think I'd like a fresh costume," Tamsin responded, glancing down at herself. "I'm feeling a little travel worn."

"That is most sensible," Aunt Sophia said. "If you'd like to come down to the drawing room about an hour before dinner, I'd be happy to take you about."

Tamsin smiled. "Thank you, I would like that. And truly, I can't thank you enough for being here. I'm sure it was a great comfort to the housekeeper to know things would be in capable hands."

"Very soon, your hands will be just as capable." Aunt Sophia winked at her.

Isaac offered Tamsin his arm. "Shall we go up?"

She clasped his arm, and he guided her into the staircase hall. As they ascended the staircase, she asked about the paintings adorning the walls. There were several landscapes but also a series of paintings depicting Isaac's great-grandfa-ther's favorite horse and dogs. "He loved animals, apparent-ly," Isaac said in response to Tamsin's question as to whether the four paintings depicted the same animals, for they looked alike.

Tamsin smiled. "Those animals in particular, I'd say. That's sweet."

They moved from the staircase into the gallery that spanned the entire first floor. She asked him about the portraits they passed, and he admitted he'd forgotten most of their names, just that they were ancestors.

When they neared the southeast corner, he opened the door to their shared sitting room. Decorated in greens and blues, the room offered a seating area as well as a small table at which they could dine, if they chose. Isaac had never done so, because he didn't wish for the servants to work that hard fetching his dinner all the way up here. He could just as easily dine downstairs, which was much closer to the kitchen.

"This is so grand," she said, looking about the room, her head tipping back slightly as she took in the high ceilings.

Isaac gestured to the left where the baron's room was located. He really ought to start thinking of it as his wife's chamber. "Your chamber is through there."

She walked to the door, and he hastened to push it open for her. Stepping inside, she sucked in a breath. "Surely this must be the baron's chamber?"

The wide four-poster hung with deep blue velvet hangings sat atop a dais his grandfather had constructed. He'd enjoyed fine things and preferred everything to excess. Perhaps that was why Isaac's father hadn't been close to him, since he'd eschewed such luxury for more basic items.

Isaac stood to the side as she walked farther into the room. "It is, but I wanted you to have it because it's more comfortable, particularly the bed."

"That is awfully kind of you," she said, looking from the bed to the pair of chairs situated before the hearth where a low fire burned. She walked to the other side of the room where three windows overlooked the rear parkland. Between them stood a tall dresser and a dressing table with mirror.

She went to the latter and ran her hand over the top of the wood. "This does not look as though it belongs to the baron."

"No, that is for the lady." It had been in the dressing room, which was now his bedchamber.

Pivoting, she inclined her head toward a door in the corner. "Where does that lead? A dressing chamber?"

There was a small room between the two bedchambers that had once been used for dressing. "It could be, though it's not very large." He went to open the door for her.

She stepped inside and glanced toward the tall armoire to the right. High on the left wall was a small window that provided light.

Another door stood before them. She paused in front of it. "And this door?"

"Through there is my chamber," he said.

Looking over her shoulder at him, she asked, "May I?"

"Certainly."

She opened the door and walked into his bedchamber, which he'd furnished with a dresser that had been in the baron's chamber, along with most of the contents of a bedchamber farther down the gallery. Isaac had tested several beds before settling on this one. While he'd found it to be the most comfortable, he supposed it was femininely dressed with pale yellow and dusky rose bedclothes.

"This is pretty," she said, glancing toward the bed on her way to the hearth where there was a high-backed chair covered in dark green fabric with a gold pattern. "But your chair doesn't match. You need something pink." When she turned to face him, he saw the teasing glint in her eyes.

"That chair is very comfortable," he said. "However, you may be right about the color being wrong."

She laughed softly, then her brow furrowed gently. "This looks like the lady's room, except that everything is mismatched." She moved toward the dresser. "This seems to belong with the furnishings in the other room."

"Er, yes. I had it moved in here because I'm used to it. If

you'd prefer to have it in your chamber, I can return it and take the one we moved in there."

"The one that's in there doesn't seem to match this bed," she said. "I'm just surprised that the lady's room would not be as well appointed as the baron's. Wouldn't your aunt have overseen all the decoration and ensure it matched?"

Blast. He hadn't wanted to explain that he'd converted this room back to a bedchamber. But why should it matter? They had a perfectly logical reason for needing two bedchambers. "Aunt Sophia and her husband shared a bedchamber—the room you will be using. They used this chamber for dressing and bathing."

Her eyes rounded briefly before she gave a quick nod of understanding. "You've moved other furniture here to create a bedchamber for yourself. Because we'll be sleeping separately."

"Yes." Just as they'd done during their journey from Cornwall. Though it had been necessary, it had been awkward, or even wrong. They were married, and on their wedding night and the nights thereafter, they'd gone to their separate beds. Isaac had lain awake each night wishing he could just hold her, but he wasn't ready to tell her the truth, to expose himself so she could decide if she wanted him in return.

Separate beds would be absolutely necessary. Perhaps for a long time.

"You went to a great deal of trouble," she said softly. "Thank you. Especially for giving me the larger room. I really wouldn't mind taking this one. The bedclothes do seem more appropriate for me."

"I can't argue with you there; however, I insist you take the larger room." He was trying to be thoughtful.

"Wasn't this the lady's chamber originally? Before your aunt and uncle refurbished it?"

"I believe so, yes."

"Then I should have it," she said firmly. "Honestly, I don't mind. I'd rather you remain where you are comfortable, where you've been residing for years now."

Put like that, it did make sense. He exhaled. "I'm rather unprepared for how to behave in a marriage."

Her lips curled into a small smile. "I think you're doing just fine. But let's have the footmen exchange the dressers." She went to sit in the green chair by the hearth. "Oh, this *is* a comfortable chair. Perhaps I could just have it re-covered to match the bedclothes."

She wriggled on the cushion, and Isaac was struck with a sudden flash of carnal lust. He imagined her on his lap doing the same thing, and his cock began to harden.

Turning away from her, he said, "I'll do that right now. I'll also make sure your trunk is brought here and your maid knows which room is yours."

"I really do appreciate all the thought and effort you put into this." She was closer behind him, so she must have left the chair.

Hopefully, she wasn't too close, for while his body had begun to cool, Isaac wasn't convinced it would stay that way. Too many times on their journey, he'd envisioned them together—whether it was a torrid imaginary encounter in the coach or a bone-melting seduction in one of the inns where they'd stayed.

But he'd kept away from her because it was necessary. He couldn't be intimate with her without telling her what he'd done. He had to think Tamsin would despise him, that she would be eager to keep their marriage in name only.

Inhaling deeply, he willed his body to relax. He turned to face her. She was closer than he'd hoped. Close enough that it would not be terribly difficult to pull her into his arms and kiss her. Not that he would. He would just imagine it. "Your comfort is my primary concern. I know this is a big change."

"It is, but I'm ready for change, I think." She smiled again. "I'm looking forward to seeing more of the house and the estate. Will you be taking me on a tour?"

He'd explained that seeing the entire estate could take a few days or even longer, depending on how much time she wanted to spend with the tenants or investigating different areas. They could spend a few hours, at least, at the sawmill alone.

"As I've just returned after several days away, I have business to attend in my study. Aunt Sophia will guide you about the house tomorrow. Seales, the steward, can take you around the estate in a few days after you're settled."

"I'd rather go with you. I'm enjoying our rediscovered friendship."

He was too. They'd shared many lively conversations during their journey, including a discussion as to which fowl tasted better, duck or pheasant. He was firmly behind duck while she wholly endorsed pheasant. They'd also debated rain and sun. Predictably, she preferred a sunny day, while Isaac enjoyed a good rainstorm. As much as he loved talking with her, he needed to focus on work.

"Then you'll have to wait for another day," he said.

Her brow puckered faintly. "I'd also like to see the bees, but I'd prefer you take me."

"Then I shall. I will let you know when it's convenient."

Her brow creased again, but not with confusion as earlier when she'd tried to make sense of the disordered furnishings. This seemed to be something different.

"Is aught wrong?" he asked.

She flattened her brow. "No, not really."

"I hope you'll feel comfortable in telling me if anything upsets you. I did promise your father that I'd ensure your happiness."

"Did you?" She smiled again. "That's nice. I suppose I'm

not very good at displaying if I'm upset, but that is likely because I rarely am. Truly, all is well."

"I'm pleased to hear it. I'll see you at dinner." He turned and went to the door.

"Isaac?"

That was the first time she'd used his given name. He'd called her Tamsin several times during their journey, and he'd said she could call him Isaac if she liked. So far, she hadn't. Why had she changed her mind now? And why did the sound of his name on her lips send a wave of heat through him?

He faced her once more, his hand on the door. "Yes?"

She stood with her hands clasped, appearing so feminine and lovely with soft brown locks brushing her temples and cheeks, her pink lips barely parted. "I wondered how long you expected our marriage to be in name only. That is, when do you anticipate wanting more than that?"

A torrent of thoughts and emotions briefly blistered through him before he tamped them down. "I haven't thought about it. We've only been wed a few days, and we've yet to settle into a routine." His voice sounded as taut as he felt. He ought to tell her the truth of why he'd put this wall between them, but he couldn't. Not yet. It seemed their secret sharing had ended with their marriage.

"I see," she responded. "I do hope you'll tell me when you're ready."

Did her queries mean she wanted more? What did she even know about the physical aspects of marriage? He assumed her to be a virgin with little knowledge, but perhaps he was wrong.

He didn't have the courage to ask, not now. At the moment, he could think of little else beyond frigging himself to find a modicum of relief, which he'd done every night since they'd wed.

In lieu of any response, he simply inclined his head before beating a hasty retreat. Once he was in his chamber, he closed the door firmly. How had he not realized there wasn't a lock? She could barge right in while he was pleasuring himself. *Blast.* This would not do. Where in the hell was he going to find satisfaction?

He thought of his companion at the Rogue's Den. She'd given him many nights of satisfaction, having learned his cock as well as a musician knew their instrument. Would he continue to see her now that he was wed?

The idea repulsed him. Even if their marriage remained in name only, Isaac would not betray his wife.

Was that due to the strict morality with which he was raised? Or was it because he cared too much for Tamsin?

Neither, he told himself. Tamsin deserved his faithfulness. He'd promised that, and he was, at the very least, a man of his word.

CHAPTER 14

On her first morning at Wood End, Tamsin woke feeling slightly overwhelmed, but also excited for what was to come. She had to admit she was relieved to have Sophia here to guide her. As someone who'd been in exactly Tamsin's place, she was uniquely and expertly equipped to provide assistance. However, she had been more prepared, having been raised in the peerage as her father was a viscount, and her brother currently held the title. Tamsin had learned all that at a very informative dinner last night.

Isaac had been quiet, but Tamsin didn't know if that was due to Sophia's near-constant talking—which was lively and entertaining—or some other reason. It was possible he was tired, for Tamsin had been after their travels. They'd retired early, each to their separate rooms.

She and Sophia had planned to meet in the late morning in a sitting room on the ground floor. Tucked behind the staircase hall, it was small, but elegantly furnished in pale greens and yellows. The writing desk, from France from the last century, was employed with a myriad of intriguing compartments. The seating area arranged near the hearth with three chairs and a cozy settee was most inviting. However, the best feature was the wide window that looked out to a line of aspen trees, whose leaves were just beginning to change color.

"Tamsin?" Sophia spoke from the doorway.

Tamsin had given her leave to use her given name last night. They were family, after all, and in truth, Tamsin was still struggling to answer to "my lady" or "Lady Droxford."

Tamsin pivoted to face Isaac's aunt. "Come in. I'm just admiring the view."

Sophia moved into the room. Dressed in a smart dove-gray day dress trimmed with dark rose, she appeared the epitome of a stylish lady of Society. She reminded Tamsin somewhat of Min, both ladies who understood fashion. Tamsin looked forward to them advising her on her London wardrobe when the time came, for she'd no idea where to begin. "It's a splendid perspective," she said. "You see why I chose this as my personal sitting room."

"I plan to do the same," Tamsin said.

Sophia grinned. "This pleases me so much. Shall we sit?" She gestured to the seating area.

Tamsin waited for the other woman to sit, noting that she chose the most worn, though still in fine condition, chair that was near the hearth. It had seemed to Tamsin that it was likely Sophia's favorite. Tamsin perched on the settee.

"I hope you passed a pleasant night," Aunt Sophia said. "If there is anything that does not meet with your approval, you must let Blunt—and me, in the absence of Mrs. Jennings—know and we'll direct its correction."

"It was most pleasant, thank you."

"I understand you decided to take the former lady's chamber," Sophia noted. "I did suggest to Droxford that you might prefer that to the larger baron's room."

Tamsin was a little surprised Sophia already knew that,

but she supposed information passed quickly and efficiently in a household such as this. It was likely Tamsin's new maid had shared that with Sophia just as she would have with Mrs. Jennings had she been here. "It seemed more appropriate. I was quite comfortable." Indeed, Tamsin had slept soundly.

"It is, however, a bit disordered." Sophia wrinkled her nose briefly. "Did you know that my husband and I used the chamber for dressing and bathing?" At Tamsin's nod, she went on. "Droxford has done his best to convert it back to a bedchamber, but I fear there is more to be done to make it worthy of the lady of the house." She gave Tamsin a commiserative smile as if they were sharing some inside information between the two of them. Except Tamsin didn't know what she meant by "worthy."

"I did notice that the furnishings were mismatched. However, they are all very comfortable and useful," Tamsin said. "Isaac said he chose them for those reasons."

"Does that mean you don't wish to change anything?" Sophia asked tentatively.

Tamsin thought of the chair that didn't match the bedclothes. "Perhaps a small thing or two, if Isaac doesn't mind." Since he'd told her she should feel free to make changes, it would likely be fine.

Sophia waved her hand with a light laugh. "I doubt he would even notice. By all accounts, he's far too focused on managing the estate to care about such changes to the house. Your husband didn't grow up thinking he would become a baron, and he knew nothing about running an estate, let alone Wood End in particular. He's completely thrown himself into his role and lived up to it quite spectacularly. I know my husband would be proud." Her lips curved into a brief, sad smile, and she looked out the window toward the aspens.

Tamsin felt the air of melancholy that had moved over Sophia. "Is it difficult for you?"

Moving her gaze back to Tamsin, Sophia asked, "Because this used to be my home?"

"More that your husband and son aren't here." Tamsin almost wished she hadn't brought it up. To lose so much was incredibly tragic.

"Yes, that." Sophia looked down at her lap. "It *is* somewhat difficult. I didn't expect to lose either of them, of course. Sometimes, I think they are just gone somewhere together, and they'll be home soon." She lifted her gaze to Tamsin's, blinking away the tears that had gathered. "But it makes me so glad to see Isaac—Droxford, I mean—here and doing so well for the estate and for himself. He had such a sad childhood." She sniffed, wiping her fingertips beneath her eyes. "I shouldn't speak of him like that. You'll think I'm a busybody."

"There is no chance of that happening," Tamsin said firmly. "I am acquainted with at least one busybody, and you are nothing like her." Unlike before, when she'd just mindlessly mentioned past tragedies, she considered what she ought to reveal to Aunt Sophia. In the end, she had so much curiosity about her husband, she decided to just say what she wanted. "Isaac and I had a rather rushed courtship. There are a great many things I don't know about him."

"Well, I'm pleased to see my nephew has wed. I wasn't sure he would, but I prayed he might find someone who would provoke him to make that choice." Sophia leaned forward slightly. "I know we've only just met, but I can see you possess a charm and lightheartedness that will be a boon to him. You are precisely the kind of wife he needed."

Tamsin warmed at Aunt Sophia's words. She of course couldn't know that Isaac wasn't "provoked" for the reasons she believed, but Tamsin wasn't going to inform her otherwise. And Tamsin wanted to believe what Sophia said about being the kind of wife Isaac needed.

"You are very kind to say such things," Tamsin said. "I can also tell you are lovely and generous. For you to come from Kent and help us—help me—during this time of transition is incredibly charitable." Especially if being here dredged up sadness for her.

"It is my absolute pleasure. Honestly, seeing the two of you reminds me of when my husband and I wed. We'd met during the Season, and we also had a somewhat hasty courtship. I don't know that we fell in love immediately, but we were quite smitten. Even so, it was an adjustment, though I don't mind telling you we decided we didn't wish to sleep separately after only a week together." She gave Tamsin a sly smile.

But Tamsin wasn't entirely sure what the woman was trying to communicate, so she merely smiled in return. She also didn't know what to say in response. Instead, she gently diverted the conversation. "How would I go about making a few changes to my bedchamber? Perhaps I would like a chair that matched the bed. I could look through the other bedchambers?" She hadn't yet toured the first floor.

"Certainly, though they haven't been cleaned or aired out. Since the baron doesn't have guests, the rooms are not in use. I think only my chamber has been slept in since my husband died. I moved there when my nephew took up residence, and I've used it a few times since, when I've come to visit."

"I didn't realize you visited regularly. That's very nice." Tamsin was glad to know that Isaac had family who cared about him.

"I intrude upon him at least once each year when I know he will be in residence." Her gaze twinkled with mischief. "Mrs. Jennings sends me letters advising me of his plans."

"He doesn't mind that you come?"

"Not at all. I don't show up without asking; I write first and ask. He always says yes." Her face creased with concern. "I do think he's almost starved for family. Growing up, his father kept him isolated. We rarely saw him. Honestly, it would have been better for Droxford to have grown up with us here at Wood End."

Another thing they shared in common, Tamsin thought. Both of them might have been better off with other relatives instead of their fathers.

"We should probably get to work," Tamsin said. "I'm sure we've a great amount to cover."

Sophia nodded. "Indeed we do. I've just learned that there will be a new tenant, which means the vacant cottage will need to be refurbished. We'll tour it soon and make a list of all that needs to be done."

"That is my responsibility?" Tamsin hadn't realized all the things she would need to do as lady of the manor, but why would she?

"I find it's best for the new tenants if a woman has a hand in things," Sophia said with a grin.

That made sense to Tamsin. "I confess I am a little intimidated, but I'm also quite excited."

"You remind me of myself," Sophia said with a hint of pride. "Shall we start with the menus?"

After spending a great deal of time with Sophia, Tamsin and she had taken lunch together. As Sophia departed to take a short respite in her chamber, Tamsin decided to find her husband. She recalled the location of his study from last night's tour. It sat adjacent to the magnificent library, in a quiet corner of the ground floor.

On her way there, she encountered the butler.

"Good afternoon, my lady. If you are on your way to see his lordship, I'm afraid he is not in his study."

Tamsin was surprised at how disappointed that made her.

But why should his absence from the study stop her from finding him? "Do you know where I can find him?"

"I do, in fact. He is with his bees."

Was he? She'd mentioned wanting to go with him, but he hadn't bothered to invite her? "Where would that be?"

"They're kept past the formal garden, just to the west at the base of a knoll in a small meadow."

That sounded easy enough to find.

"Shall I send someone for your hat and gloves?" Blunt offered.

Tamsin wanted to say no, that she could run and get them, but she knew that the retainers at Wood End were eager to help and please. She smiled instead and thanked him.

A short while later, adorned with a bonnet and gloves, Tamsin stepped out into the early-autumn day, though it still felt a bit like summer. The blue sky was dotted with white clouds, and the breeze was pleasant.

Making her way through the garden, Tamsin stopped here and there to smell the late-blooming flowers. She came upon the knoll and looked down to see a cluster of wooden structures. Isaac stood talking with a boy, but as Tamsin started her descent toward the meadow, the boy departed, moving in the opposite direction from Tamsin.

As she neared the bottom, Isaac turned toward her. She couldn't see his features at this distance, but he met her as she walked to him.

"These are your bees?" she asked, surveying the odd-looking box structures. "Where are their hives?"

"In the boxes." He gestured to one of them. "Do you want to see?"

"Is it safe?" she asked. "I was stung by a bee once when I was a child, and it was very painful."

"I've been stung many times, and it's still painful, but not horribly so. Mrs. Corwin has perfected an effective remedy."

"In addition to creating a magnificent syllabub?" Tamsin had enjoyed last night's dessert very much. "It's no wonder you kept her on along with everyone else." She looked at the box and saw a few bees buzzing around it. "Why do you come here if you are stung repeatedly?"

"I'm hardly ever stung anymore," he said. "When I first took over this endeavor a couple of years ago, I didn't know what I was doing."

"Why did you take over tending the bees?" Tamsin asked. "Wasn't there someone already doing that?"

"Yes, but I wanted to change the way we did things, and he was ready to retire anyway. He is one of the tenants, and his eldest son recently took over his lease."

"What did you change?"

Isaac moved slowly toward one of the boxes, and she followed along. "The way the honey is harvested. Bees are usually kept in skeps, which are large baskets with a hole in the top. However, there is no way to get the honeycomb out without killing the bees in order to extract the honey they've made."

Tamsin stared at him in horror. "They work hard to make all that honey, and they're killed?"

"You see why I wanted to change things. I determined there had to be a way to harvest the honey without killing all the poor bees, especially, as you pointed out, after they'd labored so long."

"Not to mention, we steal the fruits of their labor." Tamsin shook her head. "I had no idea."

"I began to research alternate ways to keep bees and harvest their honey without mass murder. The most recent development was made by a gentleman in Russia. These boxes have drawers, which we can pull out to remove the honeycomb without disturbing them. Let me show you."

He approached the nearest box and gently tugged the uppermost drawer. "You can come closer. They won't sting you."

Tamsin took small steps until she could just see the interior. Dozens of bees worked amid the bright honeycomb. They did not seem bothered by Isaac opening their home.

"What do they do when you remove the honeycomb?"

"We do it in the evening when they are tired from their day's exertions. They seem calmer, so that's what we've done. We've only done it once, to be honest. This is the first year we're using these boxes instead of the skeps, and we successfully removed a small piece of honeycomb a couple of months ago. Last year when we had skeps, I tried to remove the honey without killing the bees. That was when I sustained most of my stings," he finished wryly.

"I am sorry that happened, but I can't blame them for being angry. Except, they should have been grateful, I suppose, since you didn't kill them as had been previously done." She looked at him. "Do you suppose that is why they don't sting you now? They know you've made improvements and ensured their safety?"

He smiled—not smirked—and Tamsin thought she might melt into the ground. Did he know he was doing that?

"I don't know if they realize that I don't want to kill them, but that is a nice sentiment. I am not surprised you would think of it."

"And I am not surprised that you would go to such lengths to save the bees."

His features sobered, his gaze growing serious as he looked past her. It was as if he'd been carried away somewhere. But only for a moment. He blinked, then carefully closed the drawer.

"My mother used to save animals," he said softly. "It's one of the only things I know about her. Before my grandparents —her parents—passed on, I would visit them in Taunton. They had a dog that she'd saved as a puppy after finding him alone in a hedgerow. She also saved squirrels and kittens and, I believe, a goose."

Tamsin giggled. "I can't imagine saving a goose was easy."

The smile reappeared on his mouth. She fixed on his lips, wondering how they would feel against hers. "I can't either."

Blinking, Tamsin pushed thoughts of kissing from her mind and instead dwelled on his smile. "That's twice you've smiled out here. You never smile. Well, not never, but hardly ever. I'm not sure I've seen anything but your smirk."

"That's probably true. I meant to smile at our wedding ceremony. I'm sorry I didn't."

His words warmed her—he did care. Perhaps this was moving past being just a marriage in name only. The idea filled her with a delightful heat.

"I've just spent time with Sophia," Tamsin said.

"Yes, that was why I didn't invite you to join me. I didn't wish to interrupt." Again, his thoughtfulness made her chest swell. "How did that go?" he asked, his gaze fixed on her with genuine interest.

"If I'm to be honest, it was overwhelming. There is much for me to learn, but I am up to the task. The thing I am most daunted by is getting to know all the tenants, though I am also most looking forward to that."

His gaze moved from hers, shooting out over the meadow. "I'll arrange for Seales to take you on a tour."

Tamsin had hoped he would change his mind and accompany her himself. She couldn't help thinking he was avoiding her. But in truth, he was just busy.

"I'm back, my lord."

Tamsin turned her head toward the voice and saw the boy had returned.

Isaac gestured to Tamsin. "Oliver, this is Lady Droxford."

The boy, who looked to be around twelve, bowed awkwardly. Tamsin smiled at his effort. "I'm pleased to meet you, Oliver."

Isaac closed the drawer on the beehive. "Oliver is learning about how to care for bees. He'll be helping me harvest the honeycomb soon."

"What a brave lad you are," Tamsin said. "I don't think I could do that."

"They're fascinating creatures," Oliver said earnestly. "I like all sorts of insects."

"Then this is the perfect job for you." She could see they needed to get back to work and didn't wish to keep them. "I'll be on my way." She looked toward Isaac, whose eyes seemed to smolder as they had when they'd first become acquainted in Weston. From when their attraction had sparked. That gave her a sense of hope.

Walking back toward the knoll, Tamsin decided to take a different path and enjoy the fine day. After nearly ten minutes, she came upon a charming cottage with a thatched roof. She saw a couple on the front porch. They stood close to one another, their heads bent. The man brushed a strand of hair from the woman's forehead and caressed her cheek. Then he bent his head and kissed her. It wasn't brief, nor was it terribly long. She clasped his forearms as he cupped her head, their heads angling slightly during the kiss.

When the man stepped back, Tamsin worried she'd be caught spying. Not that she *was* spying. She'd just been unable to turn from their heartwarming display. It was obvious these people loved each other very much. Seeing them together made Tamsin's heart twist. It also made her realize love like that wasn't just a fairy tale. She wanted that closeness with someone. With Isaac, hopefully.

"Good afternoon!" the man called, and Tamsin realized it was too late to continue on her way. Still, perhaps she could act as though she hadn't seen anything.

"Good afternoon," Tamsin responded with a smile and a wave.

The man approached her, and the woman came off the porch. Tamsin saw then that she was heavy with child.

"I'm Paul Bowman," the man said when he stopped near to Tamsin. "And that is my wife, Laura."

"I'm so pleased to make your acquaintance," Tamsin said. "I'm Tamsin—" She blushed. Her new name and title would take some getting used to. "I'm Lady Droxford."

He smiled broadly. "We'd heard his lordship had gone to Cornwall to get married." He pivoted toward his wife. "Laura, this is the new Lady Droxford." Looking back to Tamsin he said, "You can go up to the cottage, if you like. There's just the two of us here, and I'm off to fetch a few things from the village."

"Thank you, I will."

Mr. Bowman inclined his head, then waved at his wife before departing.

Tamsin walked up the path to the cottage where Mrs. Bowman had returned to the porch. "I hope I'm not intruding."

"Not at all. I'm honored to meet the new lady. Would you like to come inside?" She asked almost bashfully, her cheeks coloring to a faint pink and her gaze indirect. "I don't wish to interrupt you if you're on an errand."

"You aren't interrupting me at all. I only arrived yesterday and was just taking a walk. I'd be delighted to come inside for a short while, if it doesn't trouble you." Tamsin had no wish to be a burden on this young woman, particularly in her current state.

With dark red-brown hair, warm brown eyes, a button-like nose, and a collection of freckles across her nose and the upper part of her cheeks, Mrs. Bowman appeared to be around the same age as Tamsin or close to it. She held the door open for Tamsin to come inside.

The cottage interior was a little dim as the windows were not particularly large, but it was well appointed. A parlor sat to the right of the entrance hall, and to the left a dining room, with a timbered opening to a kitchen.

"Let us sit for a few minutes," Mrs. Bowman said, resting her hand along the swell of her belly. "I am getting close to my time, and I find I need to put my feet up frequently." She sat in a chair near the hearth and set her feet up on a low footstool.

Tamsin sat on a chair nearby. "Is this your first child?"

Mrs. Bowman nodded. She stroked her belly with a sheepish smile. "I'm more than a bit nervous, I'll admit."

"I would be too." Tamsin had no experience with babies or mothers about to have them.

"I'm so glad you happened by," Mrs. Bowman said shyly. "I don't meet many girls my age." She laughed softly. "Since we are married, I suppose we are no longer girls."

Tamsin laughed with her. "I suppose we aren't." She looked about the cozy cottage and recalled what Mr. Bowman had said. "You have no one to help you here? Do you have family who will come when the babe arrives?"

Mrs. Bowman shook her head. "I have four brothers, two of whom are married, but their wives are busy with babies of their own. My mother passed away a few years ago now. I wish she were here to help me." Sad lines fanned from her eyes.

Tamsin's heart ached. "I understand how you must feel. I

lost my mother a long time ago. But I don't have any siblings at all."

"Consider yourself lucky. A house full of men is challenging. You are the odd one out, and they simply don't know what to make of you. In order to marry me off, my father took me to a matchmaking festival. That's where I met my husband a year ago last May."

"How extraordinary. I'd no idea such a thing existed."

"For hundreds of years, apparently, at least in the town of Marrywell."

Tamsin laughed. "What a fitting name. You certainly married well, or seem to have."

"Paul and I are very happy. Oh!" Mrs. Bowman stroked her belly and readjusted her weight in the chair.

"Are you all right, Mrs. Bowman?" Tamsin started to rise, to fetch…someone. But who?

"I'm fine." Mrs. Bowman gestured with her free hand for Tamsin to sit. "Just the baby testing out his legs. He's very active this time of day. And please, call me Laura. If you like," she added hastily.

"Only if you will call me Tamsin."

Laura blanched. "I couldn't, my lady. That wouldn't be right."

"I insist. I'm not yet comfortable being Lady Droxford. Besides, you are my first friend here at Wood End." She leaned forward and whispered. "I needed one of those. Please call me Tamsin?"

"If you insist." Laura smiled.

Tamsin thought of how she could help. "I hope you won't think me presumptuous, but I would be happy to come and be with you when the baby comes. If you'd like."

Laura's chocolate-brown eyes rounded. "Would you, really? There is a midwife from the village who's to come and help, but I don't know her very well. She does seem nice."

"It would be my honor to come and assist you. Or at least hold your hand. I don't have the faintest idea what to do, but I'm sure the midwife can direct me." Tamsin frowned. "How will you send for me?" Since it was just Laura and her husband here, Tamsin wondered if she could reassign someone from the household at Wood End to come and help. She would speak to Sophia.

"When it's time, my husband will run to town to fetch the midwife." Laura's brow furrowed. "Perhaps he can find someone to fetch you."

"I'm beginning to think you need a maid to be here with you until you give birth and for a few weeks after, even."

"I wouldn't want to cause any disruption, my la—Tamsin."

"I promise you it would not. We have plenty of people. I'm sure I can find someone to help you for a spell. Unless you'd rather not be disrupted yourself?" Tamsin didn't want to cause any discomfort to her new friend. She realized that while Tamsin felt this woman to be her equal, their stations were vastly different. This was one aspect of her marriage she hadn't considered.

Laura looked down at her belly and gave it a pat. "We've met a very nice person today, my sweet." She transferred her gaze to Tamsin. "I don't know what to say, but I would be grateful, thank you."

"I am glad—and eager, if you couldn't tell—to help. We must support one another, especially if we don't have family."

Laura nodded. "I need to remember that. I always try not to be a nuisance."

"Perhaps when it's my time to have a baby, you'll come and sit with me." Tamsin hoped that might happen, but sitting here with Laura made her realize how much she really wanted it.

"It would be my honor," Laura said with a dewy smile. "Paul will be so pleased." Her eyes rounded briefly as she fixed them on Tamsin. "I just realized…did you see Paul and me outside before?" Her cheeks had gone pink again.

Tamsin considered lying, but had been so cheered by their closeness. "All I saw was a couple who obviously love each other very much."

"That is true," Laura said with a laugh.

"How did you know you loved him?" Tamsin asked. She was curious what it felt like. Would she even recognize if she began to love Isaac? "Did you fall in love at first sight at the matchmaking festival?"

"Not at all. He was trying to take another young lady into the maze, but she was too cold—the evening was chilly. In fact, it rained later. I was his second choice."

Tamsin laughed. "But you must have gone with him since you're married now."

"I most certainly did not," Laura said with a glint in her eye. "I told him I was otherwise engaged. Which was a lie. Later, when it started to rain, he found me in one of the follies seeking shelter. When he noticed I was shivering, he gave me his coat. It was shocking since he was standing there in his shirtsleeves, but he was not the only man who did it. He was, however, the only one—that I could see anyway— who serenaded me with a silly song about falling in love in the rain. I think he made it up."

Captivated by the story, Tamsin asked, "Does he still sing to you?"

"He has the most beautiful voice. He sings to the babe." She stroked her belly with a wistful smile.

"That's when you fell in love with him, then? After he sang to you?"

"Not quite, but we were on our way. That was the second night of the festival. By the final day, I knew I wanted to marry him, and I was fairly certain I loved him." She shrugged. "How was I to know? Especially without my mother to advise me. I wasn't going to ask my brother who, along with our father, had come with me. My brother met his wife at the same festival."

Tamsin was curious to know how love felt, but it seemed intrusive to ask more questions. "How wonderful that you found each other."

"We are very fortunate. I know sometimes people wed because they must or it's reasonable," Laura said. "I expected I would—I just wanted to find a man who would take care of me and with whom I could have a family. To have met and fallen in love with Paul is a wonderful gift for which I am thankful every day."

Yes, Tamsin wanted that. And right now, her husband preferred a marriage in name only. How could she convince him otherwise? Was she even brave enough to do that?

He'd asked her to tell him if she was upset by anything. While she wasn't upset, she wasn't…satisfied. All her life, she'd kept any feelings of discord at bay, choosing to pursue something positive instead. Because it was easier, she realized, to avoid the difficult choices, the challenging emotions. It was why she'd never taken issue with her father's isolation or asked to live with her grandmother or pressed for him to allow her to find a husband.

But if she did nothing now, she would be waiting for Isaac to decide her future. She understood that she couldn't force him to feel things he didn't, but she hoped he would at least try. Their marriage deserved that much.

CHAPTER 15

*Y*awning, Isaac stood from his desk. He'd been working too late—and too much in general. All to avoid spending too much time with his charming, beautiful, tempting wife.

He looked at the small oval portrait of his mother that perched on the corner of his desk. He'd had it as long as he could remember, and it was his most treasured possession. He felt such love for the image, if not for the woman he'd never known. He liked to think he knew her, but the truth was that he couldn't recall a single thing about her beyond what he saw in that painting.

What he wouldn't give to have just one memory. Just one faint recollection of even sound or scent.

Wishing his mother a silent good night, he blew out the lantern, then picked up a candle to make his way upstairs. He was shocked to run into his aunt in the gallery at the top of the stairs.

"Droxford, you are prowling about rather late," she said, holding a candle of her own.

"As are you," he noted.

"Sometimes I can't fall asleep easily, and I find a walk helps tire me." She arched a blonde brow. "What is your excuse?"

"I was working."

"I should have known. You work nearly nonstop. At least you dine with Tamsin and me." She frowned at him. "You are not spending enough time with your bride. How can you expect to come to know one another?"

"I've been busy catching up on the work that accumulated while I was away." It had only been three days since they'd arrived.

Aunt Sophia looked rather skeptical. "You should not have sent Tamsin to tour the estate with Seales today. She should have met the tenants with her husband, the *baron*."

Isaac frowned, stopping himself just before he scowled. Not because his aunt was annoying him, but because she was right. And *that* annoyed him.

Aunt Sophia shook her head. "You're also working late into the night. I do not understand why when you have a lovely wife awaiting you." Her expression gentled. "I realize you did not have the benefit of a happy family life with two adoring parents, but I hope you can imagine it for yourself. You do deserve that."

Her words caused a rock to form in his throat, so he simply nodded in response.

"Well, I must inform you that you need to take Tamsin out tomorrow. The tenancy you recently let has a vacant cottage that will require refurbishment as it's been empty a couple of years now. I'd planned to take Tamsin to the cottage, but I have matters that require my attention here. So you will take her, and she can help you make a list of what needs to be done. And don't tell me you can't, because this is also necessary work."

Isaac studied his aunt a moment. Had she organized this on purpose to force him to spend time with his wife?

Of course she hadn't. It was something that needed doing. Isaac knew precisely the tenancy she meant, and it had been on his list of things to address soon. Visiting it with Tamsin should be a benefit, not a chore. If Isaac wasn't such a dreadful mope, he would allow himself to look forward to it.

"I will take her," he said.

She nodded. "I'll arrange for you to take a picnic along. Good night, then, my boy." Giving him an affectionate smile, she departed down the gallery.

A picnic? Perhaps his aunt *had* arranged for this. He wondered if Tamsin had said something about wanting to spend more time with him. But he couldn't imagine her doing that. Probably, his aunt thought they should be together more, and she wasn't entirely wrong.

Guilt weighted Isaac's legs, but he turned and went to the apartment he shared with Tamsin. Would she still be awake? The past two nights, she had not been.

His aunt was right. Tamsin *was* lovely, and she was his wife. She deserved better, even if he didn't. He would need to try. Spending time with her didn't mean the structure of their marriage had changed.

But he'd led her to believe it was temporary, and the truth was that he didn't know what he wanted anymore. He desired his wife, but he didn't want to let her inside, not past the wall he'd erected after he'd abandoned Mary. Right now, it was just easiest to avoid all of it, and so he buried himself in work.

Stepping inside, he was surprised to see Tamsin seated near the hearth, a book in her lap. She looked up, their gazes connecting. His guilt intensified.

After closing the door, Isaac moved toward her slowly. She wore a pale yellow dressing gown, and her brown hair was plaited over her shoulder, the end resting against her breast. Swallowing, Isaac forced himself to look at her face.

"I was just about to retire," she said. "I wasn't sure if I'd see you, but I wanted to try to wait up." She smiled. "I'm glad I did."

"I am too," he said, realizing he meant it. He sat in the other chair angled near the hearth, facing her. "I wanted to apologize for not being available the past few days. A great many things required my attention after being gone to Cornwall." He cringed inwardly at how that may have sounded to her, as if taking time to marry her was an inconvenience. He rushed to add, "Aunt Sophia is not able to take you to the vacant cottage tomorrow, so you will have to suffer me instead, I'm afraid."

Her eyes lit up. "Brilliant! Perhaps we could bring a picnic."

"My aunt has already arranged for that." He felt another stab of guilt at the sheer joy in her face.

She scooted forward in the chair, leaning toward him slightly. "That is very thoughtful of her."

His gaze dipped to the curve of her breast once more. A strong surge of desire crested over him, like the waves upon the beach at Weston. How he longed to pull her in his arms and kiss her.

What was he waiting for?

Before he'd come to know Tamsin, when he thought of kissing, he recalled Mary's sweet mouth, her happy sighs, her desperate whimpers. Now, when he thought of kissing, he imagined Tamsin's lips against his and her body melting in his arms. Such things led to deeper intimacy, and he wasn't ready for that.

"Isaac?" Tamsin prompted.

He gave his head a shake. "I'm sorry, I was thinking about the farm," he lied.

"I just wondered when we would go tomorrow."

"In the afternoon," he said, rising abruptly. The longer he stayed here with Tamsin, the more tempted he became. "Good night, Tamsin," he said.

"Good night, Isaac."

Isaac fled and hoped tomorrow he could continue to avoid temptation.

~

$\mathcal{A}$t some point in the night, Tamsin awoke as the world crashed down. She shrieked in fright.

Gasping for breath, she looked about and grasped her bearings. She was in her chamber at Wood End. Though it was still not entirely familiar, she knew it well. But the vantage point was different. She was lower to the ground. And somewhat crooked.

Finally, she realized the bed had collapsed. It dipped toward the floor, the middle sagging horribly, and at a bit of an angle so that she was indeed crooked.

She did not know how she was going to climb out. The dip held her amid the concave mattress and bedding.

The door to her room burst open, and light flooded the chamber. "Tamsin?"

Isaac sounded as horror-stricken as she had felt.

"I'm fine," she said from amidst the sunken bed. "I fear the bed has broken."

He moved to the end of the bed, and she looked up at his face, partially shadowed where the candle's light didn't fully reach since he held it out toward her. "Are you all right?"

"I think so. Just startled." She smiled to ease his concern.

"Only you could smile at a time like this," he said with a shake of his head. Stepping to the side of the bed, he set the candle on the nightstand. Then he leaned over and offered her his hands. "Grab hold and I'll pull you up."

She clasped his hands, and he helped her to stand on the bedding.

He leaned over farther. "Put your arms around my neck."

Twining her arms about him took her back to the day on the beach when he'd lifted her from the waves. Indeed, this was very similar as he now plucked her from the destruction of the bed's collapse.

"Just like on the beach," she murmured, as he set her down beside the bed.

She wore just her cotton night rail, and he wore a long sleeping shirt, also made of cotton. He was warm and solid against her, and she was loath to release him. So she took her time, sliding her hands down his collarbones and onto his chest. She kept her palms against him, feeling his heart beating strong and sure—and perhaps too quickly as hers was doing.

He said nothing, but his gaze burned into hers, and she had the sensation again that he might kiss her. Would he finally? Her belly clenched in anticipation.

"You can sleep in my bed," he said, taking a step back from her.

Tamsin dropped her hands, disappointed that he'd gone, but thrilled at his suggestion. Until he added, "I will sleep on the chaise in the sitting room."

"That is nowhere near long enough for your frame." She shook her head firmly. "No, you must sleep in your bed too. It's plenty large enough for the both of us. I daresay we won't even know the other is there."

She held her breath, waiting to see if he would argue. He seemed adamant they not share a bed. "Please?" she added. "It's the middle of the night, and we can easily sleep there together without disturbing one another."

"All right. If you don't mind."

She wanted to cry, *no, I don't mind!* After her conversation with Laura the other day, she'd been looking for ways to spend more time with Isaac, to recapture the attraction she was sure had sparked between them in Weston. She'd felt it earlier tonight when he'd come to the sitting room. His eyes had smoldered with a passionate heat that had stolen her breath and stoked a primal heat in the core of herself.

"I'll have the bed repaired tomorrow," he said, stepping aside and gesturing for her to move past him.

Tamsin walked from her room through the small dressing closet to the baron's room. As he entered behind her, candle-light splashed into the space, but it came nowhere close to illuminating the dark corners.

She went toward the bed, slowly walking up the pair of steps to the platform on which the four-poster sat. She'd paid no attention to where he slept when she'd chosen a side. Indeed, she'd just gone to the nearest one—closest to the door adjoining their rooms and the windows. Judging from the rumpled bedclothes, this was where Isaac slept. The other side was nearer the door to the sitting room.

"This is where you sleep," she said, pivoting. He stood at the bottom of the steps, his features stoic, but his eyes still blazing with heat.

"Yes. But do you prefer that side?"

Did he sound strained? His voice seemed…tighter some-how. "I don't have a preference." Though she had to admit, she wouldn't mind sleeping where he'd been. Would it smell like him? Would she be able to feel his warmth? No, the bedclothes would likely have gone cold by now. Still, she could imagine him there.

She shook the fanciful thoughts from her head. Realizing he'd said nothing, she asked, "Do you have a preference?"

Upon his hesitation, she decided he must. "You sleep here.

I'll move to the other side." But rather than walk around the bed, she simply climbed atop it, slipped into the bedclothes—and yes, they did smell like him—and scooted to the other side. It was not quite as large as she'd imagined now that she was inside it. If she stretched her arm out, she would touch him.

She thrilled at the thought of that happening.

And yet, she must endeavor to keep to her side. He was clearly uncomfortable with this arrangement. So uncomfortable, in fact, that she wondered if there was something else happening beyond him wanting a temporary marriage in name only so they could get to know one another. Was it possible he didn't like or want sex?

But no. Everything she knew about men indicated they were obsessed with such things. Bane had demonstrated that last year.

Isaac was no Bane, however. She hadn't married a rogue. Did it follow, then, that he simply wasn't interested in being intimate? Tamsin had a hard time accepting that, and she wasn't sure why. Perhaps it was the way he looked at her—as if she were prey and he the hunter.

She shivered as he climbed into the bed, feeling the mattress dip. Her reaction had nothing to do with any concern that it might collapse as her bed had done. No, this was entirely due to her husband, his proximity, the fact that they were barely clothed, and that they were now, at last sharing a bed.

Somehow, Tamsin managed to fall asleep, but she didn't think she slumbered heavily. At one point, she roused to feel a solid presence behind her back. Rolling so that she could see where Isaac was, she had to bite her lip when she found they were quite close. He was on his back, and his arm had been against her spine.

She couldn't really make out his features in the near darkness. Only the embers in the hearth provided a dying light.

Though she longed to snuggle close to him and put her hand on his chest, she stayed on her side, allowing a few inches between them. Smiling, she closed her eyes, glad that they'd at least come this far. Because she was always optimistic, she would believe this was the beginning of something promising.

As she was dozing off once more, she heard him mutter something. Opening her eyes, as if that would make her hear better, she held her breath to see if he would speak again. No, not speak, for she wasn't sure he was actually saying words.

Then it came again, "*Mumble, mumble,* Mary. Stay *mumble mumble* longer, Mary."

Tamsin's pulse raced. She forced herself to breathe.

Mary?

Who the devil was Mary?

CHAPTER 16

*A*fter fetching the gig from the stables, Isaac drove around to pick Tamsin up at the front of the house. She was waiting for him in an ivory day dress sprigged with flowers and wore a grass-green spencer buttoned up to the base of her throat. Her bonnet had a matching ivory ribbon that was tied beneath her jaw on the left side. She looked beautiful, but despite her fetching costume, Isaac would be hard-pressed not to think of her in just the thin night rail she'd worn last night.

When he'd awakened just after dawn, he'd watched her sleep for countless minutes. She'd even looked cheerful in repose, the corners of her lips turned up slightly as if she were dreaming of her very favorite things. Perhaps she had been.

It had taken every bit of self-control Isaac possessed to leave the bed without touching her. Even the temptation to press a simple kiss to her forehead was almost impossible to resist.

Still, he'd forced himself away, and now he would spend

the afternoon on the edge of desire and desperation. It would not be a comfortable place to be.

Tamsin carried a basket, and Isaac jumped down to take it from her and help her into the gig. She put her hand in his, and though they wore gloves, a jolt of heat pushed him closer to the edge on which he teetered.

"Aunt Sophia arranged a picnic lunch for us," she said. "Isn't that sweet?"

Isaac had walked back around the gig and climbed in beside her. "Very thoughtful of her." He drove them away from the house.

"She did have a bit of bad news, unfortunately. It appears the ropes on my bed will need to be replaced. They were completely frayed apart."

From wear? Isaac didn't think that bed was particularly ancient, but he wasn't sure. He'd ask his aunt, though he supposed it didn't matter. "I trust someone is working on that today?"

"Aunt Sophia is attending to the matter," Tamsin said. "Though she did say it may not be entirely repaired until tomorrow. I told her that was all right, that we could share your chamber again this evening." She sent him a happy smile as if she hadn't just delivered the worst news ever.

The worst, really?

Sleeping with Tamsin had not been a hardship. Not unless one considered his agitation today to be a problem. Isaac could push through it. Plenty of men set aside their lust. Isaac had certainly done so countless times.

This was different for some reason. Probably because Tamsin was his wife. He couldn't evade her forever.

"Do you mind?" Tamsin asked.

He looked over to see her watching him intently, little pleats gathered between her brows. He couldn't very well tell her he did. And why should he? They were only *sleeping* together.

"I do not," he said. He would simply work in his office until late into the night, when he could be assured that she would already be in bed asleep. Then he wouldn't see her in her alluring night clothes or have to talk to her in the intimacy of a shared bed. He'd been relieved when they'd simply gone right to sleep last night. Though, it had taken him some time to slumber—long after he'd heard her even breathing.

She relaxed against the seat and looked forward along the track they'd just turned onto. "Good."

They drove in silence for a few minutes before she pointed to the left of the track up ahead. "Is that the cottage?"

"Yes." Isaac steered onto the lane leading to the cottage.

A few moments later, he parked the gig outside the front of the sloped-roof domicile, which had a pair of dormers. Isaac walked around to help Tamsin out, then he grabbed the picnic basket.

"Our second picnic together," Tamsin said with a flash of a smile. "But this time, we're alone."

Indeed they were. Alone and rife with barely restrained lust—at least on his part.

He opened the door, and she walked past him inside. He wasn't entirely certain what to expect as he hadn't been there in some time.

It was dusty, of course, with a multitude of cobwebs and dead insects in the corners. Oliver might like to come and collect specimens, Isaac thought.

"I'd say a thorough cleaning is in order," Tamsin observed as she walked into the dining room. "This is similar to the other cottages I've seen on the estate with the staircase in the middle and a parlor to one side with the dining room and kitchen on the other. I do wonder if this has a more spacious first floor. I'll go up and look in a few minutes." She pulled a small notebook from her pocket along with a pencil and wrote some notes.

Isaac felt a foreign sense of pride watching her. "You've taken to becoming the lady of a manor with ease." He went to set the basket on the dining room table. The cottage had a great deal of furniture, much of it covered with dustcloths.

She let out a short laugh. "I can't say it is easy. There is much to remember, and I have your wonderful aunt to support me. I do take notes, especially when I am out with Seales meeting the tenants." She gave him a shy smile. "But thank you for saying that, since I was not raised to be the wife of a baron."

"Nor was I raised to be a baron," he replied, feeling guilty that he'd sent her out with Seales. He'd missed her being efficient and intelligent.

"Was that difficult?" she asked, removing her gloves and bonnet and placing them on the table near the basket. "Adjusting to inheriting Wood End, I mean."

"It was unexpected."

"I imagine it was hard having to learn all that, especially in the wake of tragedy. I do feel a little badly for relying on your aunt. I know this is difficult at times for her—being here without her husband and son. I know she's visited you, but returning to help run the household has to take her back to an earlier time when she was the lady of the manor."

Isaac nodded. He'd also felt badly. "She doesn't mind. In fact, she enjoys it—the work and feeling needed. Like you, she has maintained a level of optimism despite losing her son and husband. Those tragedies could have broken her, but they did not. It's no wonder the two of you get on so well."

"I have not suffered as much as her—or you." She regarded him as he removed his hat and set it on the table. He hesitated in taking off his gloves. The removal of clothes could continue, and that would be a problem.

She cocked her head. "I hope you won't mind my asking, but are you happy?"

It was such a straightforward question, and yet the answer felt incredibly complicated. "I am content." Happiness wasn't something he understood. He'd had fleeting happiness with Mary, but true joy had evaded him. Nor did he seek it—not like Tamsin did.

"Content is not the same thing." Her tone was playfully scolding as her eyes danced with a flirtatious mirth.

He did not want her to flirt with him. Not here. Not now. The tether on his self-control was the barest thread.

"What would make you happy?" she asked, moving to stand closer until she was right in front of him—as close as she'd been last night when they'd worn nothing but their nightclothes. She hadn't seemed to notice his erection then, and he prayed she wouldn't notice the one that was happening now.

"Wood End makes me…happy." Caring for it gave him purpose and satisfaction. Were those the same as happiness?

"What about me?" She looked up into his eyes, her expression wide open like an empty field just waiting for someone's attention.

Isaac could not look away, nor could he deny what she wanted—his attention. "We are friends," he said, sounding almost hoarse. "I am grateful for that."

She tentatively put her hand on his chest. "I look forward to when you are ready for more than that, because I am."

Invitations did not get any clearer than that.

"Tamsin, I know I told you that I wanted a marriage in name only for now, but the truth is I don't know how long that will be. I'm just not…I'm not ready to be intimate with you."

Her eyes grew huge, then she blinked. She hesitated

before speaking, and when she did, it was hardly more than a whisper. "I see. Thank you for your honesty."

He hated her confusion and disappointment. "It's nothing to do with you," he said earnestly. "I am—" He inhaled sharply. "That is, I have difficulty being close to people."

"Are you a virgin?" she asked, her eyes searching his face.

"Er, no." He wasn't going to lie about that. He was already keeping enough from her—Mary and his son—because he had to. He wouldn't expose her to his shame.

He could see her mind was churning. Her gaze had drifted from his, and her brow bore deep creases.

He blew out a breath, deciding rather suddenly that she deserved a modicum of truth, if nothing else. "I told you I'd done things in the past of which I am not proud. When I first went to Oxford, I behaved very badly. I had to rein myself in. Since then, I have kept myself firmly in check."

"You've been...celibate since then?"

"In a manner of speaking. I engage in certain activities but I, ah, I pay for the service." Heat rushed up his neck, and he looked away from her. "I probably shouldn't tell you such things."

"No, you should. I appreciate hearing the truth. Will you be paying for those services now that we are wed?"

He snapped his gaze to her. "No," he replied vehemently. "I will be faithful to you."

Isaac hated that he was practically shaking. This was more of himself than he'd ever revealed, and to see her confused and uncertain reaction did not ease his distress.

Finally, she nodded. Once. Twice. Very slowly. "I want to understand. And I want to be supportive." Her gaze found his once more, and while there was still uncertainty, there was also compassion. "I can be patient. I want you to be comfortable." She gave him a tentative smile.

"Thank you," he breathed, as an astonishing relief washed over him.

Without thinking, he brushed his lips against her forehead, closing his eyes as he inhaled her intoxicating scent. Then he kissed her temple. Her skin was so soft beneath his lips.

"I have never been kissed, Isaac."

The whispered statement was a plea, and Isaac, at last, was powerless to resist. He didn't pause to think of how long it had been since he'd done this or whether he ought to, he just lowered his head and gently swept his lips over hers.

That could be the end of it, for that was a kiss. But it wasn't enough. Not for her, and definitely not for Isaac. Now that he'd barely tasted her, he was desperate for more.

Her hands moved up to his shoulders and she angled her head, pressing her lips to his. Isaac clasped her more fiercely, pulling her against him, the suppressed desire in him taking over. He kissed her again and again, using his lips against her with increasing pressure. Then he licked along her lower lip before slipping his tongue into her mouth. She opened for him, but he realized it was a surprised reaction for she pulled slightly back against his hands.

He released her and stepped back. "My apologies," he murmured.

Her hands remained on his shoulders, and she pressed them into his coat. "Do not apologize. And don't stop. I was enjoying that. Will you please continue?"

The battle inside Isaac reached a fevered pitch. His brain told him to walk away, that they needed to take things slowly. But his body urged him to kiss her again, to give her what she wanted. What they both wanted.

"Tamsin, you must understand that I have withheld myself from you because I am a terrible rogue. The things I want to do to you are not proper. They are not bright and cheerful. They are dark and erotic and driven by my absolute need to possess you. Can you comprehend that?"

Her eyes had grown wide, and her lips had parted. The tip of her tongue peeked against her lower lip. She nodded. "I understand. And I want you to possess me."

~

*I*t took all Tamsin's self-control not to scream at her husband to keep kissing her. Was he hesitating because he was worried she would think him a rogue? Wanting physical intimacy with one's spouse was not roguery. It was what she wanted, what she *needed*. Before she could beg him—and she was quite prepared to do just that— he moved closer to her once more.

His head came down, and he kissed her again.

Tamsin's toes curled in her walking boots. Her entire body thrummed with desire as his lips molded to hers. Then his tongue glided into her mouth, which she'd been shocked to discover she liked very much. She imitated his move-ments, the sweep of his lips and the thrust of his tongue.

Something inside her unfurled and bloomed. It became a succession of kisses, each one more enchanting than the last.

She wanted to feel more of him, particularly where sensa-tion was most concentrated. Her breasts felt heavy against his chest, and a persistent throb had started between her legs. She clasped his shoulders and pressed into him, desperate for more and not quite knowing what that would be.

As her hips met his, she gasped softly, for that was what she wanted—to feel him there.

"Do you want me to stop?" he asked softly.

"No. I just want to feel you there." She felt the heat rise up her neck, both from shyness and the pulsing need within her. She wanted to remove her spencer. Taking her hands from him, she put them between them to unbutton the garment. "I'm a bit warm."

He watched intently as she opened the spencer and shrugged it from her shoulders. Then he helped her draw the garment down her arms and set it on the table. Wordlessly, he removed his own coat and put it with hers.

Tamsin recalled how he'd looked in his night shirt, the outline of his body barely visible through the lawn. She'd wanted so badly to touch him, to feel him. And now she could. But she wished he wasn't wearing so much.

They came back together with another kiss, his hand cupping her neck as he devoured her mouth. She tipped her head back, offering herself to him and greedily taking what he gave her. She began to understand what possession might mean, and she wanted that as much as he did.

He moved his lips to her jaw, and she shivered at the new sensation. She imagined him kissing her everywhere and her body began to tremble with an even greater need.

His hands had returned to her back, but now he slid one of them forward where he cupped her breast. It was difficult to feel his touch through her corset, but the pressure was divine. She wished she could strip all her garments away.

Suddenly, he picked her up and set her on the table, between two chairs. He set her feet on each of them, widening her legs and bracing her boots on the wooden seats. His gaze met hers with a dark, seductive promise. "Keep your legs just like that."

Unable to form words, Tamsin merely nodded. The throb between her legs grew.

"Forgive me," he said softly, lifting one hand to her bodice. "I would like to see you. I can loosen this, and it will drop down?"

"Yes." She wore a round gown, and the bodice would come down in the front. "You can untie that and tug it loose."

He found the small cord that gathered the bodice tightly around her and pulled so the fabric gapped open. Tamsin quickly unpinned the top of the bodice just below each shoulder and it fell to her waist, exposing her corset. It also tied in the front, as most of her garments did, a necessity when one did not have a ladies' maid.

"You can remove that too, if you like," she said, eager for him to do so.

"Perhaps it should be loosened just a bit." He pulled at the laces, so the corset came open, but he didn't remove it. His gaze was now fixed on her chest. His expression was rather stark, almost hungry.

He traced his finger from the hollow of her throat down to the space between her breasts. Tamsin's chest rose and fell rapidly as her pulse sped. She wasn't sure what to expect, but she wanted whatever he planned to do. Her breasts tingled, and she realized they were eager for his touch. She held her breath, waiting.

With slow, measured movements, he used his fingers to caress her, at the top of her breasts, above her garments, then tucking them into her corset. His hand cupped the underside of her breast, pushing her up and over the loosened garment. Then he did the same with the other, using his other hand until she was full revealed to him.

She glanced down at herself, her pale breasts resting on her open corset, the nipples hard and extended, as if they were reaching for him. He cupped her with both hands, gently, then with more pressure. His thumbs moved over her nipples, and she moaned softly as a new rush of sensation claimed her. The throb between her legs expanded and her hips twitched.

He closed his thumb and forefinger over her nipples, pressing on them and then gently tugging. Tamsin grabbed his upper arms and closed her eyes, her body quivering with a desperate urgency.

He kissed her again, briefly, but thoroughly, his hands continuing to caress her breasts until she felt nearly mindless. "Do you like this, Tamsin?" he asked against her ear before licking the outer rim.

"Yes."

"Then you will like what I am about to do even more." He kissed along her throat, his mouth moving down. She began to comprehend what would come next, but when his lips closed over her nipple, she was not entirely prepared for the jolt of arousal and the rush of pleasure.

Gasping, she moved one hand to his head, tangling her fingers in the waves of his dark hair as he licked and sucked her. He tugged on her other nipple until she cried out. Somehow, everything he did reverberated between her legs, stirring the pressure there until she thought she might weep if she didn't find relief. But what did that even mean?

Still, she could be quite happy if he simply continued what he was doing until the end of time. She clutched at his head as he moved his mouth to her other breast, treating it to the same divine torment.

But nothing lasted forever, and he moved his hand from her breast, though he continued to use his mouth on the other. She felt him lifting her skirt, exposing the flesh of her upper legs as he tucked the garment around her waist.

Lifting his head from her, he asked, "Are you ready for more, or is that enough for today?"

"More, please." She'd still no idea what that meant, just that she didn't want this to end, not until she found some sort of completion. It wouldn't just stop, would it? What would happen to that persistent throb between her legs. "I need something, Isaac. I just don't know what."

His hand moved along her inner thigh, and her muscles

tensed. "Relax, my lovely," he coaxed just before his fingers stroked along her sex. "I know what you need. I will give you a release—it's called an orgasm. You will fall apart into a thousand pieces and miraculously come back together again. And when you are finished, you will feel deliciously replete."

Tamsin liked the sound of that. She opened her eyes. "Yes, please. I would like that now."

His lips spread into a wicked smile the likes of which she had never seen—not from anyone and certainly not from him. It stirred something deep within her. She clasped the back of his neck and kissed him, copying what she'd just learned from him and thrusting her tongue deep into his mouth. He kissed her back, and for several long moments, they feasted on one another as Tamsin's arousal spiraled to new heights.

Then his fingers began moving over her folds once more, slowly at first. He massaged the top of her sex, and she liked that very much. Indeed, that seemed to be a focal point for everything she wanted. He ended the kiss and whispered, "This is your clitoris. It is where a great many of your sensations are gathered. I could perhaps make you come just from touching you here. But it will also feel good—you must tell me if it does not—when I put my fingers into you."

He cupped her, the heel of his hand pressed against her clitoris. Lights danced behind her closed eyelids as he worked her flesh. Her hips began to move with him as pleasure built inside her.

Then his finger slipped inside her. Tamsin dug her fingers into his shoulders as everything she felt intensified. She wanted more of him—more of the delicious friction he was creating with his finger stroking in and out of her.

She became fuller, and she realized he must have added a second finger. This was even better, especially because he began to move faster. Her hips bucked up from the table, thrusting against his hand, seeking that release that would set her free of this torment.

"So beautiful," he murmured before he took her nipple in her mouth once more. The pull of his lips on her flesh and the thrust of his finger sent her rushing toward the edge of something vast, something that would give her what she so desperately needed.

"Do you feel that storm building?" he asked, between licks and sucks. "Like dark clouds opening up and raining down a torrent. Your body must do the same." He stroked her faster and faster, and she felt what he'd described—a cataclysm that must be released.

But she didn't know what to do beyond savor his touch. She thought of what he said, of opening up…

"Yes, Tamsin, I can feel you're close. Come for me now."

Everything inside her tightened as a blistering ecstasy swept through her. She cried out, unable to keep anything together a moment longer. She had no choice but to let it all go. And it was glorious.

Isaac held her as he whispered softly in her ear then kissed her cheek, her temple as she gasped to regain her breath. Her body began to slow, and so did his hand. Then he left her completely, gently pulling her skirts down over her legs.

He tugged her corset up and together, covering her breasts then began to tighten the garment, as if he were her ladies' maid.

"I can do that," she said, raising her hands. But they were still shaking as her body worked to return to normal. Although, Tamsin wasn't sure she ever could, not after something like that.

He arched a brow? "Are you sure? Why don't you just let me?"

She let her hand fall to her lap and gave herself over to his care. "You've performed these duties before?" She shook her head. "Of course you have."

"Not as often as you may think. I have generally tried to abstain, but there comes a time when needs must."

"Why abstain?"

His eyes darkened. "Partly because of how my father raised me."

"And the other part?" she asked, desperate to know him.

"It's just best if I keep that aspect of myself under tight control. I have abstained from intercourse for more than a decade."

"And you call yourself a rogue," she said with a hint of a smile. "I thought men were unable to control their impulses."

"Precisely. Which is why I take care to do so. But just because I hold myself in check doesn't mean I'm not a rogue at my core."

Tamsin wasn't sure she believed that. The man she knew was kind and caring, and full of integrity. He'd gone above and beyond what was necessary to protect her reputation. "If you have abstained from sex for a decade, what services do you pay for?"

"Do you really want to know?"

She nodded several times. "Yes." She was desperately curious to learn more after what they'd just done. She felt as though she stood at the precipice of a whole new world that needed exploring.

"What we just did, for one. I can also put my mouth on your sex. I expect you'll enjoy that."

His mouth… Tamsin imagined how that would work, his tongue licking her and perhaps sliding into her sex. The throb he'd just satisfied began anew, though not quite as strong. Not yet anyway.

"What about you?" she asked. "Don't you also need to come?"

"Yes, but that isn't necessary today." He finished with the corset, and she was finally still enough to take over with the rest of her garments.

She pulled the bodice up and refastened it at the shoulders. "Would I use my hand or my mouth? Or both?"

"Whatever you like." His voice sounded strained, as if he were lifting something very heavy.

"Shall I do it now? It only seems fair." She glanced down at his pelvis and saw the distinct outline of his sex through his breeches. "It also looks necessary?"

He snorted then, not a full laugh, but it made her grin. She boldly reached for him, pressing her palm against the length of him. Their eyes connected with a sharp heat.

"Tamsin, this is not a good idea."

She stroked him through his clothing. "Why not? Am I doing something wrong? You must instruct me. You'll find I'm an excellent student."

He groaned softly. "I have no doubt. All right." With an amazing speed, he unfastened his fall and freed his sex.

Tamsin stared in awe as his shaft rose proud and hard. As her nipples had done for him earlier, it seemed to be reaching for her.

"Wrap your hand around the base," he instructed.

She complied quickly, her thumb and forefinger grazing the twin sacs beneath.

"Now stroke your hand up, not too tightly but not loosely either."

Hoping she'd found the right pressure, she moved her hand up his length, relishing in the hard smoothness of him. "Is this right?"

"Yes, now back down and up again, moving faster as you feel comfortable." He still sounded as though he were carrying giant pieces of granite.

Tamsin recalled how he'd used his fingers on her with

increasing speed and how good the friction had felt. It would be the same for him, then. She stroked slowly at first, finding the right rhythm and pressure. "How does this feel?" She didn't want to hurt him. She was eager to bring him the same pleasure he'd given her.

"Marvelous."

She lifted her gaze from her task and saw that he'd cast his head back and his eyes were closed. He was so handsome, and there was something so devilishly intoxicating about the way he looked right now. Or perhaps it was that she was making him do that.

Refocusing on what she was doing, she watched her hand move up and down his sex. His hips began to move with the rhythm, as she had done with hers. She imagined their bodies doing that together, and the heat returned to her core.

She moved her hand faster, giving him the friction he craved. He gripped her upper arms, not painfully, but firmly. His breath came fast, almost in pants as she increased her speed.

"I'm close," he said roughly, his hips thrusting toward her. "There will be a bit of a mess. I'm sorry."

She didn't care. Delighting in his pleasure, she stroked him faster and then, on a whim, used her other hand to cup the balls beneath, much in the way he'd cupped her breasts.

"Tamsin!" He grunted as warm liquid spurted from the head of his sex, coating her hands. Still, she continued because he was still thrusting. She would not stop until he did.

Soon, he slowed, and the liquid stopped coming. She thought it must be his seed. If she used her mouth on him, what would happen to that? Was she to…swallow it? She'd have to ask.

Pivoting slightly, Isaac rummaged in the picnic basket, then handed her a napkin. "So you can tidy up," he muttered.

"Thank you." She cleaned up her hand as he tucked himself back into his breeches. "I hope that was all right."

His gaze found hers, and his eyes were glittering with a remarkable intensity. "It was transcendent."

That was precisely how Tamsin would have described how she felt. She couldn't resist smiling, and even experienced a new emotion—smugness. She'd helped him *transcend*.

He looked toward the front window, and his face paled suddenly. Reaching for his coat, he said, "Put your spencer on. Seales has just arrived. I didn't realize he was coming."

Tamsin hurriedly complied. "It's good he didn't arrive earlier." She laughed softly, but really, it would have been horrifying.

"We should get to work," Isaac said. The intensity was gone from his gaze, and the aura of discovery and ecstasy that had reigned dissipated.

But Tamsin was not disappointed. She was encouraged. Today had been a big step forward, and she was eager to see where they went next.

She touched his forearm. "Isaac, thank you—for what you gave to me today and for sharing the deepest parts of yourself. I *will* be patient." She suspected she was falling in love with him, so she had no choice but to be.

He said nothing, but gave her a faint nod. Then he walked out of the cottage to greet Seales. Tamsin pulled her notebook from her pocket once more and began to make a list for the cottage. All the while, she smiled.

CHAPTER 17

*A*fter dinner, during which they'd discussed the plans for the vacant tenancy since Seales and his wife were also present, Isaac and Seales had remained in the dining room drinking port. The ladies had gone to the drawing room. It was all very domestic, and Isaac couldn't quite believe this was his life. He'd never imagined any of it—becoming a baron, managing a large estate, marrying a warm, caring woman.

And yet here he was.

The interlude with Tamsin at the cottage that afternoon had given Isaac something he didn't think he'd ever had—hope. Being with her was somehow…easy. She was sweet and supportive and even managed to make him smile. Now it seemed her optimism was perhaps rubbing off on him.

Seales cleared his throat, his hand resting at the base of his wineglass atop the table. "I hope you won't mind my saying so, but Lady Droxford is most impressive. She has taken to the estate with an astonishing zeal. You're a fortunate man."

That was not a description Isaac would ever have thought

could describe him, but he could perhaps glimpse it. And it was all because of Tamsin. She'd brought light to his darkness, joy to his sobriety, and apparently hope to his gloominess.

"I am pleased to hear you find her effectual. She is eager to meet each tenant and help in every way she can."

"Yes, she's taken a particular interest in a couple who are expecting their first child," Seales said. "I believe she's arranged for one of the housemaids to help them as they do not have any assistance and Mrs. Bowman is close to her time."

Isaac recalled Tamsin mentioning that, but since it involved a birth, he'd chosen not to pay much attention. He hadn't been present when Mary had given birth to their son, and for whatever reason, he associated all births with her and the fact that he'd missed it. And that he'd likely never experience one.

Except now, he was married. And if things with Tamsin continued, he could very well end up making her pregnant.

The idea of it sawed through him, leaving a sharp pain. He didn't deserve a happy family, not after he'd already abandoned one.

Seales interrupted Isaac's thoughts, for which he was most grateful. "Have you decided whether there will be a harvest celebration in a few weeks? A few tenants asked Lady Droxford about it, and she was keen to hear what had been done in the past."

Aunt Sophia had always held a celebration during the third week of October, after everyone was primarily finished with their harvesting work. Isaac had not continued this tradition. The first year it had seemed inappropriate in the wake of the baron's death. And after that, he simply hadn't made it a priority.

"She hasn't mentioned it to me," he said. "Did she indicate whether she planned to host it this year?"

Seales shrugged. "I am not sure what she is thinking, which is why I asked you. My wife would enthusiastically help. It has been missed."

Isaac frowned at his port before taking a drink. He hadn't realized the celebration was that important. Indeed, he hadn't thought of it at all. "I wish someone had mentioned it."

"I thought we had," Seales said hesitantly before drinking more port.

"That is possible." As was the fact that Isaac likely hadn't paid attention. Celebrations were not something he cared to attend. But that didn't mean they shouldn't have one. He stood. "Let's go speak to the ladies about it." Isaac wasn't sure if he was eager to discuss this or to see his wife. He could not stop thinking of her since that afternoon, and the need to be in her presence was a persistent demand.

Rising, Seales followed Isaac from the dining room. They made their way to the drawing room, where Tamsin, Aunt Sophia, and Mrs. Seales were seated.

Isaac noted that Tamsin was on one of the settees—alone. He sat down beside her, perhaps a little closer than necessary. But at this proximity, he could smell her floral scent. It transported him to earlier that day when he'd lavished his attention on her, relishing every inch of her tantalizing body. Now that he'd surrendered to his obsession, he could hardly wait to taste more of her. Would it be rude to ask their guests to leave?

"You weren't in the dining room long," Aunt Sophia observed with a smile. "You must have missed us."

Isaac was most definitely missing his wife, but not in a way he would share with anyone but her. "We came to ask about the harvest celebration. I have been remiss in not holding it again after the mourning period." He looked at Tamsin, her features so familiar to him now that when he saw her, he felt a pull—a deep connection he didn't entirely understand. This was not the same as what he'd shared with Mary.

Tamsin had angled herself toward him, her blue-green eyes reminding him of the sea, of where they'd become acquainted. Weston, he realized, was now a special place that had nothing to do with his friends or the Grove. She smiled, her features becoming animated. "I should love to reinstate the celebration. I'm so glad you brought it up since I'd planned to ask you about it."

"This will be wonderful for the tenants," Aunt Sophia said with a nod. "I'm so glad you're finally hosting it again."

The word *finally* rankled him a bit, but it was deserved. He looked to Tamsin. The urge to touch her somehow nearly overwhelmed him. Their activities that afternoon hadn't sated him one bit. He needed more of her. "Just let me know what you require. I trust you to plan an exceptional cele-bration."

"Thank you." She gave him a smile so full of joy that he found he was tempted to smile in return. This was fast becoming madness.

Aunt Sophia offered suggestions based on past celebra-tions, as did Mrs. Seales. The three of them—Sophie and the Seales—made plans to meet to plan everything. Thankfully, it was only a quarter hour or so before the Seales took their leave.

After they left, Aunt Sophia stood. "I shall retire now. You need all the privacy you can find, and I've been too much in your presence." She winked at them before departing.

Somehow, Isaac kept himself from leaping on Tamsin and ravaging her. He also managed to not throw her over his shoulder and carry her upstairs, where he could also ravage her.

"Will you be working in your office before coming up?" Tamsin asked.

He hated that this was her expectation, but why wouldn't it be after the last several days? "No." Isaac surrendered to his need to touch her, lifting her hand and pressing a kiss to the inside of her wrist. "I would also prefer to retire, though I wasn't planning to sleep. Not yet." He kissed her inner forearm and then the concave of her elbow, feeling her shiver beneath his lips.

"How wonderful," she murmured. "Shall we go up, then?"

Isaac moved his hand to cup her neck. "In a moment." He lowered his mouth to hers and kissed her, his lips and tongue claiming hers.

She clasped his shoulder, sliding her hand to the top of his collar. Her fingers caressed his flesh, and he was desperate to have her completely unclothed, bared to him entirely, her body his for the taking.

Breaking the kiss, he stood and pulled her up. "Now. I would carry you, but the servants would be scandalized."

"Or titillated," she said with a giggle.

Isaac pulled her against him. "I am titillated enough for the entire household at the moment." His cock raged with want as lust pulsed through him.

She slipped her hands up his front and curled them about his neck. "Perhaps you will show me upstairs."

He would show her here if it would also not scandalize everyone, for there was no lock on the drawing room door. "Come," he clipped, desire making his vision narrow and his pulse pound.

Taking her hand, he led her toward the staircase hall. He wanted to take the stairs two at a time, but recognized her gait was not that long. Still, he walked quickly, so that by the time they reached the top, she was laughing softly.

"I've never seen you so intent about something other than work," she said.

Past the point of caring about anything other than having Tamsin in his arms, Isaac swept her up and quickened his pace toward their apartment. "I am single-minded at the moment."

Clasping her arms around his neck, she pressed a kiss to the side of his jaw. "I'm enjoying this immensely."

He nearly groaned with want and with pleasure that she was as eager for him as he was for her. Carrying her into the sitting room, he closed the door, then hastened to his chamber, where he again closed the door. He did not set her down until he'd climbed the dais and stood her next to the bed.

"Shall I remove your clothing, or will you?"

She blinked, her lashes fluttering in an alluring, almost flirtatious fashion, but he'd no idea if she did it on purpose or if she was simply that enticing. He rather thought it was the latter.

"I have yet to upgrade my wardrobe, though Aunt Sophia says I must, and it is one of our upcoming projects. So, for now, I can undress myself entirely. Is that what you prefer?" She kicked her slippers off her feet. "Would you like to watch me do that?"

The carnal thoughts racing through Isaac's brain would have made her blush to crimson. He envisioned her disrobing slowly, stopping to caress herself, to taunt him with each new revelation of her tantalizing flesh. But she wouldn't know how to do such things. He could instruct her...

She began to pull pins from her hair, and the brown curls fell against her neck and shoulders. He watched, entranced, until it was completely loose, and she deposited the pins on the nightstand. "Should I take the time to plait my hair?"

"No. I want it loose," he rasped.

Moving her hands to her back, she loosened her gown. Isaac realized he could help, but he was too transfixed watching her. She wriggled and pulled until the garment came free, then she pushed it down her body.

When she bent to retrieve it, Isaac said, "Leave it. Finish."

She pushed the straps of her petticoat off each shoulder, not realizing the brush of her hand along her upper arm as the fabric slid over her flesh was perhaps the most arousing thing Isaac had ever seen. He swallowed, barely keeping himself in check. She pulled at the laces of her corset until it gapped open, then pushed it down over her hips, once again wriggling her body to work the garment off. She stepped out of the clothing piled at her feet and kicked the mass behind her.

Wearing only her chemise now, she hesitated. Was she nervous? "You've never been naked with a man before."

She shook her head. "Of course not."

"I want you naked. Is that all right?"

"Yes." She reached for the hem of her chemise, then pulled it over her head.

Now she stood before him wearing just her stockings and garters. When she reached for the first garter, he clasped her hand, stopping her. "Just wait. I'll do that." He needed to look at her a moment. She was exquisite, from the supple roundness of her breasts to the turgid pink points of her nipples. Her waist nipped in, inviting his hand to caress her there, then her hips flared out, also begging for his touch. Dark curls cloaked her sex, but he already knew she was pink and likely wet. She'd been so incredibly wet for him that afternoon.

"Is it too soon after earlier today?" He wished he'd thought to ask that sooner.

She shook her head. "I was hoping you would want to do this tonight. Whatever it is you desire. What is that anyway?"

Isaac closed the half foot between them and put his hands on her waist. Lifting her, he set her on the edge of the bed. "I'm going to put my mouth on your sex and make you come. Over and over."

She sucked in a breath. "More than once?"

"Hopefully." Now he grinned, like a wolf eyeing its prey.

She put her hands on his cheeks, her gaze holding his. "You are breathtaking when you do that. You have me completely enthralled." She dragged her nails along the bare stubble of his nascent beard.

He swept his mouth against hers in a hungry kiss. She returned it, welcoming his demand and making her own. Isaac cupped her breast, squeezing and stroking her, pinching her nipple gently. She grasped his waist, pulling him flush with the side of the bed. His cock rubbed against the edge of the mattress between her open legs.

Though he'd meant to remove her garters with an erotic slowness, he found himself pulling them from her almost greedily. When they were gone from her, he skimmed his hands up her bare legs and claimed her mouth once more.

Mindless, he kissed down her throat and chest until he found a nipple where he sucked hard, drawing a deep moan from her. He pushed her back gently until she was flat against the bed then he guided her farther onto the mattress. Now she was positioned perfectly. He grabbed a pillow and slid it beneath her hips.

"What are you doing?" she asked breathlessly.

"Preparing my feast." He pushed her legs wide, opening her sex to him. With one hand, he caressed her right breast with slow, methodical strokes punctuated by massages and tweaks of her nipple. Her body moved with his ministrations, her hips rotating.

With his other hand, he rubbed her clitoris, eliciting soft moans and whimpers from her. Her arousal was intoxicating, and he had to work to keep from rushing her to completion. He wanted to draw this out, to ensure her orgasm was like a thundercloud.

He slipped one finger into her sex, confirming his assumption that she was wet and ready. He could easily slide his cock into her. The thought of that made him groan with want. He would not do that. Not tonight. He couldn't even consider it, especially in his current state.

Reluctantly, he moved his hand from her breast and pressed it against her hip.

"I was enjoying that," she said wistfully.

He looked up at her, over the plane of her abdomen and the rise of her breasts. "You can continue that for yourself."

Her gaze met his with a moment of confusion.

"Touch your breasts, Tamsin. Hold them. Caress them. Squeeze them. Do whatever you like. You must learn to give yourself pleasure." Because of his choices, Isaac had relied heavily on the ability to do that. "You can use your hand here as I do." He pressed his thumb over her clitoris, rubbing her, then thrust his fingers into her, filling her. "You can find your own orgasm. Perhaps sometime you'll do it for me so I can watch."

Her lips had parted as he spoke, and her eyes had taken on a glassy, unfocused sheen. She put her hands on her breasts and began to fondle them, her fingers sliding over her flesh. Isaac's body throbbed with desire. He wasn't sure he'd ever been this aroused, and wondered if it was possible for him to spill his seed before he even removed his cock from his clothing.

He realized he was still completely dressed, and his coat was becoming restrictive. He quickly pulled the garment off and tossed it away.

Tamsin's eyes were closed, her fingers closing over her nipples. She moved her hips against the pillow.

"Pinch them, Tamsin," he said, then watched as she did. She moaned softly. "Yes, keep doing that. Whatever feels good."

He put his hand on her sex again, opening her folds before he licked along her crease.

She bucked up against his mouth with a sharp cry and grasped his head with one hand. He put his palm at the top of her mound, pressing her down. "Be still for just a moment," he whispered before he tongued her again. Using his thumb, he teased her clitoris while still holding her. He could feel the pent-up energy within her, the need to thrust and move, to bring herself to release.

Spreading her wide with his fingers, he thrust his tongue into her. He put his other hand beneath her, cupping her backside as he held her, unrelentingly, to his mouth.

Over and over, he licked and thrust as his thumb worked the sensitive flesh of her clitoris. She moved with him, her hips rocking as her desperate cries filled the room.

It did not take long for her to reach her climax. He felt her tense, the muscles of her thighs clenching around him. She bore down, her sex clamping around his tongue as she came in a frenzy of movement and sound.

As she rode her orgasm to completion, Isaac was all too aware of his own needs. He moved one hand down to his breeches and clumsily unbuttoned the fall. Slipping his hand inside, he encircled his cock. He closed his eyes in relief as he stroked himself.

"*Stop.*"

Isaac's eyes flew open, and he saw that Tamsin had risen to a sitting position. His hand stilled instinctively.

"You are to let me do that," she said with a surprisingly commanding tone that fueled his lust. "With my mouth. You said I could do that."

He released himself and straightened. "My apologies. I

was overcome." He was still a bit concerned that he might come without even a hand to aid him.

"You need to take your clothes off now. For me, as I did for you." She drew her legs up and sat on the bed watching him expectantly.

Isaac began with his boots and stockings, removing them with the same haste as with her stockings. He unbuttoned his waistcoat, going slightly slower, but only because his fingers were practically shaking with need. At last, the garment opened, and he divested himself of the nuisance.

Finding the end of his cravat, he pulled the knot free and slipped the silk away from his neck, dropping it to the floor. While he undressed, his gaze was fixed on Tamsin's lush body, her flesh a rosy hue from her earlier release. Her nipples were full and pink, like rosebuds about to bloom.

He needed to finish. Quickly. He whisked his shirt over his head and threw it away, then pushed his already open breeches to the floor, kicking them aside with perhaps more ferocity than was necessary. He stood before her and watched her eyes narrow, her gaze directed at his swollen cock.

"What do I do now?" she asked, her voice rough and lust-ridden.

He considered the ways she could take him. "You could kneel before me. Or I can lie on the bed. What do you prefer?"

"I can't decide, but since I am on the bed already, I suppose that's fastest." She scooted aside so he could move onto the bed.

Plucking up the pillow he'd used beneath her hips, he put it down near the headboard and set his head atop it as he lay back.

"I don't need to put the pillow under you?" she asked, moving to his side.

"Not necessarily. My cock is rather exposed for you already."

She licked her lips, and he moaned, his hips twitching. "I see that. Do you have instruction for me?"

"Not unless you want it. You were astonishingly adept with your hand earlier. I'm confident you will use your mouth to an equally successful degree."

"How formal that sounds," she said with a mischievous smile. "And I don't want to equal earlier, I want to *better* it, as you just did for me. I shall see if I can be creative."

A burst of heat rushed through him, sending blood flooding into his cock. He could not wait another moment. "Please, Tamsin. Suck me. *Now.* Move between my legs."

Climbing over him, she settled herself between his legs, her attention focused completely on his cock. She curled her hand around the base of his sex and lowered her head. Isaac clutched the coverlet in his hands in anticipation, his body tensing with need.

She licked him tentatively, and he gripped the bedclothes more tightly lest he clasp her head and thrust into her mouth. Forcing himself to take deep breaths, he surrendered to her as she slowly worked her tongue over him. She laved him completely, exploring him with her lips and tongue.

Isaac moaned, then put his hand—carefully—against her head, his fingers tangling into the soft curls of her hair. She lifted her head and stroked her hand up his length then down. Her mouth closed over the tip, and she took him in, guiding him along the rough heat of her tongue.

Thrusting gently, he held her as he moved farther into her mouth. She didn't flinch or falter, and he felt her swallow as he nudged the back of her throat.

He gripped her hair more tightly, cautious not to hurt her, as he cried out. She moved back, nearly releasing him, then devoured him once more. Over and over, she released him and sucked him in. Then faster, somehow knowing precisely what to do. Her hand moved with her mouth, pushing him to the edge of reason. His hips rose from the bed as he softly thrust into her.

Then she cupped his balls, and he completely lost control. He called her name, apologizing as his hips moved more quickly. She held him, clasping his hip as she increased her speed, accommodating his mindless frenzy until his body tightened. He hadn't told her about what would come next.

Isaac tried to pull himself away from her, but she held him fast, sucking him hard until he could no longer hold back. He came in a torrent, flooding her mouth, probably, and incapable of doing anything but holding her and letting his body release.

It was several long minutes before he lay flat against the bed, his body quivering with the remnants of his orgasm and his heart hammering. He opened his eyes and saw her wipe the edge of her mouth. She smiled at him, a cat's smile full of satisfaction and pride, along with a dash of arrogance. It was the most beautifully wicked thing he'd ever seen.

Sitting up, he pulled her to his chest and kissed her deep and fast. Then he brushed her hair back from her face and looked into her eyes. "Thank you for waiting for me."

"I am a patient person," she said simply. "And you are worth waiting for."

As Isaac fell asleep a short while later, his wife snuggled against his side, he made an effort not to think too closely about what she might have meant.

~

A series of kisses along Tamsin's shoulder roused her from sleep. Blinking her eyes open, she saw it was still quite dark. Isaac was pressed against her side.

The kisses stopped, and he muttered something. His hand snaked around her waist pulling her tighter to him.

Tamsin smiled, her body rousing to his touch. She turned toward him and kissed his forehead, placing her hand against his cheek.

He continued mumbling, but she couldn't make out what he was saying. Indeed, she wasn't sure if he was awake or not. She wasn't entirely positive *she* was awake. Perhaps this was all a lovely dream.

"We are *something, something,* Mary," he said. There was that name again.

Tamsin was awake now. She held her breath, waiting to see if he would say more.

When he did not, she, whispered, "Isaac?"

"Yes, Mary?" he said in the clearest voice he'd used yet.

How could she find out who Mary was? She needed to wake him and ask.

He nuzzled her neck. "I love you, Mary."

Tamsin froze. He kissed her throat. Then his leg twined with hers.

She didn't care if he was awake or not. "Who is Mary?"

His lips continued a path along her collarbone, and he didn't respond.

Clasping his shoulder, she tried to wake him. "Isaac. Isaac."

He made an indistinct noise and pulled away from her. Then he rolled to his other side, presenting his back.

Tamsin stared at his spine, his shoulder blades, the wave of hair against the top of his nape. Who was Mary, and why did he love her?

How could he love her? Particularly when Tamsin loved him?

The realization struck her as surely as the sun would rise. She loved this sober, mostly unsmiling, antisocial, brooding baron. Like her, he'd been lost at some point. Only, Tamsin had been found. He was still out there fighting his way back. She wanted to be here for him, to help him find what he sought—that which would make him happy.

She'd dearly hoped it would be her. It was, however, Mary, apparently.

Unable to sleep or share this bed with Isaac any longer, she slipped from the bedclothes. She collected her garments, which were strewn about and made her way quietly to her chamber. Once inside, she drew on a night rail and tidied her things, finding comfort in routine.

No, not comfort. Her brain was still rife with questions and…despair. Silent tears tracked down her cheeks unheeded.

Her bed was still broken—just like her heart—so she stoked the fire, picked up a blanket, and curled up in the chair by the hearth.

He loved someone named Mary. Not Tamsin. What was she to do?

How could she possibly find the joy in that?

CHAPTER 18

*I*saac slept later than usual and was surprised when Tamsin wasn't in his bed. He quickly dressed and made his way downstairs only to learn she'd left early to visit Mrs. Bowman. He tried not to feel disappointed, especially when he'd done a fair job of leaving her alone since they'd arrived at Wood End.

He ate breakfast at his desk and worked for a couple of hours, though he paused often to think of Tamsin and how everything had changed yesterday. He didn't have a single regret.

Glancing toward the portrait of his mother, he paused. Did he not regret keeping secrets from his wife?

He wished he could tell her that he had a child somewhere out there in the world. A boy he could never call son and whose very existence made Isaac feel as though he had utterly failed. Nothing he ever did could make up for the fact that he'd abandoned the boy and his mother. She'd had to start over as a mother somewhere new and foreign to her. Because it had been the "right" thing to do.

That was his biggest regret and would be until his dying day.

Shaking his head, he refocused on work. But it was only a short while before his mind was once again occupied with his wife. What was she doing with Mrs. Bowman today? Would she also meet with Aunt Sophia and Seales's wife about the harvest celebration? He wanted to know what she was doing every moment, so that he could determine when she was available to him. He wanted to look forward to when they would next be together.

He was turning into a lovesick swain. His friends would tease him. Or would they? No one made light of Welles-bourne's love for his wife.

Love?

Isaac froze. Where had that word come from?

A knock on the door startled him. Aunt Sophia swept into the study, her dark red skirts swirling about her ankles. Her eyes were alight with excitement. "I'm sorry to disturb you, but I am too eager to speak with you."

Isaac sat back in his chair. "Is all well?"

"Oh, yes, quite. I've found something you will want to see. I've been going through some trunks that have been stored on the uppermost floor." A brief grimace passed over her features. "I'd avoided that for some time—I just couldn't face seeing some of the things from the past, particularly items that belonged to Geoffrey."

At the mention of his cousin, Isaac's gaze flicked to the portrait of him that hung on the wall. It had been painted when Geoffrey was twenty, some ten years ago. He had the same thick brows as Isaac as well as his jawline, but Geoffrey's nose was sharper, his lips a bit fuller.

"It's always pleased me that you left his portrait there," Aunt Sophia said softly, now looking at the painting of her son.

While Isaac truly hadn't rearranged anything since he'd become the baron, in this case, he'd wanted Geoffrey's portrait there. It reminded Isaac that nothing in life was certain and that he had benefited greatly from another's tragedy. He only hoped he could preserve the legacy that was meant to be his cousin's.

Aunt Sophia looked back to Isaac. "I wish you and Geoffrey had grown up together, that you had been able to know him well."

"I would have liked that too." When Isaac contemplated that, he envisioned Geoffrey as the brother he didn't have. And when he did that, he invariably thought of his actual brother—whom he'd also lost. That led to him thinking of how many people around him had died, and he couldn't help feeling alone.

But he wasn't alone. Aunt Sophia was right in front of him, and he had Tamsin. His heart swelled, and again he had the uncharacteristic sensation of hope. And anticipation for the future.

"As I was saying," Aunt Sophia went on. "I was going through these old things, and I found a trunk that I'd completely forgotten about. The new rector in Dunster sent it after your father died. It's filled with things from the rectory."

"What kinds of things?" Isaac had no desire for anything of his father's.

"I didn't go through it entirely, but trust me when I say that you will want to see the contents for yourself." She gave him a warm, encouraging smile. "There are books and letters and a myriad other things."

Isaac still wasn't convinced, but he would look since his aunt was so enthusiastic. "Thank you for telling me."

"I've had it brought to your apartment so you can look

through it at your leisure. I imagine Tamsin will be interested in the contents too."

He would not be able to ignore it, then. Going through it with Tamsin, however, seemed not only manageable, but perhaps it would even be nice.

"Is that a smile?" Aunt Sophia asked. "You don't do that very often, though I've seen more hints of them since you wed. You could not have chosen a better wife for yourself. She is the sunshine to your clouds."

When Isaac didn't respond, she continued. "I don't mean to say you are covered in darkness or the harbinger of a storm, but you have always been somewhat melancholy, owing to your father," she added with a purse of her lips.

"You seemed to know him well—well enough, anyway—despite him living so far away and never visiting."

"Your uncle had plenty of stories from when they were young. They had a difficult time of things with their father—your grandfather. He was incredibly demanding, and he set his expectations for each son at an early age. Your father was always expected to enter the clergy, and as such, he was subjected to a different manner of education and even discipline. I always thought he married your mother because she was also a light to his darkness, much like Tamsin is for you."

Isaac had never heard any of this before, though he knew from his grandparents that they believed their daughter to be a bright and wonderful person. "I didn't realize you knew my mother well at all."

"I didn't," Aunt Sophia said with a wistful smile. "But I met her a few times, and her personality was immediately engaging. She was the kind of person who put you at ease and made you feel as if you'd been acquainted for years."

It was bittersweet to hear such things. He was grateful for the knowledge, but also sad that he would never know her himself.

"Thank you for telling me that," he said softly.

"You must ask me anything you like. About anything at all." She clasped her hands together at her waist. "I am glad to see you are finally breaking free of the past. Between your family and what happened at Oxford, you have suffered greatly."

The languid happiness that had been swirling inside Isaac crystallized into something hard and stiff. He slowly stood. "What do you know about Oxford?" His voice was low, guarded. The wall he'd constructed and that had recently begun to crumble around him rose swiftly back into place.

"You mustn't think it's common knowledge," she said. "I helped your uncle with the young woman and her delicate situation. He was not prepared to manage that on his own."

His aunt had known about Mary all this time.

"I didn't realize you knew. Why didn't you ever say anything?"

She gave him a sympathetic look. "Because I know how difficult it was for you to be parted from her. Shefford told us you wanted to marry her, but that you understood why you could not."

"Actually, I'm not sure I ever understood, but I have always done what I was told, what was expected of me." The regret that was constantly with him sharpened for a moment.

Aunt Sophia grimaced, her hands squeezing together. "But you surely know that all turned out well for your son. That has to make it a little easier?"

Why did she not mention Mary? "I had thought everything worked out well for him and his mother, that they were living somewhere in security, that she'd likely married and they'd both had a family this past decade." Anxiety pricked Isaac's skin.

"Oh dear." Aunt Sophia blanched. "I suppose you didn't

know, but Mary didn't survive the birth. Your son was adopted by a wealthy family in Northumberland. He will never have known hardship or want. And he has been loved."

Mary had *died*.

All this time, Isaac had envisioned the family he'd lost carrying on without him. But Mary hadn't survived childbirth. Like his mother, she'd given her life bringing another into the world.

"The boy lived?" Isaac whispered.

"Yes," Aunt Sophia answered quickly. "I was there. He was a strapping lad from the moment he drew breath."

She'd been there.

Isaac met her gaze frantically. "Why did no one tell me this?"

"When all this happened, you were distraught, or so my husband told me. Perhaps I should have been more involved with you personally." She looked at him with regret. "You could have used a mother's guidance. I left it to your uncle to speak with you while I was focused on ensuring your son was adopted. I'm sorry."

"And Mary?" he asked in a broken whisper. "Did she know that he lived?"

Aunt Sophia's features softened. "Yes, she held him and told him she loved him. But there was too much blood, the midwife said, and she died."

Isaac needed to be alone. He started toward the door, his body numb so that he barely felt as though he was moving.

His aunt touched his arm as he passed her. "She went peacefully, and she knew her son would be loved. I made sure she knew that."

He turned his head toward her, fearing that his expression was dark and frightening, but unable to change it. "What of me? What did you tell her about me?"

Aunt Sophia blinked. "Nothing. We didn't speak of you."

Had Mary remembered that he loved her, that he'd promised he would always love her, no matter what? Or did she only recall that he'd let her go, that he'd said he couldn't marry her, that it was beyond his control?

Turning on his heel, Isaac stalked from the study.

At least his son was being raised in a family. With love. It was more than Isaac had ever had.

~

*T*amsin's bed still wasn't fixed. She would have slept in there, but instead, she was in the baron's room waiting for Isaac. He hadn't come to dinner, and she hadn't gone to his study to look for him. The conversation she needed to have with him would wait until he joined her.

If he joined her. It was quite late.

She sat in one of the chairs near the hearth where a warm fire burned. It was a chilly night; it seemed autumn was upon them.

Anxious, Tamsin stood and walked toward the door to the sitting room, which stood open. She saw the trunk beside the seating area. Sophia had explained to her at dinner that it contained items from the rectory where Isaac had grown up. They'd been sent her after his father's death and stored upstairs, forgotten until Sophia had found them again earlier today.

Had Isaac found something upsetting inside? She hadn't opened it and wouldn't unless he invited her to. She worried his absence was due to the contents.

But she was still upset with him. She needed to know the identity of Mary, this woman he loved. That didn't mean she didn't care about him, didn't love him. And the sting of it was excruciating. Loving him and knowing he loved someone else was unbearable.

Glancing at the clock on the mantel, Tamsin saw it was after midnight. Perhaps she should just go to sleep. Except she wasn't sure she could. She'd managed to keep her agitation from Sophia, but Tamsin couldn't hide it from herself.

The outer door of the sitting room clicked open. Tamsin froze, and her pulse began to pound. She could hear the vibration in her ears.

Isaac stepped inside and closed the door. Turning, his gaze met hers, and he stopped short.

Tamsin walked into the sitting room. "I wasn't sure you were coming."

"You didn't need to wait up," he mumbled, dipping his head slightly and looking away from her. Toward the trunk.

"Was there something in the trunk that upset you?" she asked, moving slowly toward it.

His gaze snapped up to hers, but only briefly. "I haven't opened it."

Tamsin stopped. "Oh." Then what was the problem? She could see he was upset. Had he realized he'd spoken about Mary in his sleep?

She straightened her spine and summoned her courage. "I need to ask you about something. Rather, someone." She paused, waiting for him to look at her. When he did not, she continued, her frustration growing. "Who is Mary?"

His gaze shot to hers like a bolt of lightning. And the storm in his eyes was just as fierce. "How do you know about her?" His voice was low and dark, as tempestuous as his expression.

"You mentioned her in your sleep. Twice." She didn't want to ask about him loving her. Perhaps when he told her who Mary was, there would be a perfectly logical reason for why he loved her—and Tamsin wouldn't feel as though her life was over. That sounded so dramatic, but really, how was she to spend it with a man who loved someone else?

"She's no one." He raked his hand through his hair, tousling it.

She'd never seen him do that before. There was something very odd about him this evening. His mood went beyond serious or brooding. When he scowled or glowered, it was never upsetting, and she wasn't concerned for his welfare. Tonight, there was an air of something very dark—despair perhaps—about him.

"Is your bed fixed?" he asked, glancing toward her room.

"No, and I don't know why. I'll make sure it is first thing tomorrow."

He started to turn. "I need to go."

She hurried toward him and touched his arm, but quickly withdrew her hand. "I want to know who Mary is. You said you loved her."

He swung his head back toward her but didn't look at her. "You don't want to know about her. Just forget about it."

"I can't. Isaac, please tell me the truth. You owe me that, I think. Does she bring you joy?"

Now he met her gaze, and his eyes were seething with emotion. "She did, once, but now she's dead." He sounded so anguished, so ravaged that Tamsin couldn't help but move toward him.

"I'm sorry."

His lip curled. "I told you there were things in my past that would drive you away. I never wanted to taint you with them. You will regret marrying me."

Tamsin gave him an encouraging smile. "I could never do that." She reached for him, but he evaded her touch.

"But I am precisely the rogue you didn't want. I behaved abominably. Worse than Bane."

Exhaling, she fixed a serene expression on her face, though her insides were in utter turmoil. "You're going to have to tell me because I don't believe you."

"Stop being so bloody pleasant and positive!" He'd never raised his voice like that. "This is not something you can smile or cheer away." Now he advanced on her—just one step, but his features had gone completely dark. "I took up a liaison with my laundress at Oxford and got her with child. Her name was Mary, and she died giving birth to our son."

Tamsin lifted her hand to her mouth, but not before she gasped, her jaw hanging open. She didn't move; her feet were rooted to the floor. He had a son?

Taking deep breaths to try to calm her racing heart, Tamsin thought over what he'd said, both now and in his sleep. "You said you loved her."

"I did." He shifted his attention from her to some spot on the wall behind her. "She made me happier than I had ever been, but I lost control. I behaved inappropriately, and she paid the price—the ultimate price, it turns out." His voice did break then, and he clasped a hand over his mouth.

Tamsin watched as he fought to keep his emotions inside. She went to his side and touched his shoulder. "It's all right," she whispered.

He turned his face toward her, his eyes wide and wild. "How can you say that? I abandoned my family, and the mother of my son is dead. Nothing about that is right."

"I know you aren't a bad person," she said, hating the tumult he was enduring. "I can't imagine you abandoning the woman you loved."

"But I *did*. Because they told me to—Shefford, my uncle, my father. They said I couldn't marry a laundress, that she would be taken care of. My uncle said he would settle her in a town far away from Oxford and London and here. She would be a widow with a baby, and it was likely she would have married and had a happy family. Only, none of that happened."

She realized Mary had died, but what of his son? "Where

is your son now?" she asked tentatively. Perhaps he didn't know, and she should not have asked.

"He was adopted. Aunt Sophia just told me tonight." He closed his eyes briefly, his face etched in sorrow. "I wanted to marry her—Mary. I wanted us to be a family."

"I know what it's like to want a family of your own," she said quietly. "But you were young. How would you have provided for them?"

"That is what Shefford argued. He involved my uncle, hoping he would take care of Mary and the babe, which he did. But my uncle said if I married her, I would likely not be admitted to the Inns of Court. The life I wanted would not be available to me."

"You did the only thing you could," Tamsin said. "You listened to your family and friend, and you made sure Mary and the babe were cared for. You are not a bad person."

The curl of his lip said he didn't agree. "If I had never surrendered to my baser needs, to my pathetic search for something joyous, Mary would still be alive. Nothing will ever alleviate my guilt. How can you want to be with me after knowing this?"

Her heart nearly broke at the idea of a young Isaac feeling love for the first time and being told that he couldn't have that love. It was no wonder that he struggled to find joy. When he'd finally had some, it had been stripped away.

It wasn't hard to see why he'd been so tormented by this. He'd lost the woman he loved, a son, and a family he'd never had. She could understand that so clearly, having been abandoned by her own mother.

"I want to be with you because you are a good man who made a mistake. That does not make you a rogue or a bad person. When I think of all the ways this has haunted you and the things you've denied yourself as some sort of penance…" She shook her head. "You are *not* a bad person. On the contrary, you are a wonderfully feeling and caring man."

He looked at her in complete anguish. "I don't understand how you can say that now that you know the truth. I abandoned Mary and my son, just as you were abandoned by your mother."

Oh no, he couldn't think that. "They are not at all the same," she said heavily. "You were persuaded to do something that was supposedly best for her, your son, and for you. You didn't have a family and then decide it wasn't good enough." Long-buried emotion rose in Tamsin. She'd almost forgotten how she'd felt when her mother had gone. Tamsin had thought she was lacking in some way, that her mother wanted a different daughter perhaps.

Isaac blinked. He looked as if he might say something, but did not.

"You have a chance now, Isaac," she said, summoning an almost smile. "You have me. We are a family. We can have children. And we can have love."

He shook his head, slowly at first, then with more force. "I don't deserve that. I turned my back on my family. Mary died alone."

Tamsin's heart fully broke then. "But *I* deserve that. I deserve a family." All this time, she'd kept her head up and looked for joy instead of wallowing in sadness and loss. "I love you, Isaac. Let me make you happy. Let us be happy together."

He stared at her, a battle waging behind his eyes. "It's not possible," he rasped. Then he turned and stalked toward the door. "You need to leave me alone." He pulled the door open.

"I will, but just for tonight. I am fighting for you, Isaac," she called after him. But he was already gone.

Tamsin sank to the floor and surrendered to all the dark emotions she typically kept at bay. Tears streamed down her face. For the girl whose mother had left and for the boy who'd made an unimaginable choice. And, lastly, for the man who thought he didn't deserve to be loved.

CHAPTER 19

*A*fter leaving Tamsin, Isaac had gone to his study, where he'd found an old bottle of whisky that had belonged to his uncle. He'd poured a large glass and drank about half of it before he realized he didn't particularly care for it. Which was too bad because he'd been hoping to obliterate all the terrible thoughts pelting his brain.

He'd never meant for Tamsin to know the truth. But he'd apparently been talking about Mary in his sleep. How long had that been going on? No one would know since he always slept alone.

The look in Tamsin's eyes when she'd asked him about her had torn him apart. He'd already been a broken mess after learning that Mary had died. But to see Tamsin's hurt had compounded everything.

Despite that, she'd supported him. She'd given him solace and understanding. And love. She'd said she loved him.

He'd barely slept, and now he felt tired and unkempt. He was still wearing his shirt and breeches from yesterday. The rest of his clothing sat in a pile near the settee where he had tried to sleep. He didn't even fit on the piece of furniture. He either had to sit up or rest the back of his knees on the other end so his feet dangled.

Scrubbing a hand over his face, he stood. Perhaps he could steal up the servant stairs. Except he'd probably be more likely to encounter someone in the household going that way. Best to just keep his head down and make his way to the apartment.

Would he encounter Tamsin? He didn't want to. He couldn't face her, not after what he'd revealed. She had to think him the worst sort of person, even if she'd proclaimed she loved him. He'd abandoned his son and the boy's mother when they'd needed him most. How could Tamsin not fault him?

She'd said it wasn't the same as her mother leaving her. He suddenly recalled what she'd said—he'd heard it in the moment, then let his emotions overtake him.

Tamsin had said that at least he hadn't left his family after deciding they weren't good enough. Something like that. Did she believe that was why her mother left? Because Tamsin wasn't good enough?

And now he'd left her when she'd been trying to help him. She'd wanted to support him, to love him, and he'd walked away. Abandoning her.

Isaac scooped up his clothing. He needed to find her.

Rushing from the study, he practically ran toward the stairs. Oddly, he encountered no one. He took the stairs two at a time and dropped something, but he didn't stop to fetch it. He continued upward and on to the apartment. Once inside, he tossed his things down. The sitting room was empty, but the door to her room was ajar.

"Tamsin? Are you here?" He realized there could be someone in her bedchamber repairing the bed. She'd said she was going to make sure it was fixed first thing.

Isaac went into her chamber, but it was also empty. And the bed was indeed fixed. He realized he'd slept late, and apparently it had been long enough for someone to complete the repair.

But where was Tamsin?

At that moment, she walked into the chamber from the small dressing room. She wore a simple day dress of ivory muslin with blue flowers and a blue sash. Her hair was pulled back from her face, but she hadn't put it up. She looked simple and heartachingly beautiful.

"Are you all right?" she asked, her expression tentative, her gaze wary.

"No."

"Where are the rest of your clothes?"

"In the sitting room. I slept in my study. Actually, I didn't really sleep."

"I didn't either," she said softly. "I did ascertain that you were in your study. Blunt said he heard you within."

"I came to apologize." His throat was thick, his eyes stinging with emotion. Blinking, he added, "I need you to know that I would never leave you—not permanently."

A faint smile flickered over her features but was quickly gone. "I'm glad to hear that."

He shook his head. "No, not even temporarily." Driven by regret and the need to get this absolutely right, he stepped toward her. "I won't leave you. Ever. You were right—I have a family. I have you."

She pressed her lips together and nodded. "Thank you for saying so. I hope you believe it."

He wanted to say he did, but he decided he needed to be honest with her from now on. "I'm trying to. I just need you to know that I see that you were abandoned, that your mother left you. I can only imagine how that felt." He moved closer until they were nearly touching. He looked into her eyes, desperate that she felt he understood. "You were good enough. You *are* good enough. Please tell me you know that."

She nodded twice. "I do, but it's nice to hear. But don't spend any more time trying to convince me. My optimism will win out. It always does."

"I am in awe of it," he whispered. "How can you always find the bright side?"

"Because I don't know how to do anything else." She smiled, but it didn't hold her usual cheer. "I have used positivity to bury my feelings as surely as you've worked to hide yours. I focused on my father and his grief instead of thinking of myself. I realize now what drew me to you in Weston. You had a way of making me feel special, protected, as if I mattered."

He took her hands. "Of course you do. You *are* special. I will always protect you. And not just from overzealous, older would-be suitors."

She cracked a small smile. "Is that humor?"

"I think I should try to have more of that." He searched her face. "Does this mean you aren't going to be eternally optimistic anymore?"

"I don't think I can help that—it's who I am. But I need to learn to let even the darker emotions in sometimes. Perhaps you can help me with that."

He laughed. "I will gladly give you lessons in brooding and sulking. And you must teach me how not to dwell on the pain of the past."

"I can do that. In fact, we can start that right now. You should look through that trunk in the sitting room."

"Have you?" he asked.

"I did not. But I saw Aunt Sophia earlier, and she asked me if you'd reviewed the contents. When I said I didn't think you had, she was incredibly disappointed. She is adamant you will be thrilled."

"Will you look at it with me?"

She blinked in surprise. "If you want me to."

"Please." He gestured for her to precede him back to the sitting room.

Tamsin moved past him, her skirts brushing his leg. A wave of desire—sweet and lingering—swept over him. How had he been so fortunate to marry this amazing, caring woman?

He followed her into the sitting room and joined her in front of the trunk. "I remember now that this was sent here. I said I didn't care what was in it, so my aunt stored it away."

"I'm glad she found it." She looked at him, her gaze hopeful. "What if there is something wonderful inside?"

Her optimism was like a beacon, directing him through the dark in a storm. His destination was unclear, but with her guiding him, he didn't think he could end up anywhere bad.

She took his hand and knelt, drawing him down with her. "You open it."

Isaac unlatched the lid and pushed it open. Sitting on top was a book he remembered from his youth. He picked it up and smelled the spine. The scent reminded him of the rectory, of stiffness and propriety. But the book itself recalled escape and if not joy, then a fleeting rapture. "Books were one of the few things my father allowed me to possess."

"What is it?"

He opened the cover and read the title: "*The Life and Perambulation of a Mouse.*"

She smiled. "I remember this book. I loved it."

"I did too. It made me happy." When had things stopped making him happy?

After Mary. He could not blame his father for his lack of contentment, not entirely.

"Did it?" She sounded surprised, gleefully so. "That makes *me* happy."

Isaac set the book outside the trunk and plucked out several more books, all of them triggering a time and place where he'd gone to feel safe and warm. Then he found something truly shocking. Something he didn't recognize.

Tamsin picked up a painting. "Is this you?"

The portrait depicted a woman with a child sitting on her lap. She looked at him with utter adoration, and he smiled at a stuffed dog that he held. The woman had dark blonde hair, most of which was piled onto her head. However, a cluster of curls fell against one side of her neck. She wore a necklace with a small gold cross set with garnets. Isaac remembered that necklace. He could feel it between his thumb and forefinger even now.

His breath halted. "That's my mother."

"I recognize her from the portrait in your office," Tamsin said. "She was very beautiful."

This painting was much larger than the one on his desk. It could be hung, perhaps in the portrait gallery. He would find a place for it—somewhere he would see it every day.

"Do you want to hang this in your study?" Tamsin asked. "That way you will see it every day."

She'd read his mind and offered a reasonable solution. Except he hated that she saw him as being in his office every day. "You should know that I was avoiding you," he confessed. "While it's true that I tend to work hard and enjoy doing so, I was trying to keep myself from you. I knew I needed to tell you the truth about my past, but I didn't have the courage. I told you I was a rogue."

Her eyes were dark and fierce. "Loving her and trying to do the right thing does not make you a rogue. Nor does trying to protect me—though I do *not* need that. On the contrary, you are a man who cares deeply and would never knowingly cause anyone harm."

He wasn't sure he believed that, but he would try. For Tamsin. She deserved a family and the man she'd just described. "You make me want to be that man."

"To me, you already are." She brushed her lips against his then looked back at the portrait.

"As for the painting, I think I'd rather have it in our sitting room, if you don't mind."

Her features softened as she set the painting down against the side of the trunk. "I don't mind at all. Then I can talk to her and get to know her."

Isaac felt himself smile. "I think she would like that." He had no way of knowing that of course, but it felt right.

Tamsin's eyes glowed. "You're smiling."

"You seem to have a way of making me do that."

Shaking her head, Tamsin said, "No, this is entirely your mother. As it should be. I am so happy she makes you smile. What else is in here?" she wondered, turning back to the trunk and reaching inside. "More books. And some papers. These look like a child's drawings." Pulling them out, she showed them to him. "Did you draw these?"

"I might have. I find it strange my father would have kept them."

"Perhaps someone else did. Your housekeeper?"

Isaac had mentioned Mrs. Wilkes in passing to Tamsin, but he wasn't sure he'd shared anything that would have given her that impression. "I suppose she could have."

"It seems to me that she looked after you as best she could. It makes sense that she may have tucked some things away. Look and see if there's more." She nodded toward the trunk.

He peered inside and moved some books around. His

gaze fell on a stack of folded parchment tied with string. Taking them from the trunk, he sat back and loosened the packet. The string fell to the floor. He opened the first piece of paper.

The air completely left his lungs.

The handwriting was unrecognizable, of course, but he saw that it was addressed to him, then scanned to the bottom and saw, "Love, Mama." Tears stung his eyes. He could not have hoped for such a treasure.

He looked over at Tamsin who was watching him in wide-eyed trepidation. "They are letters. To me. From my mother."

"How wonderful," she said with a tender smile. "I'll leave you alone to read them."

Isaac was already reading the first letter but glanced over at her as she was standing. "Thank you."

She gave him a nod and quietly left.

$\backsim$

*J*saac didn't remember the last time he'd slept during the day. Perhaps never. But after reading the letters from his mother, he'd collapsed into bed, overcome by a bone-deep exhaustion.

When he'd awakened, it was late afternoon. He'd rung for his valet and taken a wonderfully hot and somehow healing bath. He could hardly believe how much better he felt compared with yesterday after he'd heard the truth about Mary from Aunt Sophia.

His insides still clenched when he thought of her dying, and perhaps they always would. He could only hope that Aunt Sophia was right, that his son was well and, hopefully, happy.

He realized now that telling Tamsin had been necessary.

How could he ever have wanted to keep the truth from her? How could their marriage have had a chance without honesty and trust? Had he really thought he could keep her at arm's length both physically and emotionally? A woman with whom he'd become obsessed and had probably fallen in love with the moment she'd said she didn't want to go on the boat to Steep Holm.

And she hadn't been angry with him. She'd been supportive and understanding, and she'd given him her unconditional love. Perhaps that was the difference in how he felt today. He *was* loved.

Again, he needed to find her. He went in search of her downstairs, to her sitting room. They'd have just enough time to speak before dinner.

He encountered Aunt Sophia in Tamsin's sitting room, where he'd first gone to look for his wife. She sat at the desk writing and looked up when he entered.

"Good evening, Isaac," she said hesitantly.

Moving into the room, he tried to decide what to say first. He owed her an apology. What must she think of him after his reaction yesterday regarding Mary?

Aunt Sophia rose. She smoothed her hands down the front of her skirts before her arms fell stiffly to her sides. Her entire frame appeared taut, including her features. "I need to apologize for our conversation yesterday. I should have realized you didn't know of my involvement with Mary and your son. Your uncle wanted to protect you from all of it. He believed it was most important for you to move on and not dwell on your mis—" She stopped herself. "On what happened."

"You were going to say mistake," he said quietly. "It's all right. It was a mistake. If I had not surrendered to my primal needs, Mary would be alive today."

Walking toward him, her forehead creasing with deep

furrows, Aunt Sophia lifted her hand. "You mustn't think that. How could loving someone ever be a mistake?"

She sounded like Tamsin. Still, he would perhaps always feel responsible for the way in which Mary's life had turned and then ended. "I owe you an apology for how I reacted. I should not have walked out."

She shook her head. "You were overcome—understandably. The blame lies with me. I should not have told you, not in that way. I suppose I thought that you'd moved past what happened after all this time, but I can see it was an indelible period in your life."

"It is, in large part, the reason for my cloudiness." He used her description on purpose. "But I do think the sun has finally broken through."

"Tamsin?" Aunt Sophia asked with a smile.

He nodded. "It is good that you told me what really happened. I'm glad my son has been well cared for. You're sure of that?"

"Positively," she said firmly.

He realized he could probably ask for his son's location. It seemed his aunt knew precisely where he was and with whom. But he wouldn't ask. The most important thing was that his son had a family and was loved. Isaac didn't need anything else. He would not disrupt the boy's life.

"I hope you won't have regrets," Aunt Sophia said gently. "Especially about your behavior. You did not act poorly. Plenty of young men have navigated the same or similar circumstances."

"That doesn't make it right." Isaac would always regret his behavior. He'd known better than to behave like a rogue. His entire upbringing had been centered on his father's expectation that Isaac behaved with propriety, righteousness, and responsibility. He'd utterly failed on all counts with Mary, and he would take that to his grave.

"Perhaps not," Aunt Sophia said, looking down. After a moment, she lifted her gaze, and he saw that her eyes were damp. "I am sorry for my part in things. I truly was just trying to help and settle everyone as best we could." She dashed a finger beneath one eye.

"You did your best, and I am gladder than I can say that you were with Mary when she left this world. I am confident you made her feel safe, and, more importantly, you ensured she knew her son would be well. There is no greater gift you could have given her."

Aunt Sophia sniffed as she wiped her other eye. "Thank you for saying that." She swallowed and tilted her head back. "Goodness, I'm an absolute watering pot. I don't suppose you managed to look through the trunk yet?"

"Actually, I did." The letters from his mother had brought him back from the darkness. She'd saved him. "You were right about the contents. They are immeasurably valuable to me. I can't thank you enough for finding it."

"I'm so pleased." Aunt Sophia beamed. "I saw that there were books and a portrait. Do you know where you want to hang it?"

"I do. There were letters too—from my mother."

Aunt Sophia sucked in a breath. "That is astonishing. I'm especially glad I found it."

Isaac went back to the reason he'd come in the first place. "Do you know where I can find Tamsin?"

"Oh, yes. She is at the Bowmans' assisting with the delivery of their child. She's been there several hours now. Perhaps you should go check on things?"

He couldn't help thinking of Mary and how she hadn't survived giving birth. And his mother. "I confess the notion of going near a birth fills me with dread."

"It's normal that you should feel that way, given your experience." Aunt Sophia gave him a sympathetic smile.

"However, only look at me, and your cousins. We have all survived birthing children—most women do."

"I will go." He would not give Tamsin reason to think he wasn't there for her, not after the way he'd behaved since they'd arrived at Wood End.

"Good." Aunt Sophia gave him an encouraging nod. "I am not entirely sure how your marriage began, but I am confident it is carrying on with a great deal of promise. I can see how well the two of you fit together, even if you don't know it yet."

Isaac narrowed his eyes at her. "Why did it take so long for Tamsin's bed to be repaired?"

Her eyes rounded, and she shrugged. "Did it take a long time?"

He now doubted the bed's disrepair in the first place. And his aunt's inability to escort Tamsin to the vacant cottage. The picnic gave the motivation away, but Isaac hadn't realized the lengths to which his aunt might have meddled. Would she have sawed through the ropes on Tamsin's bed? He wasn't going to ask.

In any case, he ought to be grateful. Without Aunt Sophia's gentle nudging, he and Tamsin might not be where they were today.

Or where he hoped they might be.

"Go on, then," Aunt Sophia said. "I'll let Mrs. Corwin know that you and Tamsin will dine later—assuming she returns this evening. As this is Mrs. Bowman's first child, it could take all night and even into tomorrow. Geoffrey took nearly a day. But he was worth every pain," she added with a smile before looking intently at Isaac. "I hope you know that you are very much a part of this family, and you've become most dear to me. You are loved, and I hope you will never doubt it or forget it."

Emotion welled in Isaac's chest, rising to clog his throat. He had to clear it to speak. "Thank you. I realize that now, and I won't forget it." He kissed her cheek, then turned and left the sitting room, hastening his steps to get to the stables.

He needed to be with his wife. Now and forever.

CHAPTER 20

*H*alf an hour later, Issac drove up to the Bowmans' cottage. Nothing seemed out of the ordinary. Had he expected something to be? Perhaps pandemonium as the baby was born? Calm and normal would be desired in this situation.

Bowman came out of the house just then. Closing the door, the man let out a cry and pumped his fist in the air as he leapt from the porch to the ground. He spun about, then stopped abruptly, positioned toward Isaac. "Who's there?" he called.

The sun had gone down, and just the lamps in the house along with the half moon in the dark sky provided illumination. Isaac stepped down from the gig and walked toward Bowman. "It's Droxford. Is all well?"

Now Isaac was close enough to see the man's expression. He grinned broadly—wildly, even. "I've a son, my lord!" Bowman let out another happy cry.

Isaac exhaled in relief. He'd been almost certain the man's noise and antics as he'd left the cottage were driven by joy but was glad to have confirmation. "Congratulations. This is a happy occasion indeed." He found it surprisingly easy to smile.

"Come inside and we'll toast with an ale," Bowman said, turning back toward the house.

Forcing himself forward, Isaac followed Bowman into the cottage. The sound of a baby's cries came from upstairs, and Isaac froze. Thoughts of his son, of all he'd abandoned, flooded him. He should not have come.

"Shall we go up and see him?" Bowman asked. He was already starting up the stairs, the ale forgotten, apparently.

Not that Isaac wanted ale. Or to see the babe.

He walked slowly forward, just to the base of the stairs. "I'll wait here," he said nervously, his gaze flicking toward the top where Bowman had reached.

Then she appeared. Tamsin. Carrying a baby. The sight nearly drove Isaac to his knees. How could something look so heart-stoppingly beautiful and cause such unbearable anxiety, panic, almost. There it was—the portrait of the family he could have. He'd never expected this.

She said something to Bowman that Isaac couldn't hear. Bowman bent his head to press a kiss to the babe's head, then disappeared from view.

"Isaac?" Tamsin's familiar, Cornish-tinged voice carried down to him.

"Yes."

"Come see the babe," she said with soft encouragement.

Feet encased in granite, Isaac climbed the stairs. At the top, he stopped a few feet from Tamsin and the child. He was swaddled tightly, and Tamsin held him to her chest.

"Where's Bowman?" Isaac asked.

"Gone in to tend to his wife." Tamsin smiled. "Which means I am lucky enough to hold their son for a few minutes."

"He has so much hair," Isaac noted.

"Yes, and so dark." She gently stroked the top of the babe's head. He didn't stir. His eyes were closed in slumber.

"Can I hold him?" The question surprised Isaac, and for a moment, he wondered if he'd said it aloud.

"Of course." Tamsin moved closer and held the babe toward him. "Be careful to put one hand behind his head. He needs your support."

Isaac did as she instructed. The weight of the babe and his warmth loosened something inside him. He held the boy close to his chest and looked into his sleeping face. Everything about him was so perfect. Isaac briefly closed his eyes and imagined his own son. Pain and regret surged within him, but they felt less raw than before.

"Are you all right?" Tamsin asked.

Opening his eyes, Isaac met her gaze. He gathered his courage and found a serenity he hadn't expected. "I think so. Mrs. Bowman is fine?"

"I don't know if I would say 'fine.'" Tamsin chuckled. "She is exhausted and overjoyed. The midwife says the birth went as well as one could hope."

Isaac exhaled. "That is good to hear."

Tamsin touched his arm and smiled at him. "I know how difficult this must be for you, the memories it stirs."

He nodded. "You must think me ridiculous."

"Not at all. I think you're brave to face your fears. As I said earlier, we need to embrace those emotions, for that is how we heal."

Heal. That's what he was feeling now, the pain lessening. The wound closing.

Bowman came from a chamber, where he must have gone to be with his wife. "Laura is ready for Jacob now. The midwife says she needs to try to feed him."

"Of course." Isaac transferred the babe to his father, who beamed with pride and love. "Congratulations again,

Bowman. Don't worry about what remains of your harvest. We will ensure it's taken care of."

"I can help—probably." Bowman swayed gently with his son in his arms. "We have help from the maid Lady Droxford sent. That's been a real godsend, my lady." He sent Tamsin a grateful look.

"It is our pleasure to help. You've plenty of provisions to keep you fed for the next fortnight, I should think. And we're here if you need anything else. Please tell Laura I'll check on her tomorrow."

Bowman nodded. "She'll appreciate that, my lady."

"Good night, then," Isaac said with a smile.

As Bowman went back into the bedchamber. Isaac turned and put his hand at the small of Tamsin's back. "Are you ready to go?"

"Yes. I think I may need a bath."

"We can arrange that." Isaac thought he might have joined her if he hadn't already bathed earlier. Although, why should that prevent him? He could, at the very least, aid her. A dozen lurid thoughts crowded his mind.

They left the cottage, and Isaac helped her into the gig. "Are you hungry? I can arrange to have dinner brought to the sitting room while you take your bath," Isaac offered.

"I hadn't thought of it until you just asked, but yes, I'm famished. Perhaps we could just nip into the kitchen when we arrive?"

Isaac laughed. "I suppose we could." He started driving back toward the house.

"Look at you, smiling and now laughing," Tamsin said with a cluck of her tongue. "I would scarcely recognize you."

"I scarcely recognize myself after these past two days." He thought marrying Tamsin would change his life—and it had —but facing his past and sharing it with her was the true change that had needed to happen.

She moved close to him so that their sides were touching. "You are the same man you have always been, just more open. We must remember to remain that way with each other—no holding emotions back or hiding behind scowls or smiles."

"It's clear which of us will be doing which," he said drily. He looked over at her. "Thank you for staying with me and not running away from this marriage that I forced with my roguish behavior. I should not even have been at that soiree, but I couldn't manage to stay away from you."

"Well, I am glad you couldn't, or I would have had to fight Brimble off myself." She snuggled against him. "I have no regrets about anything, Isaac. Indeed, I think we were meant to find one another."

He wanted to believe that too. Tamsin was a gift he didn't deserve, but he would spend his life trying to.

"I wanted to tell you about my mother's letters," he said, hoping he could keep the strong emotion at bay. If he could not, he would end up an even worse watering pot than his aunt.

"I was hoping you would."

"She wrote them in the final weeks of when she carried my brother. She was tired and unwell. I think she must have known the end could be near. She wrote of her love for me, of her hopes for how I would grow up. I wish I'd seen these when I was younger. Perhaps I might have been equipped with your optimism." He'd wondered why he'd never seen them. Had his father kept them from him on purpose? Or had they simply been lost to time as they'd been transferred from wherever his mother had kept them to that trunk and then to the uppermost floor at Wood End? He would never know, and perhaps that was for the best.

"They sound wonderful," Tamsin said.

"You are welcome to read them. Then you can get to know her too."

"I would like that."

Isaac drove the gig to the stable and helped Tamsin down as one of the grooms took charge. Thanking the young man, Isaac escorted Tamsin to the house. "Do you want to stop by the kitchen?"

She laughed softly. "No, I can wait. But do have dinner sent up. I don't want to dress after my bath."

"Perfect, because I don't want you to either."

Tamsin paused and turned toward him. "Are you *flirting* with me?"

"I think so," he said almost incredulously. "Is that all right?"

She put her hands on his chest and gave him a heated, seductive smile. "It's most welcome."

Issac kissed her, his lips brushing over hers with a gentle softness. He loved her so much. He couldn't wait to tell her when they were alone in their chamber. When he held her in his arms and surrendered to her completely.

~

*T*amsin had bathed in her chamber. Her maid helped to mostly dry her hair, but Tamsin's toilet was simple. She slipped into a dressing gown and tied her hair back with a ribbon.

Glancing at the now-repaired bed, she wondered where she would sleep tonight. Isaac had given clear signals that he meant for them to be intimate, but what did that mean?

She hoped she was about to find out.

Walking into the sitting room, Tamsin noted the table had been elegantly set for their dinner. Isaac stood at her chair, holding the back. He was still dressed, but he'd removed his coat. She reasoned that if he had worn his dressing gown, it was entirely possible that they would not have bothered to eat. Hungry as she was, she was even hungrier for her husband.

It wasn't just her fervent desire begging to be satisfied, it was her need to hold him, to show him how much he meant to her. How much she loved him.

She sat down, and he poured wine into their glasses. "No footman?" she asked.

He shook his head as he sat. "I preferred privacy this evening. I hope that is acceptable to you."

"Quite. I might even have preferred you in a dressing gown like I am, but I fear that may have been too distracting."

"I understand. It's taking every bit of self-control I possess to keep from stripping yours away and feasting on you instead of the dinner. But I shall save that for dessert, if you are amenable."

Heat flared through Tamsin as his words aroused her. She nearly suggested they skip the dinner after all, but he spoke, "We should eat." He removed the cover from his plate, and Tamsin did the same.

They had beef steaks as well as parsnips and peas. She giggled.

"Why are you laughing?" He looked adorably perplexed.

"Parsnips and peas. But we have no one to pelt them with."

Isaac's eyes lit with mirth, and he smiled. "That is unfortunate. However, I shall always be grateful for those vegetables since they were intrinsic to us deepening our acquaintance."

"I found you so attractive," she said. "Even then. I truly thought you might kiss me that day on the beach. And then again in the hotel garden, but you said you hadn't planned to do so."

He grimaced. "I lied. I was also attracted to you. Distractingly so. I was desperate to return to Wood End lest I find myself utterly bewitched."

She cut a piece of the beef. "Why didn't you leave?"

"Because I was entranced by you. I even agreed to go on that bloody boat just so I could be with you."

"I don't think I've ever heard you curse before," she said.

He paused, his expression contemplative. "No, I don't suppose you have. I generally don't, because my father forbade it and lectured me incessantly on the sins of swearing. It has always stuck with me."

"Until now?"

"I feel rather like a different person. No, not different, but...renewed. As if I am finally able to let the past go. I would much rather look to the future." His lips curved into a small, sweet smile before he ate a parsnip.

Tamsin's insides somersaulted with giddiness. "Tell me more about why you agreed to face your fear and go on the boat."

"It was less about facing my fear and more about spending the day in your presence," he said wryly. "But when I arrived at the dock, I realized I wasn't going to be able to do it, not without grave consequences to my composure."

"I could see how agitated you were. I didn't want you to go on the boat, not if it was going to cause you such upset."

He frowned slightly. "I hated that you didn't get to go."

She shrugged. "I much preferred to spend the day with you, or part of it, anyway." She gave him a flirtatious smile before scooping up a few peas from her plate.

They ate in silence awhile. Tamsin thought of how far they'd come since those days in Weston. She'd tucked the shell he'd given her in the pocket of her dressing gown earlier. Now, she withdrew it and set it on the table. "Why did you find this for me?"

"Because I knew it would make you happy. Rather, happier. You are always happy."

Tamsin laughed. "I seem to be, but I confess I am not always. It's just that I try to be. However, I've decided I can let myself be sad. Or frustrated. Or whatever I want to be that isn't happy. I know that happiness is always there for me when I need it. Especially now," she added almost shyly. She felt such an overwhelming love for him. But she didn't want to expect the same in return.

"You don't need to be happy for me," he said with a very serious tone, his gaze direct. "I suspect you did that for your father, to ease his sadness after your mother left. Is that wrong?"

Tamsin hadn't thought of it that way, but she knew he was right. "No. My father was never effusive, but he was different after my mother left. I'm not sure I noticed it right away, but over time, I just accepted that he was morose, and it was up to me to provide a sense of lightness and cheer."

"That is a great responsibility for a young person to shoulder."

"Perhaps, but it came somewhat naturally to me, so I didn't mind." They fell silent again as they ate, and Tamsin paused to sip her wine, a dark red that was richer than anything she'd tried before.

Isaac drank his wine too, and he sat back in his chair, his gaze sweeping over her with a heat she felt deep in her core. She suddenly wanted to be done with their dinner so he could sweep her into his arms and carry her to bed. There, he would hopefully dine on her instead, as he'd said he wanted to do. Or perhaps he might even take things further. How she longed to feel him inside her—his sex, not his fingers. Though, she would take anything he offered.

He startled her from the increasingly carnal nature of her thoughts by speaking. "I wanted to tell you that I think I must have been falling in love with you in Weston. Why else would that Bumble cretin have made me so infuriatingly jealous?" He exhaled. "I should not have hit him, but I did warn him."

Tamsin set her wine down carefully lest she spill it every-where. Had she just heard him right?

Isaac put his glass down and rose. He came around the table and took her hand, guiding her to her feet. "I have no regrets about that evening, not even hitting Bumble."

She giggled. "You keep calling him Bumble."

"That isn't his name?" He shrugged. "I'm just glad I didn't leave before that soiree. If I had, I would surely be filled with regret for not pursuing what might have been between us. All because I was afraid."

Tamsin could hardly breathe listening to his revelations. She was beyond ecstatic. "I'm not sure you were afraid, just set in a certain way of thinking. You needed to see for yourself that you deserve happiness, that you deserve love. I lo—"

He put his finger on her lips. "No. Don't say it. Not until I do. I love you so deeply, Tamsin, more than I ever expected to love anyone. More than I knew was possible. You fill me with light and hope, and an indescribable joy. I will be forever grateful that you came into my life."

She kissed the pad of his finger. "I love you too." Then she licked him.

Isaac moaned softly. "I hope you're done eating."

"So done."

He lowered his head and kissed her. Their lips and tongues met in a passionate dance. Each kiss grew hotter and deeper. Tamsin tugged his cravat loose and pulled it from his neck, letting it fall to the floor. Then she began to unbutton his waistcoat.

When the garment was open and she began to push it from his shoulders, he took a step back. They were both breathing heavily, and Tamsin curled her hands around the edges of his waistcoat, prepared to drag him back to her.

"I have to say one more thing," he said, his voice taut with desire. "As much as I love you and as different as I feel today, I am still, in some ways, the man I was. I don't know that I'm ready to have a child. It's going to take me some time to accept that this is my life, that I deserve this. Also, if I'm honest, I'm a little afraid to be a father. I did not have a good role model, and I've already abandoned one son."

"Would you prefer to wait?" she asked. "You've made it clear we can satisfy one another in plenty of ways without risking a child."

His nostrils flared. "God, you are an incomparable woman. You really don't mind?"

"I can be patient," she said with a broad smile.

"Oh, I'm definitely putting my cock in you tonight. I need to feel you around me."

Heat flooded Tamsin's core. She nearly whimpered with want. "But how can we do that?"

"I'll be careful not to come inside you. If I don't put my seed in you, there won't be a baby. However, that isn't fool-proof. I know that sometimes it can happen anyway. I can live with that chance."

She pushed the waistcoat from his shoulders. "Then let's get started."

He rapidly unfastened her dressing gown and pushed it open, baring her breasts and her sex. Putting his hands on her, he squeezed her nipples then slid his hands to her back and cupped her backside, his fingers digging into her flesh and parting her cheeks slightly as he lifted her. "Put your hands around my neck and wrap your legs about my waist."

Tamsin did as he bade, loving the press of his hands on her backside as she felt his cock against her sex. She kissed him, spearing her tongue into his mouth as he walked toward the bedroom, carrying her.

When they crossed the threshold, he kicked the door closed before continuing toward the bed. After climbing the stairs of the dais, he set Tamsin on the edge of the bed.

"Can I demand you take your clothes off?" she asked as she shrugged out of her dressing gown.

In answer, he began to remove his boots, and everything else followed in quick succession until he was nude and glorious before her. He moved to stand between her open legs and kissed her. She wrapped her legs around him once more, and his cock pressed against her sex. Sensation leapt within her, sending a spike of lust straight to her core.

He gripped her hair where she had it tied with the ribbon and held her head while he plundered her mouth. She ground her hips against his, her sex aching for more.

Tearing his mouth from hers, he dragged his tongue down her throat and cupped her breast before taking her nipple between his lips. He lightly grazed her with his teeth, then sucked hard, pulling on her flesh as she cried out.

Isaac wrapped his arms around her and lifted her farther onto the bed. Then he followed her onto the mattress as she lay back, his body moving between her legs.

He stroked her sex, moving his fingers along her crease until he reached her clitoris. Rubbing her, he bent his head to suckle her breast once more. Tamsin gripped his head, desperate for the release building inside her, but also not wanting this wicked pleasure to end.

She moaned as he kissed and licked his way down to her sex, his tongue flicking her clitoris. He kept one hand on her breast, his fingers twisting her nipple. She thought she might come before he even put his cock inside her.

But then his tongue was there, laving her sex, a series of

fierce licks before he sucked on her clitoris. His fingers slid into her, filling her.

"I want your cock," she managed to rasp as her climax barreled down upon her. She wasn't ready. She wanted him fully inside her.

Tamsin wriggled her hips away and reached between his legs for his sex. Finding his shaft, she encircled his girth and stroked him from base to tip. Isaac groaned as he moved against her, his cock brushing against her opening.

"Put me inside you," he ground out, his hand covering hers. "Together."

The tip of him slid into her sheath, and she immediately felt a rush of ecstasy. As she stretched around him, she arched her head back, moaning and whimpering.

"Wrap your legs around me, Tam." He held her hips as he thrust all the way into her.

Tamsin did as he instructed and rested her heels against his backside. He filled her completely, and her body throbbed with unquenched desire. She'd been so close to her orgasm, but now it seemed further away.

Isaac began to move. The friction of his thrusts stirred her again and brought a torrent of pleasure as he stroked faster and faster. She clasped his shoulders, digging her fingers into his flesh. Her hips rose from the bed to meet him, their bodies coming harshly together as they chased rapture.

He put his hand between them and massaged her clitoris again, taking her right back to where she'd been. "Come now, Tamsin. I need you to come. I'll have to pull out before I do, so you come *now*."

Her release was already upon her, having started as he was commanding her to do so. She gripped him tightly with her legs as her body clenched with the power of her orgasm. Over and over, she cried out as unimaginable pleasure crested over her. She'd never known such a glorious satisfaction, such a boundless joy.

She hadn't quite reached the ground again before he was gone from her. She opened her eyes and watched as he stroked his cock, his head cast back. Scrambling, she turned herself so she could give him aid. She put her hand over his and worked his shaft but then licked the tip where a bit of liquid had pooled. It was thick and salty, and she swallowed it down.

"Tamsin," he ground out, his hips thrusting wildly as she took him in her mouth. "You can't," he protested.

Instead of arguing, Tamsin simply pushed his hand away and took command, sucking him deep into her mouth and cupping his balls. He jerked, and a warm gush of liquid washed over her tongue. She didn't cease, just kept holding him and working her tongue on his flesh as he came apart.

She swallowed everything he gave her, and when his hips slowed, she finally released him. Falling back on the bed, she gasped for breath, her chest heaving. A smile curved her lips, and she didn't think she'd ever been happier in her life.

He fell down beside her—they were angled sideways on the bed. Turning toward her, he kissed her jaw, her cheek, beneath her ear. "Did you taste yourself on my cock?" he whispered.

She thought she had, but she wasn't sure. "Does that arouse you?" She'd heard the thrill in his voice.

"Yes."

"Then I shall do it again." She turned toward him and brushed her lips against his.

He caressed her cheek and pushed a lock of hair behind her ear that had come loose. "Now that I know how adventurous and eager you are, we'll discuss other ways we can pleasure each other, including a method of intercourse that will never result in a child."

"What is that?" she asked, enthralled, her body stirring again.

He whispered the answer in her ear, shocking her. But also titillating her. "If you are amenable," he added. "I won't mind if you aren't."

"I am open to anything I may share with you. Shall we try it now?"

Chuckling, he kissed her, his tongue stroking hers. "No, my love, you should rest. We will need to work toward that particular endeavor. I will begin with my finger and eventually, again if you are still amenable, you can take my cock."

She shivered with anticipation. "Does this mean we're going to sleep now?"

He laughed. "I do believe that was a verbal pout." He moved over her, flattening her to the mattress. He stared down at her, his eyes dark and dangerously seductive. "I take it you aren't quite finished."

"Can I have another orgasm?" she asked, her sex already throbbing with want.

"Let's find out." He arched his brow, then lowered his lips to hers once more.

As it happened, she was able to have two more orgasms, one of which she shared with him while he taught her how they could pleasure each other at the same time with their mouths.

All in all, it was a marvelous evening, and as she lay in his arms much later, she fell asleep to the memory of his laughter and the countless times he'd said, "I love you."

CHAPTER 21

The following evening, Tamsin accompanied Isaac to watch him harvest the honey. It was a cool but clear evening, perfect for their task. The sun was low on the horizon, the days growing shorter as they moved toward the solstice.

Isaac worked meticulously, with two tenants, including Oliver, helping, removing the drawers and extracting the honeycomb. Tamsin observed from a distance, seated on a blanket at the base of the knoll nearby.

When they were finished, Isaac thanked Oliver and the other tenant for their assistance. They then departed with the honeycomb, which the tenant's wife would process, separating the honey from the wax.

Isaac approached Tamsin on the blanket, noting her expression was apprehensive. "Not a single sting," he proclaimed, hoping to put her at ease. "More importantly, all the bees are alive."

She relaxed, her features loosening and her lips spreading in a wide, proud smile. "This is a remarkable achievement.

What will you do to persuade more people to revise their manner of harvesting?"

He sat down beside her on the blanket. "I hadn't considered it, but I suppose I could write something for publication or some sort of distribution." He arched a brow at her. "Are you encouraging me to work more?" That morning, he'd promised her he wouldn't spend so much time away from her. He didn't think he could anyhow. Indeed, every moment he'd spent apart from her today had been torture.

Tamsin laughed. "I can sit in your study while you write. I'll read. Or embroider."

He nuzzled her neck, kissing her sweetly scented skin. "That won't be distracting at all. Five minutes won't pass before I toss up your skirts and have my way with you."

"Promise?" She turned her head, her gaze burning with desire, and kissed him with a fiery passion.

She pushed him onto his back and straddled him, arranging her skirts so she was bare against him—her sex against his thickening cock through his breeches. Leaning forward, she kissed him again.

Isaac cupped her nape and lifted his hand to stroke her breast through the frustrating layers of her garments. If they were not so exposed, he would loosen them and give them both what they sought.

It was several minutes before she took her mouth from his. Sighing, she straightened. "I like the view from up here."

"Good. I think you need to ride me like this later. You can control the speed and the thrusts, taking me as deep as you like—or not. And your lovely clitoris will be open for my ministrations." He waggled his brows at her. "I plan to drive you mad."

Her lips were parted, and he could see her pulse thudding in her throat. "Let's go now."

"We have dinner with Aunt Sophia first." As he spoke, he slipped his hand beneath her skirts and found her wet heat.

She gasped softly, then rose up slightly, widening her stance so he could easily stroke her. "Is this wise?" she asked in a ragged whisper.

"You'll have to keep your eyes open and look out for anyone approaching from the house." She had the right vantage point. The only thing he could see was the delightful rise and fall of her breasts as they strained against her gown.

Isaac stroked her clitoris, then thrust his fingers into her ready sheath. She ground down on him, her hips rotating.

"Keep my eyes open," she breathed as she fisted her hands around the edges of his lapels.

He watched as her eyes narrowed to slits, her hips moving as he impaled her with his fingers. He moved faster, knowing they should hurry. He doubted anyone would come upon them, but he didn't want his bee helpers to return for any reason. So he worked her faster and harder, holding her hip with his other hand.

He felt her muscles clench as her sex clamped around him. "Don't scream." She'd done that once last night, and he'd had to swallow it as best he could with a kiss.

"This is so hard," she said through clenched teeth. Her eyes closed then, and her head fell back.

Isaac guided her through her orgasm, then withdrew his hand from her skirts. She pulled her leg over his body and sat heavily on the blanket, her breath coming fast. Sitting up, he licked his fingers, and Tamsin's eyes rounded.

He shrugged. "You taste divine."

"That was naughty," she said breathlessly, her hands smoothing her skirts, but she wasn't at all untidy. "Anyone could have happened upon us."

"It was unlikely. And you were looking out—until the end, anyway."

She blushed. "I did try. But see if you can survive an orgasm with your eyes open. I'll wager it's impossible."

"Hmm. I haven't tried. I shall have to conduct an experiment later. Would you care to assist me?"

She leaned over and kissed him. "Count on it."

He helped her to her feet, and she picked up the blanket to fold it. He took it from her, and they walked back to the house, hand in hand.

Isaac had never been so happy in his entire life. He'd never even imagined this level of joy was possible. To think he would have this every day was incredibly humbling.

And he couldn't help thinking it wasn't fair, that poor Mary, whom he'd loved and cared for, wouldn't have this or anything at all. He would not dwell on such maudlin things. There was nothing he could do except try to find the optimism in what had happened. Yes, she'd died, but she'd also been able to hold her son, to tell him she loved him, to know that he would be safe and cared for.

Isaac had only been able to do the latter, and he knew he could accept, in time, that it was enough. The pain was still raw, but it was less than yesterday, and he knew, with Tamsin's love and support, it would continue to ease. But he would never forget them—Mary or his son.

Tamsin had read his mother's letters this morning. She'd wept, but they'd been happy tears as she'd exalted in the joy that finding them brought.

"I received a letter from my grandmother this afternoon," she said, interrupting his thoughts. "She is delighted to spend Christmas here with us and thanked us for the invitation. I wonder if Somerton and his mother will be disappointed that she won't be spending it with them."

"Do we need to invite them too?" Isaac asked. While the idea of having so many people didn't enthuse him, he would manage it. Somerton being his friend helped matters.

"I can ask my grandmother when I respond, but I think his sisters might come to Winterstoke, and if they came here instead, that would be a great many people. I think the last thing you want, particularly for our first Christmas, is a Yuletide house party."

He smiled at her, their eyes meeting as they paused in their walk. "You already know me so well."

They began walking again, and she said, "Someday, I may ask to host a house party, but no time soon. I am just learning to plan this harvest celebration. Aunt Sophia says it is good practice for when I host things in London. I am most relieved that she spends the latter part of the Season in London."

Isaac was so grateful that his wife and aunt had formed a bond. He truly did have a family, and it was even more than just the three of them. It was his aunt's daughters and their families, Tamsin's grandmother, Somerton and his family, even his other friends, Shefford and Price. But not Bane. He'd forfeited that closeness when he'd ruined Tamsin's friend. Isaac thought he might like the man even less now that he'd wed Tamsin.

"You're brooding," Tamsin said.

"I'm not. I'm woolgathering. I was thinking of my extended family, actually. Of how they'd really always been there. I just didn't see them that way. And I should have, especially with Shefford."

"I confess I wondered why you weren't angry with him for his involvement with Mary," Tamsin said. "But he is a good and loyal friend, and I determined you must have realized that."

"Oh, I was angry with him for some time after that. But you are right that I didn't hold a grudge. I think I may be doing that with Bane, however. I can't bring myself to think of him in the same manner as my other friends." He stopped again, and she faced him. "The worst part is that I am not much better than he is."

"You made sure Mary was cared for. You didn't run away instead of accept responsibility. You are not a rogue," Tamsin said firmly, stepping closer to him. She released his hand and touched his face. "I have broken nearly every rogue rule with you, and I would do so again and again, especially the one where I show you my heart, for it belongs to you entirely, Isaac. Whether you want it or not."

"Oh, I want it." He gathered her in his arms. "Along with every other part of your body."

She twined her arms around his neck. "I love you, Isaac. You have all of me."

"I love you, my darling Tamsin—you are all that I am and all that I hope to be. Thank you for bringing me joy and hope."

The sun dipped into the west as he kissed her, and happiness settled deep into his soul.

EPILOGUE

London, April 1816

Isaac walked into the private sitting room he shared with Tamsin in their London house after bidding good evening to the last of his straggling guests. "I'd say your first dinner party was an unqualified success." He unknotted his cravat as he took in his wife. She'd already divested herself of her evening finery and was wrapped in a cozy dressing gown, her feet propped up on a footstool.

Tamsin yawned. "I hope so. I do think it turned out well."

Tossing his cravat onto a chair, Isaac removed his coat before kneeling beside the footstool. He picked up one of Tamsin's feet and began massaging the arch. "Forgive me, but you look exhausted."

She let out a satisfied moan as she wriggled her toes. "That feels lovely. Please don't stop. And yes, I'm tired. It's been a long day."

"I shall let you go directly to sleep, then," he said, moving to her other foot.

"I'm not *that* tired," she said wryly.

They'd been married six months, and they had not changed their minds about bearing a child. If it happened, they would be happy, but they weren't seeking it. Perhaps someday that would change, but for now, he was content to share his life—and all the love in his heart—with Tamsin.

"Are you ready for Almack's next week?" she asked.

He released her foot and sat in the other chair, loosening his cravat. "No. But I'll go. For you."

"Not for me, for Gwen. She's horribly nervous. She's afraid no one will ask her to dance, that she'll be dubbed a wallflower before the night is through."

"That won't happen. Her father has a prominent position, and she's pretty."

Tamsin rolled her eyes. "Spoken like a rogue, or a man with rogues as friends. She is bookish, and that can be off-putting to some men. Since coming to London, I've learned they don't like when women are too smart." Tamsin made a face.

Isaac scowled. It remained one of his favorite expressions. "Those men are dolts. I pity them. But chances are, they aren't very smart themselves. They are intimidated by a woman who will outwit them."

"Gwen can most definitely do that. I hope no one challenges her to a game of chess. She's absolutely terrifying."

Tamsin rose from her chair and moved to sit on his lap. She smoothed his brow. "No scowling in our bedchamber. Only laughing."

"Just laughing?" he asked as he kissed her neck.

"It was good to see our friends tonight," she said with a sigh. "But I wish Pandora was in London."

Apparently, she was in Bath. But her sister and Wellesbourne had been here. As had Evan Price, his parents, and his sister Gwen, who was embarking on her Season. Somerton and Shefford had not been present.

"We won't see her until we're in Weston in August?" he asked, continuing to kiss her neck and paying special attention to the hollow of her throat.

"Yes, unless she changes her mind and comes to London, though I know she won't. She is venturing out a bit more in Bath, however, so that's something. Speaking of Weston, do you mind staying with my grandmother instead of at the Grove?"

"There is nowhere I would rather be." Isaac pushed the edge of her dressing gown aside so he could kiss her collarbone.

She shivered beneath his mouth. "I just want to be with you, wherever that is."

"I suppose we should go out of our way to thank Mrs. Loose-Lips, though we can also do that if we encounter her in London." He'd learned her new moniker and agreed it suited her perfectly.

"Absolutely not," Tamsin said firmly with a shake of her head. "I don't care that we do owe her everything. If I see her, I plan to give her the cut direct." Grimacing, she put her hand to her lips briefly. "Goodness, that is rather uncharitable of me. Don't tell anyone that I am not always nice."

This provoked Isaac to laugh, which in turn provoked his wife to comb her fingers through his hair. "You know what happens to me when you laugh." Her eyes had darkened with desire, and Isaac's body responded with a flare of heat.

"I do. And I swear I don't do it on purpose." He tipped his head. "Very often."

"I don't care why or how you do it, just never stop." She kissed him, and he felt all the love and joy she possessed, basking him in a light that had forever driven away the darkness.

He was the luckiest man indeed.

Don't miss the next Rogue Rules: When the Viscount Seduces featuring Gwen Price and Lazarus, Lord Somerton!

When a bookish bluestocking must recover from social disaster, she accepts help from her brother's friend—an unserious rogue who needs a favor of his own...

Would you like to know when my next book is available and to hear about sales and deals? **Sign up for my VIP newsletter** which is the only place you can get bonus books and material such as the short prequel to the Phoenix Club series, INVITATION, and the exciting prequel to Legendary Rogues, THE LEGEND OF A ROGUE.

Join me on social media!

Facebook: https://facebook.com/DarcyBurkeFans
Instagram at darcyburkeauthor
Pinterest at darcyburkewrite

And follow me on Bookbub to receive updates on pre-orders, new releases, and deals!

Need more Regency romance? Check out my other historical series:

The Phoenix Club
Society's most exclusive invitation...

Welcome to the Phoenix Club, where London's most audacious, disreputable, and intriguing ladies and gentlemen find scandal, redemption, and second chances.

Matchmaking Chronicles
The course of true love never runs smooth. Sometimes a little matchmaking is required. When couples meet at a house party, provocative flirtation, secret rendezvous, and falling in love abound!

The Untouchables
Swoon over twelve of Society's most eligible and elusive bachelor peers and the bluestockings, wallflowers, and outcasts who bring them to their knees!

The Untouchables: The Spitfire Society
Meet the smart, independent women who've decided they don't need Society's rules, their families' expectations, or, most importantly, a husband. But just because they don't need a man doesn't mean they might not *want* one...

The Untouchables: The Pretenders
Set in the captivating world of The Untouchables, follow the saga of a trio of siblings who excel at being something they're not. Can a dauntless Bow Street Runner, a devastated viscount, and a disillusioned Society miss unravel their secrets?

Marrywell Brides
Come to Marrywell, England where the annual May Day Matchmaking Festival has been bringing hopeful romantics

together for hundreds of years. The dukes and rogues of the Regency will meet their matches with spirited and captivating ladies who may very well steal their hearts.

Wicked Dukes Club
Six books written by me and my BFF, NYT Bestselling Author Erica Ridley. Meet the unforgettable men of London's most notorious tavern, The Wicked Duke. Seductively handsome, with charm and wit to spare, one night with these rakes and rogues will never be enough...

Love is All Around
Heartwarming Regency-set retellings of classic Christmas stories (written after the Regency!) featuring a cozy village, three siblings, and the best gift of all: love.

Secrets and Scandals
Six epic stories set in London's glittering ballrooms and England's lush countryside.

Legendary Rogues
Five intrepid heroines and adventurous heroes embark on exciting quests across the Georgian Highlands and Regency England and Wales!

If you like contemporary romance, I hope you'll check out my **Ribbon Ridge** series available from Avon Impulse, and the continuation of Ribbon Ridge in **So Hot**.

I hope you'll consider leaving a review at your favorite online vendor or networking site!

I appreciate my readers so much. Thank you, thank you, *thank you.*

ALSO BY DARCY BURKE

Historical Romance

Rogue Rules

If the Duke Dares

Because the Baron Broods

When the Viscount Seduces

As the Earl Likes

The Phoenix Club

Improper

Impassioned

Intolerable

Indecent

Impossible

Irresistible

Impeccable

Insatiable

Marrywell Brides

Beguiling the Duke

Romancing the Heiress

Matching the Marquess

The Matchmaking Chronicles

Yule Be My Duke

The Rigid Duke

The Bachelor Earl (also prequel to *The Untouchables*)

The Runaway Viscount

The Make-Believe Widow

The Untouchables

The Bachelor Earl (prequel)

The Forbidden Duke

The Duke of Daring

The Duke of Deception

The Duke of Desire

The Duke of Defiance

The Duke of Danger

The Duke of Ice

The Duke of Ruin

The Duke of Lies

The Duke of Seduction

The Duke of Kisses

The Duke of Distraction

The Untouchables: The Spitfire Society

Never Have I Ever with a Duke

A Duke is Never Enough

A Duke Will Never Do

The Untouchables: The Pretenders

A Secret Surrender

A Scandalous Bargain

A Rogue to Ruin

Love is All Around

(A Regency Holiday Trilogy)
The Red Hot Earl
The Gift of the Marquess
Joy to the Duke

Wicked Dukes Club

One Night for Seduction by Erica Ridley
One Night of Surrender by Darcy Burke
One Night of Passion by Erica Ridley
One Night of Scandal by Darcy Burke
One Night to Remember by Erica Ridley
One Night of Temptation by Darcy Burke

Secrets and Scandals

Her Wicked Ways
His Wicked Heart
To Seduce a Scoundrel
To Love a Thief (a novella)
Never Love a Scoundrel
Scoundrel Ever After

Legendary Rogues

Lady of Desire
Romancing the Earl
Lord of Fortune
Captivating the Scoundrel

Contemporary Romance

Ribbon Ridge

Where the Heart Is (a prequel novella)

Only in My Dreams

Yours to Hold

When Love Happens

The Idea of You

When We Kiss

You're Still the One

Ribbon Ridge: So Hot

So Good

So Right

So Wrong

ABOUT THE AUTHOR

Darcy Burke is the USA Today Bestselling Author of sexy, emotional historical and contemporary romance. Darcy wrote her first book at age 11, a happily ever after about a swan addicted to magic and the female swan who loved him, with exceedingly poor illustrations. Join her Reader Club newsletter for the latest updates from Darcy.

A native Oregonian, Darcy lives on the edge of wine country with her guitar-strumming husband, incredibly talented artist daughter, and imaginative, Japanese-speaking son who will almost certainly out-write her one day (that may be tomorrow). They're a crazy cat family with two Bengal cats, a small, fame-seeking cat named after a fruit, an older rescue Maine Coon with attitude to spare, an adorable former stray who wandered onto their deck and into their hearts, and two bonded boys who used to belong to (separate) neighbors but chose them instead. You can find Darcy in her comfy writing chair balancing her laptop and a cat or three, attempting yoga, folding laundry (which she loves), or wildlife spotting and playing games with her family. She loves traveling to the UK and visiting her cousins in Denmark. Visit Darcy online at www.darcyburke.com and follow her on social media.

facebook.com/DarcyBurkeFans

instagram.com/darcyburkeauthor

pinterest.com/darcyburkewrites

goodreads.com/darcyburke

bookbub.com/authors/darcy-burke

amazon.com/author/darcyburke

threads.net/@darcyburkeauthor

tiktok.com/@darcyburkeauthor

Printed in the USA
CPSIA information can be obtained
at www.ICGtesting.com
LVHW040556120524
779803LV00005B/683